THE SCORPION TRAIL

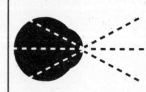

A JOSIAH WOLFE, TEXAS RANGER NOVEL

THE SCORPION TRAIL

LARRY D. SWEAZY

THORNDIKE PRESS
A part of Gale, Cengage Learning

Detroit • New York • San Francisco • New Haven, Conn • Waterville, Maine • London

GALE
CENGAGE Learning™

LIBRARY OF CONGRESS CATALOGING-IN-PUBLICATION DATA

Sweazy, Larry D.
    The scorpion trail : a Josiah Wolfe, Texas Ranger novel / by
Larry D. Sweazy.
        p. cm.
    ISBN-13: 978-1-4104-3030-4 (hardcover)
    ISBN-10: 1-4104-3030-8 (hardcover)
    1. Texas Rangers—Fiction. 2. Large type books. I. Title.
PS3619.W438S94 2010
813'.6—dc22   2010021273

Published in 2010 by arrangement with The Berkley Publishing Group,
a member of Penguin Group (USA) Inc.

Printed in the United States of America
1 2 3 4 5 6 7 14 13 12 11 10

To Cherry: For never giving up on me.

ACKNOWLEDGMENTS

This book would not have been possible without the help of a number of people.

Special thanks, as always, goes to John Duncklee for helping me with the Spanish translations. *Gracias, mi amigo.* Any mistakes are my own.

I can't thank Sandra Harding enough for her encouragement to see this novel through from beginning to the end. One of the great pleasures of writing this series was working with you. A special thanks to Faith Black for stepping in and carrying on.

Thanks also goes to some special friends who have encouraged me along the writing path. Some of them are: Steve and Judy, Patrick and Gina, Phil, Tom, and Chris of the old writer's group, Mark and Carla, Liz and Chris, Jim Huang of The Mystery Company, Jaci for your help with publicity, Loren and Deb, Johnny, Robert, Dusty, Bill, Terry, and all of my WWA and MWA friends. No one ever achieves anything worthwhile on his own, and you're all proof of that.

And finally, to my first reader, best friend, wife, and fellow passenger on this crazy journey we set out on together, Rose, who sees all of the open wounds, struggles, frustrations, and pure joy that no one else ever sees during the writing process — and keeps coming back for more. Thank you for all that you do.

AUTHOR'S NOTE

The Lost Valley fight that occurred between Major John B. Jones, Texas Ranger Company B, and a band of Kiowa and Comanche Indians in July of 1874 is portrayed in this book as closely to historical accounts as possible. Liberty has been taken with the time line and actual events for the purposes of storytelling.

For historical works concerning the Texas Rangers and the Frontier Battalion, the following books have served me well: *Lone Star Justice: The First Century of the Texas Rangers* by Robert M. Utley (Berkley, 2002); *The Texas Rangers: Wearing the Cinco Peso, 1821–1900* by Mike Cox (Forge, 2008); *Six Years with the Texas Rangers, 1875–1881* by James B. Gillet (Bison Books, 1976); and *A Private in the Texas Rangers: A. T. Miller of Company B, Frontier Battalion* by John Miller Morris (Texas A&M Press, 2001).

Online resources such as the *Handbook of Texas* and the *Texas Ranger Dispatch* magazine have also been helpful in portraying the Texas Rangers as accurately, and honorably, as possible.

PROLOGUE

September 1852

Twelve-year-old Josiah Wolfe was acutely aware of every sound in the woods. The long gun he carried was his father's — and it was the first time he had ever been allowed to carry it away from the house on his own. Beyond target practice behind the cabin, away from the barn, he had almost never handled the gun, much less hunted with it, but his father was ill, struck with a fever that had lingered longer than anyone thought it would, and the meat in the larder was growing thin.

His ma had given him the charge to bring home some squirrels or rabbits, something, anything, to get them through until his father recovered.

There was an anxiousness in his ma's blue eyes that he'd never seen before, a tenseness in her voice when she saw him off and said, "Now, you be careful out there on your own, Josiah. I need you to come back whole. I need you to come back," she'd repeated with fear frozen in her throat. His father coughed from the bed behind her, too weak to raise his head. "I couldn't bear to be like those Parkers." She watched him until he disappeared down the lane.

There was not a child in East Texas who did not know the names of Cynthia Ann and John Richard Parker. Fort Parker had been built by the eldest Parker in 1834, and it was surrounded by twelve-foot walls that enclosed four acres, with six cabins inside. Most of the inhabitants were extended family from Illinois. The raid in which the Parker children — Cynthia, age eight, and John, age five — were taken was quick and bloody — conducted by a large party of Indians, mostly Comanche, but there were also Kiowa, Caddo, and Wichita involved.

Fort Parker was less than a day's ride from Seerville, the closest town to the Wolfes' small parcel of farmland, and even though the massacre had taken place four years before Josiah's birth, he carried a healthy fear, mistrust, and curiosity about anything that had to do with Indians. Sometimes he thought the kidnapping was just lore, a spooky story used to correct bad behavior. But there were still Indians that refused to give up the raiding, and some strays stole cattle and traded with the Mexicans down south.

The story went that John Richard had been ransomed back from the Comanche, but had run off to rejoin them not long after. No one had ever seen or heard from Cynthia Ann again — though there were newspaper reports that she'd been spotted trading with a companion, a Comanche, on the Canadian River. The memory of her white life had been stolen from her, and most folks believed that Cynthia Ann would have been better off dead than living among the Indians.

Just the utterance of the word "Comanche" made Josiah shiver, even though Indian Territory was a long way away, and the Comanche and other tribes had been all but run out of East Texas. No child wanted to be the next Cynthia Ann or John Richard — and no parent in the vicinity was fully confident that such an attack could never happen again.

With the world on his shoulders, and surely not wanting to disappoint his father or his sweet but forever nervous ma, Josiah had headed out into the woods, assuming the role of provider, of doing for others what they could not do for themselves.

At first, he was confident and prideful, but as the morning edged along, and he got farther from home, the more fearful he became. He had shot one scrawny little gray cat squirrel that barely covered the bottom of his satchel. Fox squirrels are bigger and forage later in the morning than the gray cats, so there was still hope, but the need for meat took Josiah deeper into the forest than he had ever been on his own.

He wished it was spring instead of fall.

Then there'd have been plenty of cat squirrels bouncing around the hardwood forest, not yet a mile from the cabin; the fox squirrels favored the river bottoms, farther away. But all of the wishing in the world wouldn't turn back time. There was a chill in the air that Josiah could not disagree with, and the recent days had been regularly overcast and growing shorter. Now that the corn harvest was in, he'd been obliged to return to school — which did not make him too happy.

A game trail caught his attention, and he eased down a hidden, winding path that cascaded into a steep ravine.

He clung to his father's long gun tightly and navigated his way through the towering hardwoods, a thick grove of pines, then into a floodplain that was dried up and sandy.

Silt covered the first six feet of the base of every tree along the meandering river that was at the end of the trail, remnants of the spring floods. A red-bellied woodpecker chortled three times as it lit out overhead, then landed on a nearby tree and started to work, quickly hammering away, in search of ants or other insects to eat.

Every creature on earth must be hungry, Josiah thought. He stopped and caught his breath. He could feel his heart beating in his chest, and another pang of hunger gurgled in his belly — breakfast had been a bit of grease-soaked bread.

After he stood still for five minutes or so, a big squirrel buck jumped from one tree to another. But it was nearly a hundred yards away. Josiah raised the gun, steadied himself, and tried to balance his weight so he wouldn't go tumbling backward once he pulled the long gun's trigger. The light was dim under the canopy of leaves that had yet to fall, and the sky above was roiling gray, the clouds tossing and turning in a north wind that seemed to be growing stronger by the minute.

The buck was busy jumping from one tree to the next, and with each jump it was farther away from Josiah, and the certainty of a piece of meat was quickly running out of range. Josiah took a deep breath, sighted the squirrel as best he could, and pulled the trigger. The blast shattered the peaceful silence that blanketed the river bottom. The squirrel fell to the ground with a loud thud. The shot was square on.

The discharge had propelled Josiah back a bit, but he did not fall — he'd known what to expect. The smell of black powder tickled his nose, and it gave him a feeling of satisfaction and comfort. He'd have two squirrels in his bag — a couple more and he could head home and present his parents with a few days' worth of meals. Hopefully, his father would recover quickly and they could go hunting together.

He made his way to the squirrel, unconcerned about how much noise he made. All of the creatures had now been alerted to his presence and intention. The buck was truly the biggest squirrel Josiah had ever seen. It had to weigh three or four pounds. It made the gray cat look like a mouse when he tossed the buck in the satchel with it.

Blood covered the fingers of his right hand, so Josiah went to the river to clean himself up. He had laid the long gun down on the ground behind him, but he clutched the satchel tightly between his arm and ribs. He could smell the squirrels, the blood, and it quelled his appetite, almost made him queasy, but he would not part with the kills for a second — some critter might grab them and run off.

Bent over, staring down at the water, washing his hands, then his face, Josiah could see the reflection of the clouds overhead — but after a second, after wiping the last bit of water from his face, he nearly quit breathing.

There was a man in the reflection, a man standing over him with his father's long gun in his hands. Even worse, setting panic free to scream through his veins, was the realization that the man was an Indian. Josiah was almost certain he was a Comanche.

Josiah froze until the Indian nudged him from behind with his foot. "Up," the Indian demanded. "Up."

Josiah did as he was told. He was trembling, and he was afraid he was going to pee himself like a little baby, but he didn't. He turned and faced the Indian.

The Indian had shoulder-length black hair, a buckskin shirt, and a breechcloth with leggings. There were streaks of paint on his face, black curvy lines trailing from his hard eyes, and Josiah didn't know what they meant. All he knew about was war paint. But why would a lone Indian be here in war paint? he wondered. That would mean there were more Indians. He broke out in a sweat at the thought.

The Indian motioned for Josiah's black-powder bag and for his cartridges, too. Josiah instinctively shook his head no and started to back up. He stopped when he was ankle-deep in the water, not taking his eyes off the Indian. It was then that he noticed the blood running down the Indian's thigh, noticed the gaping bullet hole, and the scowl of pain that was marbled across the man's face.

"Give," the Indian demanded, motioning again for the ammunition.

Josiah shook his head no again, squared his shoulders, and stood firm, but before he realized what was happening, the Indian swung his father's long gun at him. The butt crashed into the side of his head before he could move, before he could scream. He only felt a brief burst of pain before everything went black.

Josiah slowly came to a little while later, lying on the bank of the river. A loud sound had startled him awake. His head ached with pain, and he could taste a bit of blood. It was late afternoon now — the sky was grayer than it had been in the morning; a cold rain sprinkled down from the sky, and a fierce wind was rattling the leaf canopy overhead. It sounded like a train was running over the tops of the trees. Josiah sat up, rubbing his head, his eyes searching every turn for the Comanche.

But he was gone . . . along with his father's long gun and the satchel of squirrels. Josiah stood up slowly then, gathered his bearings, made sure that he was correct — that everything was gone, including the Indian.

He began to run, run as fast as he could, toward home, toward his father and his ma, as far away from the woods, and the Indian, as possible.

He could only hope the Indian was alone, and not waiting for him, or waiting to follow him home. And then fear broke loose in Josiah Wolfe's twelve-year-old soul when he realized that his mother could not protect herself any better than he could, or the Parkers had, when they were overwhelmed by angry, raiding Indians.

He ran home faster than he had ever run before in his life.

CHAPTER 1

July 1874

"Ofelia, have you seen my boots?" Josiah Wolfe demanded.

Morning light bathed the porch in a warm glow from the rising sun. It was a small comfort that the house faced east, toward Tyler, toward Seerville, toward what had been, until recently, home.

Ofelia Martinez smiled and ignored Josiah. She was sitting on a porch swing holding Josiah's two-year-old son, Lyle, on her lap, playing pat-a-cake. *"Acariciar a una torta, acariciar a una torta, hombre del panadero."*

Breakfast had already been cooked, eaten, and cleaned up. There was still a lingering aroma of Arbuckle's and bacon wafting out from inside the small clapboard house.

Lyle squealed with laughter, then said, "Pat-a-cake, pat-a-cake, baker's man!"

"Sí," Ofelia said, giving Lyle a hearty hug.

"Ofelia!"

"*¿Qué, señor?* What?"

Josiah was standing in the doorway. His face was red, an odd contrast to his cornflower blue eyes and the thick shock of straw-colored hair that stood uncombed on the top of his head. He was tall and lanky, and his head nearly bumped the top of the door frame when he came and went. He had to watch his head when he had a hat on or he would knock it off. One more thing to get used to in this house.

"Where are my boots?"

Ofelia broke into a healthy laugh. She was short, what some might call squat; her dark brown Mexican face was lined with wrinkles, and her hair was grizzled and unruly, gray refusing to turn white, even though it probably should have years before.

Josiah had known Ofelia since he was a boy, and she was the closest thing to family he had left in his life. She had been a midwife in East Texas almost her entire life. Mostly to Mexicans like herself, but Josiah's father and ma didn't carry around much prejudice — Mexicans came and went frequently on their little farm, helping out for what wages they could earn, and what wages Josiah's family could pay.

The Wolfes never owned a slave. Josiah's father found the practice distasteful — even though he never said so outside the confines of his own home — but that did not stop Josiah from signing up with the Texas Brigade when the War Between the States came to the state. He was a son of Texas, and there was an expectation that he fight like the rest of the Wolfe family had in the earlier skirmishes of the land, like the Cherokee War his father had fought in, and become a hero in, before Josiah was born. Josiah was more than happy to carry on the fighting tradition when the time came.

Ofelia had been with the family during happy times and sad. After the war, when Josiah had returned broken, he was rescued by Lily, the girl of his dreams, giving him a family, and new hope. Ofelia had been there, too, when both of Josiah's parents died and were buried on the back forty of the Seerville farm. Most importantly, and most recently, Ofelia had been there when the fevers came and took Josiah's three little girls and, ultimately, his wife, Lily, in childbirth, leaving a newborn baby, Lyle, in the arms of a man who knew nothing about child-rearing. Ofelia had been there through it all. So when Josiah decided to move to Austin, he was more than a little relieved when Ofelia agreed to come along and watch after Lyle while Josiah continued on

Rangering. He owed her the world.

"They are on your feet, Señor Josiah." Ofelia laughed again, so much so, her whole body shook from head to toe.

Lyle joined in, even though it was obvious that the little boy, who favored his mother, with curly dark hair and brown eyes, didn't know why he was laughing. He looked at Josiah and Ofelia quickly, from one to the other, trying to determine, it seemed, if he was causing the laughter. Lyle was too young to know the past, or understand the present, and Josiah was intent on keeping it that way for as long as possible.

Josiah burst into laughter then, once he looked down and found his boots exactly where he had put them. "Well, that figures, doesn't it?"

"It does, señor, it surely does."

"My apologies, Ofelia."

"No need, señor, you know that."

"It's just hard . . . to leave so soon."

Ofelia nodded, wiped the tears from her eyes that had accumulated from laughing so hard, and stood up, lugging Lyle up with her. She easily handled the boy, like he was a sack of potatoes, balanced on her hip like he was a commodity that fit perfectly against her body.

"It will be easier to get the house in order

without you underfoot. Besides, it is best to get you back where you belong . . . among the living. I will be fine here. The city has much allure, and I have some distant relatives here as well. It is not like I will be all alone, señor."

"I don't know how I'll ever be able to repay you."

Josiah held out his hands a few inches from Lyle. The boy eagerly jumped into his father's arms.

"We have already discussed this, señor. I will stay until it is time for me to leave. We will settle up then."

Josiah nodded. "It's a deal. All right. No more of that, I promise."

"Bueno."

"Good!" Lyle shouted. "Good!"

Josiah and Ofelia both broke into a hearty round of laughter again.

One thing was for sure, Lyle would be much better at speaking more than one language than Josiah was.

All things considered, since he was obviously going to be raised a city boy instead of a country boy, it was a good thing for Lyle as far as Josiah was concerned. The world was changing faster than he could keep up with.

"Bueno. Bueno," Lyle continued, as Josiah

walked back into the house, followed by Ofelia, readying himself to finally leave.

Josiah Wolfe had been in a new city more than once in his life, but it was still nearly impossible for him to conceive that his recent move to Austin was now a permanent one. He was no longer a visitor, or a Texas Ranger riding into town on business just to leave again when trouble was quelled or an arrest made.

The Texas capital was now his home, and it was a far cry from living on the land he was born on in East Texas, where he knew exactly what to expect with the seasons and weather, where every step he took could be retraced to his boyhood, to his own painful — and joyful — memories. The new scenery was a relief from the tragedy he'd left behind.

City life was going to take some time to get accustomed to, if he ever did, but it was the choice he'd made and he knew he'd have to live with that decision.

It was for the best, he was sure of it, even though his heart caught in his throat as he tightened the saddle on his horse's back.

Clipper, his Appaloosa stallion, stood firm. Josiah and the horse had been through a lot together, too. Outside of Ofelia, there was no other creature on earth Josiah trusted more than Clipper.

He climbed up on the horse, took a deep breath, settled himself in, then nodded solemnly at Ofelia, who was standing on the porch with Lyle still attached to her hip.

"Adiós, Papa. *Adiós."*

Josiah waved, then turned and rode off slowly without saying good-bye. He had promised Lyle and Ofelia that he would be back soon. That was as close to saying good-bye as it came for Josiah Wolfe.

Austin was a crowded, noisy town. Josiah missed the whip-poor-wills at night, even the baying of a lone coyote — all replaced with flat-out citified silence, at night anyway.

Daytime in Austin was louder than ever, day in, day out, people coming and going, horses whinnying, train whistles blowing. It was the trains that unsettled Josiah the most. His house was less than a block away from the tracks, and it shook regularly.

He would be glad for the reprieve from the noise, from the shaking house, he thought, as he made his way through town at an easy pace on Clipper's back, taking in the coming day, in no huge hurry to get where he was going.

There was a lot to take in, a lot to learn about his new home, but Josiah knew enough to kind of understand what was happening around him, and that was important as far as he was concerned.

The Houston and Texas Central Railway had come to Austin in late 1871, a Christmas present to businessmen and those eager to take advantage of the new opportunities the railway afforded. The capital city became the westernmost railroad terminus in Texas, and the only railroad town in almost any direction. Construction boomed, and the population, helped along with an influx of freed slaves, had doubled since the first steam engine roared into town.

Along with the growing communities of Negroes, there were Mexicans living near Shoal Creek, and a healthy mix of Germans, Irish, and Europeans were scattered about the city in small enclaves.

All of the new residents were separated, knowingly or otherwise, as decided by the old guard of Anglos who had seen the bloody birth of Texas and the building of the capital. However, a new governor, Richard Coke, had been elected and taken his seat in January, and there seemed to be a new leaf turned. The past, specifically Reconstruction, was thought to be over and finished, but old social lines were still not crossed.

Change washed over a city like Austin more like water on a rock — one slow, tiny, layer at a time. But there was a new optimism in Austin, and that was not lost on Josiah. Unlike him, the recent immigrants to the city seemed like they were used to living in close quarters, and to city life as a whole. Josiah could tell this by the way the newcomers navigated through the streets, offering food and goods from their homelands to one another without fretting, like they had moved from across the river instead of the ocean.

There were spicy smells of tacos and tortillas, German sausages, and Irish soda bread in the air, almost at every turn. Josiah admired and envied the immigrants for their apparent ease of adjustment, but he knew, deep in his heart, they were just like him: They could not return to their old home any more than he could.

Even such a thing as the newly installed gas street lamps perplexed Josiah.

The streets were well lit at night, making it seem like the day never ended. And it didn't, not in places like "Little Mexico," the quadrant of streets and businesses just off Republic Square that very few Anglos dared venture into — even at midday. Josiah had visited there once at night, before moving to Austin, and made the brief acquaintance of a woman, Suzanne del Toro, but he had not visited her since moving to Austin permanently. He didn't have the courage to make the return visit. Though he did search the crowds for her face, hoping to get a glance at her — no matter how guilty the search or the thought of her made him feel.

The Anglos had their own section of town just across the river that was just as dangerous as "Little Mexico" and was certainly off-limits to the majority of polite folk in the city. Most big cities had their own version of Hell's Half Acre, and Austin was no exception.

Josiah had not explored all of Austin, but he figured he would have to eventually.

Even a Yankee had his place in the city — on the outside of the proper social circles, the hardest enclave to penetrate, if that were ever achieved. Money or fame usually broke down those doors, or at least wore them down — opened them if there was enough of both. Josiah had neither.

The only thing he had going for him was his Texan birthright, his stature as a Texas Ranger, installed as a sergeant in the newly formed Frontier Battalion. He had connections to the powerful, but was reluctant to use them, or even acknowledge them in public.

There was no mistaking that he was welcome in the home of the now deceased Captain Hiram Fikes — at least by the captain's daughter, Pearl, but not by the captain's widow. Pearl's mother feared Josiah as a potential suitor, and though she may have been right, Josiah was well aware that the new captain of his company, Pete Feders, had asked Pearl to marry him. She had used her grief and mourning to hold the decision at bay, and Josiah was glad of that, but he knew he stood no chance of winning the girl's heart, and he wasn't entirely sure he was ready to try. Though he thought she was the most beautiful girl — more of a woman, really — in the living world.

Josiah eased Clipper to a stop near the center of the capital city. He was a few blocks away from the democratic operations of Richard Coke and could have easily taken another route to the Red River camp where his company of fellow Rangers was assembled for training, but he hadn't.

He had one last stop to make before leaving town.

CHAPTER 2

For most lawmen, finding Juan Carlos was like looking at a fish in the water: One second he was there and the next second he was gone, like he never existed at all. But Josiah knew most of the man's haunts, where he felt safe, where he could blend in — and it wasn't in Little Mexico, like everyone thought, but on the other side of Republic Square, in the livery that served the local sheriff, Rory Farnsworth.

Juan Carlos was a mouse living right under a cat's food bowl. A courageous and crazy ploy that left Josiah shaking his head every time the two men met in the light of day. The old Mexican was a wanted man, had a bounty on his head from at least one jurisdiction down south that Josiah knew of, in San Antonio, and there were probably more.

As a Ranger, it was his duty to see Juan Carlos escorted to the jail and set behind bars, but even Sheriff Farnsworth showed little concern over the Mexican's capture. The charges were bogus and everybody in Texas with half a brain damn well knew it.

Juan Carlos loved living in the shadows, and for the most part served the law in one form or another while he was there, whether as a spy or a snitch, it depended on the need. Juan Carlos's half brother was once a Texas Ranger, the now-deceased Captain Hiram Fikes, gunned down in cold blood escorting a criminal to trial. Fikes was a dead hero, and Juan Carlos was on the run, again — still — for saving an Anglo's life in the process.

That Anglo was Josiah, and he had benefited from Juan Carlos's adept knife skills. He was forever in the Mexican's debt — well, half-Mexican, but in Texas, one drop of Spanish blood spoiled the rest, no matter the darkness or lightness of a person's skin.

Juan Carlos was a Mexican through and through, the identity of his father, and the gift of his father's last name, null and void, because it was never given to him. Juan was born out of wedlock, never allowed the privileges of his father's Anglo name. You'd never know by looking at the old man that there was a drop of Anglo blood in his body — he'd embraced the Mexican culture from the serapes he wore, to the food he ate, to the words he spoke. Most men in his situation would have tried their best to pass themselves off as Anglo — life would certainly have been easier — but not Juan Carlos. For some reason unknown to Josiah, the man had rejected the way of the white man.

When Josiah arrived at the livery, it was almost full of horses. Two stable boys were running around furiously, tending to the horses and their chores.

Josiah grabbed one of the boys by the shoulder as he tried to hurry by. The kid was tall, with a head full of greasy black hair, and he smelled of horse manure. His boots were clogged with wet mud, and all four feed buckets he carried were empty. A horse whinnied in the distance and kicked the stall. The other stable boy hurried past, as quick as he could, without saying anything to either Josiah or the first boy.

"Where's the old Mexican?" Josiah asked.

"Ain't no Mexicans here, mister." It sounded like the boy said *Mesh-e-kins;* his words seemed slurred.

The tone in the boy's voice struck Josiah as strange, so he looked him up and down, and noticed a bead of sweat on his fuzzy lip and a bit of nervousness in his eyes — like he'd stolen the last loaf of bread fresh out of the oven.

"I got to go, mister."

The kid pulled away from Josiah, but Josiah snatched him back in a hurry. He was beginning to think the sweat was nervous sweat, not work sweat. The air inside the stable suddenly felt thick — like something was wrong.

"Not so fast there, boy."

The kid, who was probably no older than fourteen, obviously didn't have the patience to wait — he stomped down on Josiah's boot as hard as he could.

Josiah let out a yell, raised his foot, staggered back against a stall, and let his grip on the boy fall away.

The boy disappeared around the corner, and Josiah was left to wonder what the hell had just happened, and what the hell was going on inside the livery barn.

All of the horses were reacting to the strange goings-on. Restless kicking and grunting suddenly filled the air. And now that the boy had disappeared, Josiah could see no other human inside the livery. It was oddly vacant.

Before he saw the fire, he smelled the smoke, and he knew full well the quick trail a flame would take in there, consuming all the hay, straw, and oats in its path.

"Juan Carlos!" Josiah shouted, eyeing his way out of the livery.

There was no answer, just the sizzle and rush of a growing fire.

The fire had started at the back of the livery, and a wall of flames jumped up wildly from the straw-covered dirt floor, climbing up the back wall, and spreading across the rafters like a hungry swarm of locusts chewing saw grass as fast as they could.

The flames reached out at Josiah with hungry, hot fingers, almost in the blink of an eye.

"Juan Carlos!" he shouted. He was answered the same way as the first time — with nothing but silence.

He pulled his bandanna up over his mouth. He had never seen flames spread so quickly. Smoke turned his throat raw before he could yell out again.

He could feel the heat, feel the hair on his arms singeing. Josiah had no choice but to flee, even though he was worried about Juan Carlos.

As he hurried toward the door and to the street, he opened all the stalls that held horses. His own horse, Clipper, was tied to a post in front of the sheriff's office, so his trusted mount was safe for the moment. The nervousness of the fire would surely set Clipper off, though.

Every horse had fear in its eyes as they all ran out into the street. Most of them kept on running. The escaping animals were a blur, a moving wall of muscle and sweat, and Josiah nearly got trampled.

There was no sign of the stable boys, no sign of anybody, once the horses emptied out of the livery.

By the time Josiah got outside, the roof was ablaze, and a crowd had gathered across the street to watch the fire.

Thick gray smoke obscured the sun, instantly making the day dreary and overcast. A storm of fire and ash began to fall from the sky instead of rain.

Josiah's lungs felt like they were burning from the inside out. Bells were clanging, people were shouting, and it was all nearly too much to take in. He fell to his knees and tried to gather his breath. He coughed and hacked, drawing some attention to himself.

Someone tapped him on the shoulder and asked him if he was all right.

He nodded that he was. The person ran off then, and Josiah never got a good look to see who it was. A stranger, he surmised, searching the crowd for a face he recognized in between coughs.

His vision was blurry, and his eyes stung like somebody had thrown acid in them. There was no sign of Juan Carlos. He could only hope the Mexican had found his way out of the livery before the fire started.

The flames had engulfed the entire building now, and a rush of fire carts had arrived. There was not enough water to save the livery, so there was a line of men passing buckets to coat the sheriff's office and jail, trying to keep the fire from jumping over from the livery's roof. Luckily, there wasn't much wind, so there was a good chance the fire could be contained.

Josiah was starting to regain his regular capacity to breathe. He had stood up, ready to join the fire line, when he heard someone shout his name.

"Wolfe, what the hell are you doing here?" Sheriff Rory Farnsworth was striding toward him. Farnsworth was a spritely man, nearly five years younger than Josiah, with a finely waxed mustache. The sheriff was not quite thirty years old and had attended some fancy college out east that gave him some odd ideas, before returning home to Texas to pursue a career in keeping the law. Unlike Josiah, Farnsworth had missed fighting in the War Between the States. The difference in the men, in the way they carried themselves, how they saw the law, was extreme — as it was between most men who had witnessed true battle, and lost a friend or two along the way to an angry bullet, and those who hadn't.

Josiah had spent time with the Texas Brigade, the 1st Infantry. They were first in the advance, and then the rear guard in retreat. First in, last out. Only the bravest of the brave could withstand a life of that kind of fighting.

He had spent his entire enlistment in the Brigade. When Josiah came back to Texas a broken man, he had found love with Lily, started a family, and ridden with Hiram Fikes as a Ranger, even after they were disbanded and turned into a weak arm of the then governor in the State Police. When Coke took office and created the Frontier Battalion, it was the second time the Rangers had saved Josiah's life, by giving him reason to sit up on a horse and ride for the sake of justice.

Josiah was certain that Sheriff Farnsworth was a good man, but the difference between their experiences as lawmen was palpable.

Farnsworth obviously had higher aspirations than being a sheriff, situated as he was in the state capital, and Josiah always kept that in mind when he dealt with the sheriff. His days as a soldier had taught him to respect a man who had ambitions and was willing to work toward them, but to be leery of a man who was just flat-out ambitious.

It wasn't that he didn't like Farnsworth — the sheriff was genial enough — it was just that Josiah knew a politician when he saw one, and he questioned the man's backbone in a gunfight.

"At the moment I think I'm trying to breathe," Josiah said, answering Farnsworth's question about his presence in front of the burning livery.

"What in the blue blazes is going on here?"

"Looks like a fire, Sheriff."

"Well, do tell."

Josiah hunched his shoulders with uncertainty. "I figure somebody started that fire. I stopped by to see . . ." He stopped midsentence, looked around him at the flurry of activity, and decided quickly that nobody was paying any attention to him and Farnsworth. ". . . to see a friend before leaving town, and all of a sudden the fire jumped on the wall and took off from there. I can't imagine why anybody would set the livery on fire with intention. I suppose a horse could have knocked over a lamp, except it's straight-up daylight. You ought to ask the two stable boys what they saw."

"Stable boys?" the sheriff said, looking over Josiah's shoulders, eyeing the crowd. "Clive Werner doesn't have a regular stable boy that I know of, just a couple of Mexicans that help out every so often." He stared Josiah in the eye, and Josiah understood that Farnsworth was referring to Juan Carlos.

"That's strange then. One boy was carrying four empty buckets. The other hurried off when he saw me. I didn't think anything about it. I just thought they were busy with their chores."

"I'm sure glad it's not windy today. Looks like the jail is safe."

"Anybody in there worth busting out?" Josiah asked.

Rory Farnsworth shook his head no. "Not a soul but our trustee and a couple hooligans sleeping off a night of whiskey and women. Once they wake up, they'll be free to go."

"I thought there might be some malicious cause, a distraction?"

"No reason that I can think of. The Wells Fargo isn't due in for a couple of days to make a delivery. Banks are safe as far as I know. If this was a distraction for a robbery, I think I would know, or be hearing something by now. Probably just an accident,

41

though your mention of stable boys is odd, a bit of a worry. Ever seen them before?"

Josiah shook his head no. "I haven't spent much time in Austin, Sheriff, and have not been around the livery much at all. Been trying to get my house in order so I can head off to the Red River and join the other Rangers. I never saw those boys before in my life. But even at that, I thought they were nervous. Might not be anything to it at all. Fires happen."

"They do, all too often," Farnsworth said. "Well, I need to find Clive Werner and get these horses rounded up. You probably ought to get on to where you're going."

"I'd be glad to help with the horses."

"Suit yourself."

Josiah watched Rory Farnsworth saunter into the crowd, his manner calm, not as concerned about the fire as Josiah thought he ought to be. At least not showing it. *Maybe that's what a good politician is,* Josiah thought, *somebody who hides what he's really thinking.*

Something told him that he was wrong about the sheriff. What you saw was what you got with that man.

He shrugged off his doubt, settling with the fact that the problems in Austin were mostly Farnsworth's to carry, not his.

The authority of Rangers was broad, especially now that Governor Coke had made them an official unit of the government. But the whole organization was still new, still rebuilding their reputation under the guise of the Frontier Battalion.

Josiah was a sergeant, not a captain, so his authority didn't branch out too far from his own company. And even that level of command was not fully established yet. He had spent little time in the company of his fellow Rangers since rejoining. Life and duties past had intervened.

Josiah brushed himself off and made his way to Clipper. He was more than a little concerned about Juan Carlos, but the Mexican had gotten through some major scrapes in his life, so his concern was troubling, but minimal.

The encounter with the fire had slowed Josiah's progress. His intent was to be out of Austin by noon and fully on his way to the Ranger camp. It was past time he rode with the company of Rangers he'd joined up with.

The fire line had proven effective, and the fire was nearly under control. The sun had recaptured the sky from the billowing clouds, calming Josiah, encouraging him that there was time enough to be a good distance from Austin before night fell.

He mounted Clipper, then caught sight of an odd movement of men. Sheriff Farnsworth, specifically, was leading a group of men and easing into the smoldering front section of the livery.

About the same time a breeze kicked up, then shifted, and the raw, pungent smell of charred human flesh touched Josiah's nose.

It was a familiar smell, though buried deep in his past, in the recesses of his mind that he had hoped had been sealed off forever. The battle in Chickamauga came rushing back to him, and he felt like he was standing in the middle of battle watching a cadre of men burning to death after an explosion in an ammunition dump. He could still hear the men screaming and writhing in terrible, unstoppable pain. Even Yankees didn't deserve to die such a horrible death, perishing in a true, living, burning hell.

Josiah lowered his head, looked away from the livery, and covered his face with his bandanna.

"There's a body over here," one of the men called out.

CHAPTER 3

The flesh was burned off the face, leaving hardly anything but a skeleton. The body itself was nothing but charred meat, crispy black strands barely hanging on to bones that would turn instantly to dust if touched.

All of the bones were intact, but completely blackened by the fire, ashes still smoldering on the ground underneath. If the smell of a human burned to death was strong and repugnant at a distance, it was nearly unapproachable close up.

Josiah was standing in the stall where the body, if it could be called that, had been found. He stared at the fully intact skeleton and decided it had been stuffed in the corner, bent over as if the person had fallen forward.

There was a little bit of cloth on one of the legs and both arms, a remnant of a boot heel, and some metal buttons lying under the breastbone. There was no sign of a gun belt, or a gun. The ground was scorched darker underneath the bones, like maybe the fire had been hotter there, like maybe that's where the fire had started. It was surely a sight Josiah would just as soon forget, but he doubted that would happen anytime soon.

As soon as Sheriff Farnsworth caught a glimpse of the bones and digested the smell, he immediately exited the livery.

There was nothing that Josiah could see to identify the body — even to tell if it was a man or a woman. He had assumed it was a man as soon as he saw it. The boot heel and the height of the skeleton, if it could be imagined standing up, seemed more in line with the size of a man than a woman. But there was just no way to tell for sure.

More than anything else, what Josiah found most troubling was that there was no way to figure out whether the bones belonged to Juan Carlos or not. He sure hoped the Mexican hadn't come to such a bad end.

"Look there," a man standing next to Josiah said, pointing at the skull. The man wore a deputy badge, so Josiah assumed he was one of the sheriff's men, a deputy he hadn't met.

Not being from Austin originally had its drawbacks, and not knowing the roster of lawmen was one of them. He was certain he'd know more of the deputies once he'd lived in the capital for more than a month, but he was at a loss at the moment. He thought he'd heard Farnsworth call this man Pence, but he wasn't sure.

Josiah followed the point of the man's index figure, and his gaze landed on exactly what the deputy saw — a hole about the size of a silver dollar, square in the back of the skull. It was like a hole in the ice, jagged edges, dangerous, the cause uncertain other than the obvious assumption that the injury hadn't been an accident.

"Could it be a bullet hole?" Josiah asked Pence.

The man nodded yes. He was young but old enough to grow a mature mustache. One that fell freely over his clasped mouth, dark brown like his hair, free of gray and wax like Farnsworth's. "Maybe," he said, then crouched on his knees, his sharp blue eyes keen on the skull as he edged close enough to see inside the hole. He put his hand over his mouth, caught a gag in his throat, then shook it off. "But there ain't no bullet," he said as he pulled back to Josiah.

"Well the man's dead, that's certain. I guess it's up to the sheriff to figure out who it is and what happened," Josiah said.

"How do you know it's a man?"

"I don't," Josiah said. "Just makes sense that it is."

"You thinkin' it might be somebody you know?"

"Could be. I came here looking for somebody. He's not here — but bad trouble has a way of finding him."

"Lord, have mercy, I ain't never seen a man burned to death. Smells like a rotted cow set on fire. I'm gonna be eating a plate full of corn and bread for the next couple of days and no meat, that's for sure. I'll be helping the sheriff figure this one out. Not too often we have a full-fledged killin' on our hands that doesn't have a certain killer at the other end of a gun."

Josiah headed toward the door, taking in as much of the sight and smell as he could, leaving Pence to consider the remains. There was nothing left for him to do there. He could only hope the burned remains didn't belong to Juan Carlos, but there was no way to be sure.

"Looks like a man, but hard to say," Josiah said to Sheriff Farnsworth. "Hard to know whether it was an Anglo, Indian . . . Mexican."

"No Indians in town that I know of. Not ones that aren't tamed, anyway. Mexicans . . . well, you never know. I haven't found Clive Werner yet, and he should have been here."

"You'll get word to me once you figure out who the bones belong to?"

"Why should I do that?"

"Consider it a favor. I'm a little concerned for a friend of mine . . . a friend of ours."

Sheriff Farnsworth studied Josiah's face, saw the concern and uneasiness that must have been in his eyes, too, then nodded. "I can do that . . . if it's someone you might know. I'll send word."

"I appreciate that."

There was still plenty of activity going on around the livery, and Josiah had to make his way through the crowd to get to Clipper.

For the most part, no one knew who he was, and since Texas Rangers didn't wear a badge or a special uniform, he blended in like any other man who had come to help put out the fire. He heard one man say to another that he thought the fire was set on purpose, that he'd seen two boys running away from the livery right before the smoke came out of the roof. Josiah stopped and listened, but the men noticed him and walked on.

He took a deep breath and wondered if

the two stable boys could have killed the person in the stall, then set him on fire to conceal their crime — or if they were running away just because there was a fire. What would prompt such a heinous act . . . from boys, who may have killed a man? he wondered, then quickly hoped he was wrong. Hoped he was dead wrong, as he was worried that the skeleton was Juan Carlos.

The sheriff needed to find those boys . . . and Josiah needed to know if the old Mexican, his friend and protector, was still alive. He owed Juan Carlos that much.

He owed Juan Carlos his life.

There were two places he knew to look, and even though he was expected at the Ranger camp by morning, he knew he didn't have a choice but to find out if his worst fear was true.

Captain Hiram Fikes had lived a long and interesting life. He was a Texas Ranger, of both the old days and of the recent Frontier Battalion. He was a veteran of the War Between the States and had served in the State Police. He was a hero and had lived and died for his beloved state. Almost all of Austin had turned out for his funeral, on this very land. The governor and his state senators were there. Even President Grant had sent a representative to the funeral. Captain Fikes was the first Texas Ranger to die in the line of duty since the forming of the Frontier Battalion. It was a big to-do and the biggest funeral Josiah had ever attended.

For a man of property, Captain Fikes had had more adventures in his life than most . . . and he was away from his estate more than he lived there. It could be called that, since the house itself was huge, a two-storey red brick mansion that had as many rooms as nearly any hotel Josiah had ever been in, with the exception of the Menger in San Antonio.

Fikes had had many secrets, too. A few Josiah knew, after spending so much time with the man.

The first time Josiah had set foot on the captain's land was when he'd returned the dead man's body. Now he was returning for the first time since the funeral, since moving to Austin. He had avoided the house, and the complication that lived inside, specifically the captain's daughter, Pearl.

A long lane eased up to the massive entrance of the house. Someone had seen him coming and was waiting for him.

It was Pedro, the houseman, a porter and

manservant of sorts for Madam Fikes, the captain's widow. The Madam was a hard nut to crack. She had the personality of a badger, and Josiah often wondered, after meeting the woman, if she was the reason the captain had spent so much time away from the house. It would have been understandable. Her family had made a lot of money in the silver mines, and she was most definitely accustomed to getting her own way. She looked at Josiah like he was dirt on her shoe, an uneducated sergeant who didn't belong in her good graces or presence just because of his lowly beginnings. He was not fond of the woman, but showed her as much respect as possible since she had been the captain's wife.

Pearl, on the other hand, treated him like he was a man of means. Too much so as far as he was concerned . . . which was one of the reasons he had avoided returning to the estate.

In an odd way, Pedro looked a little like Juan Carlos, but his speech was more Anglo, his Mexican accent less defined, almost impossible to detect. He spoke proper English, like he had been schooled in the same places of higher learning back east as Sheriff Farnsworth. Pedro was a tall man, his nose angular, and his skin dark, not leathery, but lustrous in the afternoon light. He wore a long black frock coat, a hard-starched white shirt, white gloves, and shiny black boots, his pants tucked at the knees.

"It is good to see you again, Señor Wolfe. Miss Pearl has often wondered aloud why you have not returned to spend time in her company," Pedro said, taking Clipper's lead and tying it to a post in front of the house, as Josiah dismounted.

Josiah didn't know what to say. He hadn't really considered the implications of his actions, or his lack of actions, concerning Pearl. The last he knew of her situation was that the new captain of Company B, his captain and fellow Ranger, had asked Pearl to marry him. It was just after the funeral of her father, and she had put Pete off, but there was no way Josiah was going to get in the middle of that. Besides, Madam Fikes favored Pete. He had standing, being a captain and all.

"I should apologize, Pedro. I have been getting settled in."

"That is understandable, señor."

"I was leaving town, as it was, but something occurred that caused me to delay a bit."

"Nothing of dire consequence, I hope," Pedro said.

"Dire enough, I think. Have you seen Juan Carlos lately?"

"Juan Carlos? *¿Qué apuro él ahora trae?*"

Josiah hesitated, saw a shadow fall across Pedro's face. "I don't speak your language."

Pedro shook his head. "My apologies, Señor Wolfe, I rarely speak in my native tongue, but Juan Carlos forces me to lose control of myself. What trouble does he bring us now?"

"I'm not sure that he has brought trouble on anyone. Anyone but himself. I fear he is dead."

Pedro's brown eyes were hard, and he jerked a bit when he heard the door behind him. "Please, señor, enough has befallen us."

"Josiah? Josiah Wolfe, is that you?" a female voice said.

He broke the gaze he and Pedro were holding. He understood the man's plea; he just wasn't sure he could oblige.

Pearl Fikes was one of the most beautiful women Josiah had seen in a long time. She rivaled his Lily, even the memory of her. Pearl had shoulder-length blond hair, a soft-featured face, and an hourglass figure easily encased in a long dress made of black fabric. She was still in mourning, casual as it might be, for her father.

She rushed to him, stopping just inches

from him so they stood nearly face-to-face. Pearl was only an inch or so shorter than Josiah.

He could smell a familiar flowery fragrance, toilet water, a choice that he did not understand, another part of the feminine mystery that Josiah Wolfe was fully aware he sorely lacked any knowledge of. It was, however, a great relief to replace the smell of a charred human being with the presence and fragrance of a beautiful woman — even one that made him feel a pang of guilt, like Pearl did.

His wife, Lily, had never been afforded the opportunity to wear toilet water. Instead, she'd smelled of their sparse land, of the pine cabin, of their children, and of living. Josiah knew how to react to that scent, even though he had almost lost all of his memory of it now. Hanging on to that and living, walking forward, complicated his life in ways he did not know how to deal with.

"I thought I heard your voice," Pearl said.

Pedro eased away, disappearing past Clipper, but not before he made eye contact with Josiah, then nodded, silently demanding that the message about Juan Carlos would not go any further.

Pedro obviously did not know the extent of all of Pearl's relationships. But it was also obvious that the porter did not have any personal use for Juan Carlos. Josiah found that curious.

"It is good to see you, Pearl. I apologize for not calling on you, but I did not think it would be appropriate."

Pearl had not moved, and she stood stiffly before him. Josiah had to look away from her eyes. They were deep blue. What he imagined the ocean to look like, or a fair day in summer, perfect and calm . . . a day you never wanted to end, a day you could get lost in, that could make you believe in happiness once again.

"Appropriate? Why should you worry about appropriate? You are always welcome here. You were favored by my father. He thought highly of you," Pearl said.

"Thank you. That is very kind of you to say."

"Only because it is true."

"Your mother is less fond of me."

"She is an angry woman. You must pay her no mind."

"That's easy for you to say."

"Hardly."

They let her words linger between them. Pearl smiled first, then Josiah followed suit, both of them finally letting go and laughing.

Josiah wanted nothing more at that moment than to pull Pearl close to him and kiss her, wanted to touch her more than anything, but he restrained himself, almost forcibly. For a moment, he forgot why he was there, why he'd come to the Fikes estate in the first place, but once he remembered, the smile fell quickly from his face.

"Is something the matter?" Pearl asked.

"I'm not sure. Have you seen Juan Carlos recently?"

Pearl's soft face tensed, and her skin tightened up like canvas drying quickly in the sun. She took a deep breath, then looked past Josiah. "You know how Juan Carlos is, one minute he is here, then the next he is gone. Tell me something tragic has not happened to him, too? I'm not sure I could take it."

"I don't know. I have reason to believe something may have happened, but I can't be sure. When was the last time you saw him?" Josiah was not going to tell Pearl his fear, like he had Pedro, that Juan Carlos was dead. He felt responsible for her heart in an odd way, and it was obvious that losing her uncle would have a demoralizing effect on her grief.

"Three nights ago. He 'borrowed' a horse. I thought nothing of it since he has done that before. But now that I think about it, he seemed more nervous than I had ever seen him, in a hurry to flee into the darkness. I had the sense that someone was after him . . . but again, that would not be so unusual. I have not seen or heard from him since."

Josiah nodded. "You have no clue where he was staying or what he might have been involved in?"

Pearl shook her head no. "All I know is that he told me if I ever needed him that I was to send word through Pedro to a woman named Suzanne del Toro."

Josiah flinched at the mention of the woman's name and looked away from Pearl to the ground.

"Do you know this woman?" Pearl asked.

"I do," Josiah said. "I surely do . . . even though I wish I didn't."

CHAPTER 4

Every large town worth its salt, and even small ones, has a section of town that is typically off-limits to folks of the polite persuasion. Austin was no exception. Hell's Half Acre was what most folks called it, or the Acre, but it wasn't an official name like in Fort Worth or Tascosa.

There were usually only two reasons to venture into such a place: for excitement in the company of a female, or for trouble of the other sort — a fight or a brawl to blow off steam.

Josiah had a third reason: to find someone. He hoped to at least find out that Juan Carlos was on an adventure, alive and well, and had been miles away from the livery when it burned. He couldn't bear the thought that the skeleton with the hole in its skull was his friend.

He had made no mention of the grim discovery to Pearl. He left her quickly, before she could ask any more questions. There was a look of confusion on her face, a desire for something more that Josiah was uncertain about, so he avoided her eyes and dashed away. He really had to restrain himself in Pearl Fikes's presence. The air between them felt like lightning dancing out of a thundercloud.

The ride into town from the Fikes estate was a fast one.

Little Mexico was situated in the confines of Austin's city limits, and was tougher than most towns in Texas, even along the border. It was a courageous Anglo who would venture uninvited into the small section of town, even in broad daylight, without the escort of a Mexican.

Josiah didn't need an invitation . . . or an escort.

He had been to Little Mexico before, long into the night, in one of his weaker moments, he thought — though the visit had awakened him, torn him away from his hunched-over, guilt-stricken walk in grief, and set him straight up into life again, at least the pursuit of it, living with a future purpose. For that he was grateful.

The memory of his visit to Little Mexico, however, left him burdened with a load of guilt that surprised him. He felt something for Suzanne del Toro that he could not identify, that on most days he refused to acknowledge. It was a different attraction than he had felt for Pearl.

Oddly, Josiah didn't feel like he had to restrain one ounce of himself when he was with Suzanne. There was nothing fragile about Suzanne del Toro. She had seen things and done things in her life that would make most men cringe and turn their head, but not Josiah. He liked her, even though he knew any kind of a relationship that stretched on beyond one night was impossible. They could never walk down the street in Austin arm in arm; it just wasn't acceptable with a woman of her means and race . . . especially for a Ranger.

So far he had avoided Little Mexico since settling in Austin, but there was no avoiding his return, or facing Suzanne, now.

Dusk was coming on, and Josiah was only too aware of the fact that he was skirting his original trip, turning his back on his sworn duties. He hoped he would not be stripped of his responsibilities as a Ranger for lack of presence at the camp, but he felt it was far too important to find out as much as he could about the welfare of Juan Carlos. His gut told him that his friend was in serious peril.

61

His promotion to sergeant was surely on the line, but he was certain he could survive if he was banished from the company of Texas Rangers. He could find work as a lawman in Austin, or one of the surrounding towns, if it came to that . . . but he hoped it wouldn't. He was truly excited about the new possibilities surrounding the Rangers and the Frontier Battalion.

The captain of his company, Pete Feders, would surely understand his desire to find out what had happened to Juan Carlos, Captain Fikes's half brother. Pete knew Juan Carlos, too. Probably owed him more than one favor himself. Pete Feders had ridden with Captain Fikes for as long as Josiah had, if not longer.

Josiah garnered a few uncertain looks from those that walked the boardwalk in Little Mexico. It was like he had crossed an imaginary river into another land. Like he had walked square into a foreign country, where he did not understand the language or many of the customs — which, of course, was true. It was like stepping into Mexico itself, brightly colored with a brilliant red sunset, loud music, and a spice in the air that made his nose twitch.

The sign over the entrance said: "Hotel del Paraíso."

Josiah knew enough Spanish to know that the name of the place was the Paradise Hotel, and he knew its proprietor was the woman he had hoped to never see again, Suzanne del Toro. "Fat Susie" to Captain Hiram Fikes, and many other men who knew her as a shrewd businesswoman and keeper of fancy girls who were loose with their bodies and ideas of love — for a price. Her clientele was usually Mexican, but Suzanne didn't discriminate toward race or religion. Anglos were welcome if they were brave enough to enter her establishment. Her favorite color was gold.

The music was loud even though night had yet to fall. Beefsteak sizzled in the kitchen behind the bar, the unmistakable smell wafting out into the saloon, mixing with cigar and tobacco smoke and the damp smell of vaqueros just off the trail. The piano player switched songs to one with a faster melody when he noticed Josiah walk in the door. The volume of voices dropped noticeably.

There were several tables strewn about with men sitting, either eating or immersed in a game of cards, gambling away their wages. Most men played poker, but not being a gambling man himself, Josiah wasn't certain about the intricacies or names of the other games he saw being played, nor did he care. He only had one thing on his mind.

Josiah strode up to the bar, a long cherry affair that looked hand-carved and was highly polished. The Paradise was hardly a hole-in-the-wall like some of the Mexican saloons — cantinas — Josiah had had the misfortune of being in at one time or another. It was a first-class establishment, which was no surprise.

"What can I get for you, senõr?" the barkeep asked, keeping himself busy cleaning the bar, not making eye contact with Josiah. The barkeep was a full-blooded Mexican, skinny as a post, with shiny black hair, a thin, waxed mustache, and wearing a heavily starched white shirt that was a testament to a Chinaman's laundry.

"I'm looking for Suzanne del Toro," Josiah said.

The barkeep wiped the bar with a towel. "To drink, senõr? What can I get for you to drink?"

He motioned for Josiah to sit on a bar stool, but he remained standing.

"I'm looking for Suzanne. For Fat Susie."

"There is no one here by that name. You must be mistaken." The barkeep shifted his eyes to both sides, once to the front door and then to the back door, as if he was looking for an escape route.

Josiah leaned in closer, checked the exits with his peripheral vision. "I am not mistaken, sir. Where is the owner of this establishment?" It was not a question, but a demand. A loud demand.

The music suddenly stopped playing, and the saloon became quiet, save for the rattle of gun belts and the scoot of chairs.

Josiah felt a hot breath on the back of his neck, smelled it, too. The barkeep was looking over his shoulder, and Josiah had to calculate quickly whether he had time to pull his gun, a Colt .45 Peacemaker, on whoever was standing mere inches behind him.

"*Necesitas irse. En una prisa,*" a man's voice said.

"I don't speak Spanish. *No hablo español.*"

"Then you are in the wrong place, and you need to leave. In a hurry. Now. Pronto." It was the same voice, the same man. A rustle of cloth drew Josiah's attention to the reflection in the mirror behind the bar. He didn't move, stayed frozen in place, but he searched for a clue to who the man behind him was and found a reflection of two men standing on either side, their guns drawn.

One man had swept his duster open and exposed a rifle in his other hand. Both men were Mexicans, bulky and accustomed to handling trouble with the sheer volume of their size and the guns they carried.

"I'm not leaving until I get what I came for."

"Senõr, please . . ." the barkeep pleaded. "These are serious men." It was difficult to understand the barkeep's English, but there was no mistaking the seriousness of the situation. Sweat had formed on the barkeep's forehead.

"So am I," Josiah said. He hesitated for just a second, then jumped straight back, knocking the closest man off balance with the hard hit, followed by a swift thrust of his elbow into the man's gut.

He heard the hammer of a pistol cock, felt his own heartbeat rise, sensed the rush of adrenaline pulse through his veins, pushing away any fear that might have existed as he swung around, grabbing the grip of his gun and pulling it straight out of the holster.

The man directly behind him had collapsed, fallen to his knees, but the man assigned to be backup, a huge boulder of a man, who had the skin of a buckskin horse and the breath of a dead pig, was ready for Josiah to make a foolish move.

"Drop the gun," the man said in perfectly understandable English as he stepped calmly forward and pushed the barrel of his six-shooter square in the center of Josiah's forehead. "Before I lose my patience."

Josiah took a deep breath, scanned the room for an escape, for any aid, and saw none.

If the man pulled the trigger and blasted his brains out, the whole saloon would probably cheer. They had no idea he was a Texas Ranger, not that it would have mattered, and he wasn't about to tell them. The fact was, his position might have been more of a hindrance than a help. The Rangers had a mixed reputation among Mexicans. There had been little time to erase the sins of the State Police with the broader reach of the law that the new Rangers promised.

There was no way out.

"Don't make me ask again," the man holding the gun said.

"I am looking for Fat Susie," Josiah said through clenched teeth.

"I heard you the first time when you asked the barkeep. What's your business with her?"

"She's a friend . . ." The barrel of the man's six-shooter was still pressed firmly into Josiah's forehead, and when he said "friend," the man pushed a little harder.

". . . of a friend," he added.

"Who is this friend of a friend that would bring you all alone into a place where you are not welcome?"

"Juan Carlos. Juan Carlos Montegné."

"Juan Carlos, you say?"

"Yes. He saved my life, now he is missing, and I am trying to find him."

The man pulled the six-shooter away from Josiah's forehead. "You have come to the wrong place. Your friend is not here. But I, too, am concerned about his welfare."

"Can I see Suzanne now?"

"I am afraid that is impossible, senõr. No one has seen or heard from her in the last three days. I do not know where she is at."

CHAPTER 5

The man's name turned out to be Emilio del Toro. He was Suzanne's brother and the keeper of the peace at the Paradise Hotel. The only outward sign that Josiah could see that Emilio and Suzanne were related was the forcefulness of their personalities. Both were take-charge kind of people, and it was obvious why Suzanne had chosen Emilio to make sure her establishment was properly looked after in her absence.

Anyone in his right mind would not have crossed the bulking man. He was as tall as Josiah, his muscles as hard as any rock found in Texas, and he did not suffer fools gladly. Josiah felt lucky that he did not have a hole in his head instead of a glass of fresh water in his hand and a comfortable seat in an office that was situated between the bar and the kitchen.

Emilio sat directly across from Josiah. "Tell me how you know my sister. She has never mentioned being, um, hombres with a Texas Ranger besides Captain Hiram Fikes. It is not in her character to take up with more than one man at a time."

"She hasn't taken up with me," Josiah said. "I do not want to dishonor your sister. Or the captain for that matter."

"There is no need to explain to me the torrid details. My sister is a private woman. I stay out of her business unless it affects our business," Emilio said.

"The hotel?"

"*Sí,* it belongs to us both as much as it does to anyone else, but I would rather not be accountable for anything other than keeping the vaqueros from killing each other, holding down the trouble to a whisper. That is usually not a problem, unless some cowboys wander in off the trail, looking for a fight. We try to keep to ourselves."

Josiah nodded. "What do you know of Juan Carlos, then?"

"He is the *bastardo* brother of my sister's dead lover. Of course, I know of him. He has spent many nights in the rooms above the tavern — for pleasure and his own safety. That is why I am very worried that he and my sister might have fallen into some trouble together. She trusted his counsel. He is like an uncle to her, but Juan Carlos is always playing games with people, playing on both sides of the fence, either with the Rangers as a spy or for the *bandidos,* south, who rustle cattle across the river, trying to make some fast money outwitting the same Rangers Juan Carlos is amigos with. One minute he is Anglo, the next he is Mexican, the next he is vamoose, gone like he never existed. I did not worry for him until Suzanne came up missing, too. The more Juan Carlos is gone, the better off we are. *Yo no confío en él.* I don't trust him."

The office was small, and the smell of simmering stew, *menudo,* and meat cooking on an open grill was distracting Josiah. The day had gotten away from him. "I need to go," he said, standing.

"Why did you think you would find Juan Carlos here?" Emilio asked.

"It wasn't that I thought I would. It was that I was *hoping* I would. I figured your sister might know how to get in touch with him."

"Why?"

"Because he told Pearl, his niece, the captain's daughter, to contact him through her."

"Interesting."

"I thought so, too," Josiah said. "Something had him concerned, or he would not have laid out a path for Pearl to ever en-counter Suzanne. He knew of the discreet relationship that his brother had with your sister, and I think he would protect that, unless it was absolutely necessary to expose Pearl to the truth."

"Is this Pearl fragile? I have little reason to venture out of the confines of the Paraiso, so I have never seen this grand house the captain avoided so desperately, or met his family. His Anglo life was none of my concern, though I liked him a great deal."

"I don't think Pearl was aware of how her father lived most of his life. He was away a lot."

Emilio tapped his fingers on the desk he was sitting at. "Captain Fikes is dead and buried for a couple of months. I do not think this has anything to do with him."

"I don't think so, either," Josiah said. "The livery in Austin burned down this morning. There was a body in the rubble. A body with a hole in the skull. I think it was there before the fire started."

"Juan Carlos?"

"I hope not. I went there to see him before I left town, to ask him to keep an eye on my house, on my son, Lyle."

"He was staying at the livery, next to the jail?"

"Does that surprise you?"

"Not considering all that I know about Juan Carlos. Sometimes I think he is plumb loco," Emilio said.

Josiah forced a smile. "He is brave."

"He is *bobo.* If he has brought harm to my sister or caused her any pain, I will kill him. As sure as I am sitting here, I will kill him."

Josiah cocked his eyebrow and shrugged his shoulders. "I don't doubt that." He hesitated, thought about leaving again, but couldn't just yet. "When was the last time you saw Suzanne?"

"The night before she disappeared. She closed the bar, oversaw the cleanup, and settled her accounts. It was a normal night. The next morning I went looking for her, and she was just gone. Her bed had not been slept in, and she did not have any travel plans. Everything was in its place."

"Except Suzanne," Josiah said.

Emilio nodded. "I have put the word out in the community that I have not seen her, but I have heard nothing in return. She was in no trouble that I can detect. But now that you've brought me this information concerning the fire, and the body, I am starting to become very worried."

"Me, too. Me, too," Josiah said.

■ ■ ■ ■

Night had settled in, and the air was moist and muggy, an unusual occurrence in Austin as far as Josiah knew. His clothes stuck to his skin, and the summer night was warm, almost hot. His lungs felt heavy and wet even though he was doing nothing but sitting on his horse, navigating his way toward the Red River.

He knew little about the weather in this part of Texas, if it was that different from his home place in Tyler, but he was glad there were only a few clouds in the night sky, a slight breeze, and a waning moon, just past full, to light his way.

Clipper, his Appaloosa, eased along the trail out of Austin with no great urgency, since Josiah's grasp was slack on the reins.

It had taken him far longer to leave the capital than he'd thought it would, but there was nothing he could do now but join the rest of the Ranger company and speak with his captain, Pete Feders, about what was going on in Austin. Feders might know something about what was happening since he spent a great deal of time in the capital city himself.

Josiah was conflicted about leaving, of

course, but he felt there was nothing left for him to do. He had to see to his own duties. The problem of the dead body at the livery was Rory Farnsworth's to contend with. Finding the killer, if there was one, and the identity of the body itself all also fell under the jurisdiction of the sheriff.

Josiah could only hope the body didn't belong to Juan Carlos. And he was certain that the whereabouts of a woman like Suzanne del Toro was of no interest to Farnsworth. Her welfare was in Emilio's hands. Something told Josiah it wasn't the first time that had happened, that Emilio'd had to rescue his sister, Suzanne, from some sort of trouble.

Frustrated, he trotted along, trying to clear his mind.

He kept his ears open for any sign of ambush, outlaw or Indian, but he wasn't too concerned about either.

He always kept an ear out for Indians, especially heading toward the Territory. An incident with an Indian when he was a boy had always made him uneasy about redskins. He figured there were good and bad ones, just like the Mexicans, or even Anglos, but still, there was something buried deep in him, a fear of sorts, that kept him alert on the trail.

After a while, maybe an hour or so, Josiah decided he had gone as far as he could and should stop and make camp.

The moon burned brightly overhead, and in the distance, a couple of coyotes yipped with enthusiasm. He could have kept on, but he was tired. It would be easier to find the Ranger camp in the daylight, and he would be better suited to a day of exercises after a good night's sleep. He had dozed off a couple of times already. Clipper would have kept on going, and who knows where they would have ended up if he had fallen asleep.

There was plenty of light to gather up some firewood. He had stopped in a spot that skirted a grove of towering oak trees on one side of the trail and on the other side a scrub-filled ravine that eased down to a stream that was running weakly. He could barely hear the trickle of water over some exposed rocks. The area wasn't drought-stricken, but it probably hadn't seen any rain in a good while.

He tied Clipper to a tree, but his lead was loose, allowing him to chew on some grass. Josiah built only a small cooking fire, since there was no need to keep himself warm, and fixed a meal of beans and johnnycakes. After spending a bit of time in the camp, he grew comfortable enough to take off his gun belt and set it aside on the bedroll he had laid out.

His rifle, a new model Winchester '73, was still in the scabbard on his saddle. He'd carried a Sharps rifle for a lot of years, but his sign-on money from the Rangers had allowed him to buy himself a new rifle. He was still getting accustomed to the weapon. It was the first time he had owned a repeating rifle, so he wasn't as proficient with it as some of the other Rangers who'd carried the rifle for a longer time. He was confident of his shooting skills, though. Confident that he would be just as good as any man in his company by the time the need arose.

Being a man that neither smoked tobacco nor drank alcohol, Josiah was left few vices to pass the time. Sometimes, he hummed, but he dared not sing out loud. He sounded worse than a mule braying in an empty barn. He lay down on the bedroll, on his back, and stared at the moonlit sky. It was almost so bright that he couldn't see any stars. He'd thought about counting them, knowing full well it wouldn't take long for him to fall into a deep sleep.

Counting stars was a far better use of his time than thinking about his life, his past. Of course, he worried about Lyle and hoped

Ofelia was getting along all right — but that was a small worry. The Mexican woman was more kin to him than she was a wet nurse, and he was certain she could handle any situation that arose. What he really hoped to avoid was thinking about Lily. If it had not been for their son, born at Lily's death, then Josiah would have prayed to die himself then, even though he wasn't a praying man. No . . . he wanted to avoid thinking about the family he no longer had, his beautiful wife and three daughters, all gone in the blink of an eye, no killer to blame except something that floated unseen in the air — a disease, a sickness. He wasn't a doctor, but he knew he was lucky — and had learned once again just how precarious life was in the first place.

Any thought of sleep was quickly dashed when he heard the rush of a horse's hooves heading toward him on the trail.

By the time Josiah had slapped on his gun belt and grabbed the Winchester out of the scabbard, he could see the silhouette of a man on a horse, rushing toward him at great speed.

There was no sign that the approaching man posed a threat, but it was late into the night, and there could have been more men coming; a gang would not have surprised

Josiah, since he had managed to make more than a few enemies over the years. He didn't know what to expect, but there was no use hiding. The camp was visible in the brightness of the moon, and the cooking fire still smoldered — nothing but a bed of glowing orange embers, but an indication of his presence.

Both of his weapons were loaded and ready.

Sweat beaded on his lip, and just for safety's sake, he edged up next to a big oak tree to give himself some cover.

The rider slowed once he spotted the camp, and shouted, "Hello, there! Anybody here?"

Josiah recognized the voice at once, lowered his rifle, and slid the Peacemaker back into his holster. "Over here, Elliot. Over here."

"Damn it, Wolfe, I was afeared you was dead. Captain Feders sent me to look for you. There's more Indian tussles brewin' up north, and Feders wants you along. Major Jones is headin' there, too, from what I understand, itchin' to see some action and prove his worth. Where the hell you been?"

Scrap Elliot was a young Ranger who had signed on with the Frontier Battalion under Captain Fikes nearly two months prior. He was still green behind the ears, not old enough to grow anything but fuzz on his lip, twenty years old if he was that, and he was, at most times, an annoyance to Josiah. But there was no mistaking that Elliot was an excellent horseman and a better shot than men twice his age. He might have been scrawny and rambunctious, but Scrap Elliot had proven his worth in the scuffle that had been fatal to Captain Fikes. In the end, he'd backed up the other Rangers to bring down the scoundrel, Charlie Langdon, who'd killed the captain.

"Rest your horse, Elliot. We're not going anywhere straightaway."

"But the captain said . . ."

"I'll handle the captain."

"But . . ."

"Don't push it, Elliot."

After a loud exhale, Scrap Elliot climbed off his horse and said, "Is those beans I smell, Wolfe?"

Josiah nodded. "They are. Help yourself." He slid the Winchester into the scabbard, then tossed a log on the fire. It blazed up almost instantly.

Scrap had already produced a metal plate out of his saddlebag and was shoveling beans into his mouth like he hadn't had a decent meal all week. Josiah smiled, then looked away. Regardless of how much Elliot annoyed him, it was good to see a familiar face after the kind of day he'd had.

CHAPTER 6

Josiah and Scrap were on the trail before the sun broke the horizon. The wind had shifted from the northwest, and the mugginess of the previous day had blown away. There was a taste of rain in the air, sweet moisture that had all of the trees and plants standing on end, like they were waiting for water to drop on their tongues, to sate their thirst.

"Be faster to run the Chisholm. I came down thata way — it's just a couple miles east."

Josiah nodded. "We'll skirt it, stay out of the way of herds. Cows might wander over this way anyhow. This route looks to have been used by more than one herd recently the way it is. I can still smell them."

"Can't follow a trail that ain't rightly there like a street in Austin. I'm just lucky I stumbled on to you," Scrap said.

"You are. We better speed it up, I need to

make up some time."

"You can say that again. Captain Feders said you'd better be dead or next to dyin' when I found you. At least have a good excuse for staying out of camp."

"I think I do, but what Pete Feders thinks is not up to me. He's yet to show himself, show what kind of captain he will be. He's got some deep boots to fill."

Scrap agreed, then said, "I can't say I've missed your contrariness, Wolfe. You always remind me of a longhorn and why I never aimed to be a cowboy. Those cattle can be sweet as a lamb one second and mean as a badger the next. You, too." He paused, saw the hard look lock itself on Josiah's face, making his strong jaw jut out even a little farther than normal. "But," Scrap added, "it'll be nice to have you in the company where you belong. Camp wasn't the same without you around."

Josiah thought that was a compliment, but he wasn't sure. It was always hard to tell whether Scrap was being sincere or was adding a dash of sarcasm to the conversation. Didn't really matter, he finally decided, relaxing a bit. He was just glad to be on the trail with somebody he trusted.

Scrap's horse was a blue roan mare named Missy. He handled Missy with an unspoken gentleness, and they seemed to know each other well, readily able to compensate for shifts in weight and direction, to understand the press of one leg or the other like it was a request and not a command.

Josiah had seen Scrap and Missy do some amazing riding, and he was secretly envious of the boy's skill. Not that Clipper and Josiah didn't have a relationship of sorts. Clipper had alerted Josiah to more than one dangerous incident and had gotten him out of some scrapes that he wouldn't have otherwise escaped. It was just that their relationship was different. Maybe, Josiah decided, it was just the difference in age. Scrap was willing to risk more of himself, run harder, ride faster, than anyone else. Josiah remembered those days, though they seemed like a long time ago. Risk was definitely more appropriate for the young ones to take, and that left him wondering if he should have left Lyle in the first place. Maybe his place wasn't on the trail but at home, making sure his son could see somebody that was kin to him on a daily basis. Maybe, just maybe, his time for adventures had come to an end. It sure was something to consider . . . but he was not turning back; he still had something to prove to himself, even though he wasn't quite sure what that something was just yet.

"You ready to ride?" Josiah said aloud.

Scrap looked over at him and nodded, then urged Missy on by loosening the reins, leaning forward, and pressing hard enough with his boots to let her know she had the right to run, to put her head to the wind.

Josiah smiled, and he and Clipper followed suit, riding full-out as the sun crested the horizon in the east.

If they were lucky, they'd make Waco by nightfall.

There were some kerosene lamps burning dimly in a few windows of the section of town they'd come to, but the streets were clear, no horses coming and going, no coaches sitting in wait. Everyone, it seemed, was inside. Which was a surprise, given that the warmth of the day was still palpable.

There were muted voices to be heard, music in the distance, but Waco, or this part of Waco, didn't appear to be set for an extreme amount of rowdiness. Of course, there had been few herds on the trail riding up from Austin, very little cattle moving through. The heat of summer normally quelled a lot of that commerce, but not all of it. There had to be a steady supply of cows for the growing population in the plains and the frontier.

It was just after nightfall, and Josiah and Scrap were covered with dust.

The promise of rain earlier in the day had never fulfilled itself. The clouds never grew big enough to fully let loose, to satisfy the thirst of the ground and the plants that lived off it. A strong wind finally blew the clouds off to the east, bringing behind it a wave of air so hot it was like sticking your nose as close as you could to one of those lamps in the windows.

Hot summer days were normal in Texas, and the weather had a habit of changing whenever it decided to, on a whim, or like a malevolent child, a long stewing of anger suddenly unleashed. The run north had been hampered only by the sheer force of the heat. Rain would have been more welcome, though it would have muddied the trail and slowed their progress.

They had skirted the Chisholm until they closed in on Waco, wanting to avoid the slight backup of herds that had made it this far and were waiting to cross the suspension bridge over the Brazos River.

It would be a short wait, considering the time of year, but Josiah was in no mood to deal with a mass of stinking cows, or to take the chance of getting hung up. He didn't think they had time, nor was it in his plans to pay a toll to cross the bridge. He'd made the trip recently, from Austin to Waco, so he wasn't entirely unsure of where he was going, though he knew he was taking a risk by spending the night in a less than desirable section of town.

He'd led them into a section of Waco he would have surely hoped to avoid under most any other circumstances — but his experiences leaving Austin and his uncertainty about the fate of Juan Carlos and Suzanne del Toro forced him to go places he would not normally go.

He and Scrap had arrived directly in the Reservation, a section of the city similar to Austin's Hell's Half Acre. Prostitution was not regulated or endorsed by the city, though most men thought it a fair and accountable business, so long as it was far enough away from the proper side of society to flourish. The business side of the street in the Reservation was large enough to accommodate all the cowboys and trail drivers that wandered in off the Chisholm, as well as treat the regular population of Waco to a night out on the town if it was so desired. The whole of the area was located between Washington Street and Jefferson Avenue and ran on to Third Street all the way down to the river.

High-priced prostitutes did their business and lived in fine houses, perfectly white-washed and tended to, on Third Street. A couple of saloons and markets sat between the houses and the river. The girls of lower aspirations worked the river, or as close to it as they could, taking advantage of the traffic crossing the bridge. The river's edge was lined with shacks and was accessed only by walking down a meandering, often muddy path, where you'd have to watch for critters of a bad attitude — snakes, scorpions, and humans — who meant to survive any way they could.

Josiah and Scrap had come to a stop just off Third Street, and if it was possible that night, Josiah thought he would ask around about Suzanne del Toro and Juan Carlos.

He was certain that if there was any news to discover, it would be found in the better part of the Reservation, knowing Suzanne del Toro's taste for the finer things in life.

Stopping off in the Reservation was a logical choice, rather bold of Josiah, but not out of hand or character, since he could not get either of his Mexican friends and their welfare off his mind. His only fault was not sharing the information, or the cause of his decision, with Scrap Elliot. The less the boy knew about his choices, the better. He did worry, though, about exposing Scrap to the Reservation, but something told Josiah that Scrap had visited the inside of a whorehouse more than once already in his short life. If not, it was likely to happen soon. Rangers might be men of high morals, but they were still men spending most of their time in the company of other men. The touch of a woman's skin was the cure to a lot of ills, a thirst some men could never quench, and a desire held even by those of the strictest mind. Josiah felt he was the latter, and his brief tryst with Suzanne del Toro, less than two months prior, had pulled him out of a grieving funk so deep he thought at one point he would never be able to pull himself out of it without dying. He owed her a certain amount of credit for his current state, and to settle the bill he aimed to find out what had happened to her.

"You need to find a livery. There should be one close by," Josiah said to Scrap, dismounting easily off the saddle and patting Clipper as he did. The Appaloosa snorted in kind.

"You sure you want to stop here, Wolfe? You know where we are, don't ya?"

"I know where we are."

"I never figured you as the type."

"The type for what?"

"The kind who likes the ladies who charge for a . . . service."

"Who said that was my aim?"

"Well, if it ain't, there are places to stay in town that might be a little quieter."

"I've had enough quiet lately."

"Whatever you say." Scrap sat comfortably atop Missy, a big smile on his face, looking down at Josiah. "Won't bother me none. I still got some coin in my pocket."

"You'd be wise to hang on to your wages."

"I better see if I can sleep in the livery then."

"That might not be a bad idea, but I doubt you'd be welcome."

"When do we get to be equals, Wolfe? When do you get to stop treating me like a child?"

"When you stop acting like one."

"I ain't a lost sheep, and I sure as hell don't need to be bossed around by you."

Josiah took a deep breath. "You'd save yourself a whole lot of trouble if you'd just go do what I asked you to do."

"And if I don't?"

"Then I'll order you, seeing as I'm your sergeant. But I'd rather not. I'll just wait here until you come back. Looks like there's probably a livery up there and around the corner. I just saw a few horsemen slow and turn."

Scrap scowled at Josiah, who had pointed to the corner, grabbed Missy's reins tightly, and hurried off down the street without saying another word.

Josiah stood there shaking his head, regretting his relief when he first saw Scrap Elliot ride up on the trail. At the moment, he'd just as soon have been alone.

Chapter 7

The foyer inside the house was less than grand, but well appointed nonetheless. Josiah and Scrap stood waiting after ringing a bell at the counter. The inside of the place was thick with the smell of perfume, not real flowery, a smell Josiah couldn't identify, nor did he think he wanted to. Air heavy with toilet water was foreign to him. He'd prefer to be surrounded by the gassy excrement of a livery full of horses, which Scrap had found around the corner. It surprised him that Scrap had made a beeline back to the hotel. He had figured Scrap would find a distraction of the female variety or two along the way.

Scrap quickly plopped down in a highback chair covered in purple velvet and brass buttons to hold the tucks at the sides and back. Josiah was sure it was just a matter of time before his fellow Ranger's impatience and immaturity brought them a dose of trouble — again.

Red-and-gold striped wallpaper covered the walls, and on top of the polished wood-slat floors was a rug that looked like it had come from far across the seas, maybe the East, from China — it had intricate hand-woven designs that looked like the language marks Josiah had seen in a laundry once. The foyer itself could not compare to a fancy hotel like the Menger in San Antonio, but it was big enough to accommodate a fully stocked bar with six stools, two sitting tables for card playing, and a staircase that shot straight up to the second floor. No curves or fancy banisters, just a utilitarian means of access to the upstairs. The counter was nothing more than a hole, the size of a large picture, cut into the wall. The front door and the stairway were the only ways out if it became necessary.

Josiah stood stiffly, his hand next to the bell on the counter. He could hear a low mumble of voices coming from the back room. Female to female. Blocked by walls and a heavy tapestry curtain, too far away to understand any words. He didn't want to seem impatient, so he waited before ringing the bell again. A newspaper lay on the counter, the *Waco Daily Examiner.* It was yesterday's paper.

Scrap sat in the chair, shifting his weight constantly and tapping his fingers nervously. Maybe he was wrong, Josiah thought. Maybe Scrap had never been in a whorehouse before. Josiah found the conclusion a little surprising, then picked up the newspaper before him and perused it:

George Axley is in proud ownership of a new horse. The training is going remarkably well, though one of the excellencies which George must contend with is that the spirited stallion will not let anyone approach him or mount him except his owner and master. George is willing to lend his new horse to anybody, but there are two of them to consult, George and the horse itself, and without the horse's consent, it is not worth taking the chance.

The Mite Society meets at Mrs. Cooley's by night.

The old Advance Office, at the corner of Austin and Fourth streets, is in the process of being torn down so it can be replaced by an elegant, new three-storey brick building to house the office. Viva la progress.

Masonic News: *The following members of Waco Lodge No. 92, A F & A M, have been appointed to a committee to visit and attend to the sick and infirmed during the month of July: J.P. Macy, F.L. Harris, A.P. Hills, J.T. Jones and B.M. Powell. By order of the W.M. — L.L. Chestwater, Secretary.*

A deadly row *occurred on the riverfront two nights ago, and two men were left dead. Abe Henson was killed and stabbed in three places, one of them being the neck, and shot once in the chest. Tom Kennedy was killed by being hit in the head with a heavy object. His body was found just inside a shack that had been set on fire. Witnesses, who chose to remain nameless, saw a man and a woman, both of Mexican descent, fleeing from the fire. Neither has been seen since or questioned in connection with the killings. The shack burned to the ground. Like they all should.*

Josiah set the paper down, not wanting to read anymore, and drew a deep, concerned breath.

Footsteps approached from behind the heavy curtain.

"Come on, Scrap, let's go." Josiah headed for the door just as a tall, curvy blond woman dressed in a tight-fitting green satin dress appeared from behind the tapestry that separated the lobby and counter from the back rooms of the whorehouse.

"What can I do for you gentlemen?" The woman's voice was soft and buttery.

Scrap bolted up from the fancy chair, his jaw agape as he stared at the woman.

"Sorry, ma'am, we made a mistake. We have no business here," Josiah said, pushing open the door to leave.

Scrap was frozen in place, his eyes glued to the woman's chest. The satin dress was cut low, and the view for Scrap was full, since nearly three-quarters of the woman's healthy breasts were exposed.

"Looks to me like at least one of you has found what he was looking for." The woman locked eyes with Scrap, smiled in a naughty way, then winked at the boy. "You look like lots of fun, boy."

"Scrap, let's go. Now."

"Another time, ma'am," Scrap said, doffing his hat and heading for the door.

"Oh," she purred, "what a shame. You look like you have some pent-up spirit."

Scrap stopped. "Oh, I got spirit all right."

Josiah reached out and grabbed Scrap by the shirt collar and pulled him out the door.

"Damn it, Wolfe, what in the Sam Hill are

you doing? I thought you wanted to see the happy side of Waco, not the angry side of loco. Come on, what are you thinking?" he said, slapping Josiah's grip away from his shirt and stumbling off the front steps. "That girl was pretty. Downright pretty enough to let loose a week's wages, don't you think?"

"We need to go."

"Where to?"

"Down to the riverfront."

"Hot damn," Scrap whistled and followed after Josiah, his step enthusiastic, the disappointed look on his face replaced with curiosity and anticipation.

The path that led down to the riverfront was only visible because of the waning full moon. The night before, the moon had allowed Josiah to travel into the night and had made it possible for Scrap to find him.

On this night, the light from the sky was not quite as bright, but bright enough to lead them both down a path that was, to say the least, precarious and full of uncertainty. There was no mistaking the need for Josiah to go down to the riverfront, to see for himself the burned shack and perhaps pick up on the trail of Juan Carlos and Suzanne del Toro. The newspaper had set him on the path, and he thought it a stroke of luck to find the mention without exposing Scrap to more temptation than he already had.

There was no description of the two Mexicans, and Josiah sure hoped he was wrong . . . hoped Suzanne and Juan Carlos were south, far from Waco, and not involved in the deadly row, as the paper had called it. All things considered, though, he had to assume the two mentioned in the newspaper were his friends.

Josiah had hoped to gain some information, perhaps even find them in Waco, but he had hoped it would be in a better and safer circumstance than where he was being led. It looked like trouble continued to follow Suzanne and Juan Carlos, and the events that surrounded their presence in this town eerily echoed the events Josiah had left in Austin.

Was it possible that they were on a spree of madness? Living like outlaws? If so, what was their motive? Josiah wondered. What would cause them to stand outside the law in such a cavalier and open way, committing murder? For what gain? The entire list of questions and assumptions made no sense to Josiah — mostly because he could not see either of them, Juan Carlos or Suzanne del Toro, as cold-blooded killers.

Scrap would find out soon enough what was going on, what Josiah's true aims were in taking them down to the riverfront, once Wolfe started asking questions. For now, his main objective, other than pushing out of his mind any thought about joining the Ranger camp as soon as possible, was traversing the path as carefully as he could.

There was a raw smell to the air, fishy and rank, rising upward from the river. The thickness of the air also carried the smell of coal oil, and it took Josiah a moment to adjust to the putrid environment, the combination of all the smells.

He could see torches burning in the distance, reflecting off the river. The water looked black, smooth as ice, with the moon lying on the surface like it had fallen from the sky into the river, drowned, and then been left to float on its own, unnoticed or unattended. The current didn't look like it was moving at all. The water on the surface was still, the pull of it underneath, hidden by the darkness.

"Damn it," Scrap said.

Josiah stopped, quickly edged his hand to the Peacemaker, and gripped it, ready. "What's the matter?"

"I stepped in a hole."

Josiah turned to face Scrap. They were in a thicket of trees, and the path was lined with waist-high nettles and ivies. "Are you all right?"

"I think so."

"Walk it off."

"I twisted my ankle."

"So you can't walk?"

Scrap limped forward. "Not very easy. It hurts like hell."

"You think you broke it?"

"Nah, the hole was deep, and I wasn't paying no attention. I just twisted it, like I said."

"You're lucky you didn't get bit by a snake or a badger."

"Leave it to you, Wolfe. Always looking on the bright side of things, while I can't hardly stand up."

Josiah had eased his hand off the Peacemaker once he realized there was no threat, other than Scrap's lack of sense. He stooped and allowed Scrap to throw his arm over his shoulder. He was none too thrilled to be used as a crutch. They started walking onward, down toward the shacks that lined the riverfront. Josiah was going to dump Scrap on the first logical sitting place he came to, a bench hopefully.

"Did you have any older brothers?" Josiah asked.

Scrap shook his head no. "Just a sister. I done told you that, Wolfe, why?"

Josiah had forgotten that Scrap had a sister, since he tried to ignore the kid's rage about the Comanche attack on his home. "Never mind."

"What, Wolfe?" Scrap limped along. Their pace was methodical and slow. The boy looked like he should be light as a feather, unless he was hanging on you. He must have been all muscle and bone. Luckily, they didn't have far to go. They were about halfway down the trail.

"I said, never mind. I was thinking you needed toughening up as a child, but I should have just kept my mouth shut. I forgot about your unfortunate circumstances. My apologies."

"Ain't nothing. It's been a long time. I sure am anxious to get back north and face down some of those redskins, though."

"Vengeance might likely get you killed. Instead of stepping in a hole, you might come face-to-face with a Comanche."

"What would you know about that?"

"I have my own tales from when I was a boy," Josiah said.

A hard silence fell between the two men.

They walked forward, a limp and a swing at a time. The first shack was in sight, about twenty yards down the path. A torch burned brightly, stuck in the ground just outside the open door. A silhouette of a woman stood waiting, still, like a statue.

A crew of voices caught Josiah's attention. He stopped, and Scrap looked to him to protest, but his attention was drawn to the voices as well.

Three men came around the corner in between the first shack and the second and walked toward them quickly, spurs clanking, dusters flying open, the moonlight catching the full stock of bullets in their belts, rifles tight in their hands, their faces hidden in the shadows cast off their hats. Each of the men wore a badge, a silver five-pointed star, and that didn't fully surprise Josiah.

It was like three angry steers had been cut loose from the herd and were taking to the trail on their own, and nothing was going to deter them. Anything in their way was going to get trounced, smashed under the weight and heft of their intention.

Josiah was not one to be intimidated, but he knew Scrap was more of a detriment than a help, and would have been even if he hadn't twisted his ankle, so he eased off the trail, pushing his way in the nettle as gently as he could.

The men didn't acknowledge Josiah or Scrap as they approached, just marched forward, eyes to the top of the trail, to the buildings of finer Waco that looked down over the river. Whatever their mission was, it was urgent. They were just short of trotting.

"Keep your mouth shut," Josiah whispered to Scrap, as the three men neared them.

Scrap started to say something, then restrained himself.

Josiah was impressed but was too interested in the three men to acknowledge the restraint, even silently.

It was hard to make out any of their features, but as the men passed, the one on the far side of the trail slowed and squinted at Josiah, who had caught sight of the man in the moonlight and recognized him, too. Or thought he did. The man didn't seem certain of the recognition himself.

Josiah looked down and tapped his hat forward as softly and indiscriminately as he could. The man must have decided that Josiah's face wasn't worth checking into further, and he quickly regained his pace, a look of uncertainty molded on his face.

" 'Tis going to be a black day when we

103

catch those two," the man said.

His voice had a lilt, an Irish lilt, and in the cast of light from the moon, Josiah was sure the man's skin was fair and his hair the color of rage and anger — red as the fire burning in front of the shack.

"Shut up, O'Reilly," the man in the middle said.

Then Josiah knew for certain that the man was who he'd thought he was. The man was a scoundrel, an outlaw, a man who not two months prior had set Josiah on a path to match wits with another outlaw who was holding his son hostage — the spark that precipitated the permanent move to Austin after it was all said and done. The outlaw, Charlie Langdon, was a dead man, hanged in Tyler . . . but Liam O'Reilly had escaped the shoot-out that had brought Langdon to justice.

And now he had obviously collected a new set of friends, who wore badges on their chests, set on doing harm wherever they went. Of that, Josiah was certain. A man like Liam O'Reilly only wanted to help himself, and no one else.

CHAPTER 8

"Come on," Josiah said, pulling Scrap down the trail as fast as he could limp. "We need to get out of here."

"You see a ghost?"

"Something like that."

They stopped just before reaching the first shack. The silhouette of the waiting woman was no longer visible. Once the three men hurried past, the door of the shack had eased shut. A crack of flickering light shone out onto the ground, a sliver. Josiah was certain that he and Scrap were being watched, judged as potential customers for the wares offered on the riverfront, or as two lawmen looking to shake things up. As far as he was concerned, they were neither at the moment.

Scrap was panting and reached down to rub away the pain in his leg. "Damn it."

"Try walking."

"Now?"

"Look, if you were a horse I just might have to shoot you. We need to get out of here as quick as we can."

"Why is that, Wolfe? You're not making any sense to me at all. Why in the hell did we come down here in the first place? Not for a visit with the ladies, was it?"

Josiah shook his head no. "Why would I do that?"

"If you have to ask . . ."

"I don't," Josiah snapped. "And you'd do us both a fine favor to walk off that limp and leave any notion about the ladies behind."

Scrap shot a look at Josiah that could only be interpreted as hateful, but he did what he was told. At first, his steps were tepid, pain grimacing across his face, but after making a short, wobbly circle around Josiah, the boy started to walk a bit more normally, the pain falling slowly from his face. He still limped, though, and took uncertain steps, like it was the first time he'd set foot on the earth, like he lacked the confidence for any kind of journey — which, of course, was unfortunate, since they still had a great distance to travel to join up with their company of Rangers.

"Good. Looks like I won't have to shoot you," Josiah said.

"Funny, Wolfe."

Scrap came to a stop. They were standing shoulder to shoulder.

"You think you need to see the doc while we're here in Waco?" Josiah asked. His tone of voice had changed, modified from tense to concerned. It was probably going to be a brief modification, but Josiah hated to see anyone, or anything, in pain.

"Nah, I'll be right as rain come tomorrow. I told you I just twisted it." Scrap paused and followed Josiah's gaze up the trail. "Now, are you gonna tell me what in the heck is going on or not?"

"Not much that you have to worry about. I just think we need to get out of Waco as soon as possible."

"Why's that?"

"Is 'why' your favorite word?"

"It is when I'm left in the dark. When I'm treated like I'm still on the teat."

"You're not?"

"I think my shooting saved your skin once. I don't deserve to be treated like a little tot. Why are you being so skittish, Wolfe? It ain't like you at all. Not that you're ever the most pleasant riding companion, but I think I'm in good company when you have a gun in your hand and my back's your cause and yours is mine. But ever since we met up on

107

the trail, you've been acting stranger than usual, like a man with a secret, and to be real honest with you, I'm not sure that I appreciate the way you're treatin' me. We're both Rangers, Wolfe . . . and you've got rank. I know that. You don't have to go rubbin' my face in it all the damn time."

Josiah took a deep breath, then spent a second considering what Scrap had just said. He'd pretty much been laid out, and he had to accept, for once, that Scrap Elliot just might be more grown-up than Josiah had thought possible.

"You're right," Josiah finally said. "OK . . . I think I recognized one of those lawmen, only the last time I saw him, he was on the other side of the law. And I think our friend Juan Carlos might be in trouble. But we're outmanned here. If anything is going to come of this, we'll need help. Ranger help. I don't think we can trust the local law."

"Juan Carlos is your friend, not mine. That Mexican's nothing but trouble if you ask me. I don't trust him."

Josiah wasn't sure if Scrap knew the truth about Juan Carlos — that he was only half-Mexican and the brother to his lost hero, Captain Fikes. He wasn't going to be the one to tell him. The heritage of blood was not the issue at the moment, anyway. Far from it. Those entanglements were of the past, however recent, and Josiah was certain that the mixed blood that ran through Juan Carlos's veins was not contributing to the situation at hand. He hoped not, anyway.

"That's my mistake, then, assuming Juan Carlos is your friend," Josiah said. "But regardless, there was a killing down here a night ago that's gone unsolved."

"Makes sense why the law is out in force, then."

"It does. If the law is in the right hands."

"Not our jurisdiction," Scrap said.

"Not at the moment. There was a similar killing in Austin before I left. May just be a coincidence, but I don't think so. Not now, not since I saw the Irishman."

"The outlaw?"

"The outlaw, Liam O'Reilly."

"He rode with Charlie Langdon and his gang."

"He did."

"Why would he be wearin' a badge now?"

"Don't know," Josiah said. "But I need to get word to the sheriff. And we need to get to camp. We're going to need more Rangers than just the two of us to sort this thing out if my hunches are correct. The whole town of Waco might just be set for more trouble than they're aware of."

"We can't let that happen."

"I don't think we can, either. But we have to be careful not to put ourselves in a corner."

"Especially if that lawman really was Liam O'Reilly."

"That's something to consider. It might not have been him. If it was, he might have recognized me and maybe not. I think he would have stopped and confronted us if he had truly been aware of my presence."

"You think he's on his own?"

"Charlie Langdon was hanged for all his misdeeds, but he had a lot of friends that scattered once he was brought to justice. All three of those fellas could have been associates in the cause of that meanness — or not. It's hard to say."

"How'd you know about the killings?"

"Saw the aftermath of one with my own eyes. Read about the other one in the newspaper while we were standing in that whorehouse in town."

"That's why we scurried out of there?"

Josiah nodded. "It is."

"And all that time, I thought we were up for some fun," Scrap said.

"Now's not the time for fun."

"I suppose not," Scrap answered. He walked around in a circle again, this time planting his feet more confidently.

"You think you're up to walking on your own?"

"Yup."

"Good, I want to take a look at that burned shack."

"Ain't going to be anything there but ashes."

"Maybe so, but I still want to take a look."

"You ain't worried about O'Reilly circling up behind us?"

"I'm always worried about that. But you got my back, right?"

"I do," Scrap said, a smile growing quickly on his face. "That I do."

Two torches burned brightly next to the ruins of the burned-out shack. The path was narrow, not as wide as a street, but wide enough to get a wagon down if necessary. All told there were probably twenty shacks lined up at the river. The bridge was close, reflecting on the surface of the water in the distance. There was no one making passage this late in the night, but there was a herd of cows close, probably waiting to cross in the morning. Their low moos were infrequent, but highly identifiable.

The fishy smell of the river grew stronger the closer Josiah and Scrap got to the water, and the ground was moist, not arid and cracked like a lot of the trail had been along the way.

No one approached them. They were left to themselves. Josiah had expected someone to approach them, especially from the first shack — he was certain they were being watched from there — but they weren't even propositioned or called on to view any of the girls standing in wait just inside the shacks. It was like the word had been put out that they were diseased, to be avoided. That was just fine with Josiah. He wanted a quick look at the shack, then they'd be off.

It was easy enough to find since, as Scrap had predicted, it was nothing more than a pile of ashes and a few charred beams that had not burned completely through. It was a ten-by-twenty square of nothingness; everything that had been there prior was lost. The smell reminded Josiah of the livery fire, with the exception of the burnt remains of a human being. There was nothing here that could compare with that smell — it was unforgettable, and thankfully absent from this aftermath.

Both shacks on either side of the ash pile were dark, empty, with the exception of a man, his back to the wall of one of them, his head down, covered with a sombrero, his knees pulled in tight, like he was sleeping. His face was hidden, but there was no question he was alive. A loud snore escaped out from under the floppy Mexican hat on occasion. Other than that, the man could have been a statue he was so still.

Josiah paid the man no mind. The shack he sat in front of was the closest to the river, with the sound of running water slightly discernible, but there was no activity inside it.

In the distance, someone laughed. A little closer, someone strummed a guitar. Life was returning to the riverfront, now that the lawmen were gone, along with the uncertainty about their origin. It was obviously a relief.

A door opened in a shack two doors farther on, and Josiah looked up in time to see a young woman walk outside. She was a head shorter than Scrap and wore a loose dress with no shoes, and it was easy to discern from the light of the torches and moonlight that the woman wore no undergarments. She lit a cigarette, exhaled a puff of smoke, and looked away.

Josiah did the same, looked away and tried to ignore her, hoping she would stay where she was at. He turned his attention back to the rubble, hoping she hadn't noticed him, or didn't care about his presence.

"What in tarnation do you think you're gonna find, Wolfe?"

"Go grab one of those torches."

Scrap scowled, then eased over to the torch, treating his ankle like it were made out of fine porcelain, taking assured but soft steps. He grabbed the torch and swung it toward Josiah, casting a new ray of light on the burned shack. The man under the sombrero snored loudly, coughed, then moved, turning his back to the light.

Josiah looked up at the noise, at the man moving, then went about walking through the ashes, slowly. "Don't know what I'll find. Just looking for anything that might tell me what happened. Or if it's like the fire in Austin."

Scrap stopped at the edge of the rubble and held the torch steadily. "I ain't coming near that mess."

"No need."

"I'll kind of be glad to get out of here."

"Why do you say that?" Josiah asked, stopping, looking over his shoulder.

"Because I'm not feelin' real welcome at the moment," Scrap answered.

Josiah looked up toward Scrap, then froze. It was like he had looked up and suddenly found himself in a nest of snakes, or in the middle of a storm he hadn't seen coming.

The woman who had stepped out of the shack a moment earlier was standing behind Scrap, a little gun pressed firmly to the back of the young Ranger's head.

The gun was probably a .22 that could be concealed easy enough, but there was no place to tuck it, and besides, the woman didn't look like she was in the mood to hide — or sell — anything.

"You boys are pokin' around someplace you shouldn't be," the woman said. "Don't you move, there." She nodded at Josiah.

"No worry, ma'am," Josiah said. "Just take it easy."

"I take it any way I can. Now, tell me what you're looking for."

Before Josiah could say anything, Scrap jumped in and said, "We're Rangers, lady. We ain't outlaws."

"Rangers. Really? Texas Rangers in Waco wanderin' around at night on the riverfront. Is that right?" the woman said.

"It is," Josiah said.

"New Rangers?" the woman asked, her eyebrow cocked up.

Josiah nodded. "That we are, ma'am, both of us are with the Frontier Battalion. I'm out of Austin myself. We're on our way up north to join our company, up Red River way."

"You got a long way to go."

"We do."

Josiah eyed Scrap forcefully, silently pleading with the boy to keep his mouth shut and let him do all the talking.

"What's your name?"

"Wolfe. Josiah Wolfe. That there is Scrap Elliot."

The woman pulled the gun away from Scrap's head, and it disappeared quickly back under her dress. "Well, why didn't you say so?"

CHAPTER 9

Josiah carefully made his way out of the rubble — curious and unconvinced that the woman's sudden show of hospitality was genuine. His Peacemaker was holstered, but he wore a swivel rig, which allowed him to shoot the gun without drawing it out of the holster if the need arose. He'd not likely shoot to kill the woman, but he'd do what he had to in order to protect Scrap, so he watched his step among the ashes, but he never took his eyes off the whore, either.

Scrap sighed loudly, like he was relieved and angry all at once. He turned to the woman, his teeth clasped together forcefully. "You could have got yourself killed."

The woman was barely more than a girl.

She looked like she was eighteen if she was lucky, even though her hard blue eyes suggested she had lived twice that long. There was a flitter of softness about her, though, now that she had relaxed and stepped away from Scrap, situating herself directly between him and the front door of her shack. It was obvious that her short life had not been a happy one. A smile would have changed her demeanor from sour to golden in a quick shake, but it sure didn't look like she had much to smile about or had practiced a happy facial expression in quite some time.

There was no sign of the little .22 she carried, but Josiah was certain she had her own wariness to contend with. The stingy gun was within reach, he was sure of that.

"Killed by the likes of you?" the girl said with a chuckle. "I've seen rats that are mean, boy, trust me. Rats that'll tear your eyes out if you let 'em get near you. You ain't a rat. At least not that kind."

"By one of us, then. Either one of us could have mistook you for an enemy and shot first, then asked questions," Scrap answered. "Rangers have been known to do such things and be justified for the safety of the action."

Josiah couldn't keep his eyes off her. It wasn't that the girl didn't have some fine attributes. She did. They were just difficult to see in the moonlight, under the hard shell she wore, at least as far as Josiah was concerned.

He made his way to Scrap and eyed him with a glare, a silent suggestion to shut his mouth, even though there was serious doubt that Scrap could read facial expressions any more than he could take a direct order.

"You know of us, then?" Josiah said.

"I know of you. Word's out that you're on the hunt for some information about a mutual acquaintance that we both share."

There was a hint of an accent in her voice that wasn't Texan but more like Tennessee or Kentucky. Josiah had fought in both places in the War Between the States, and all of the accents of that region ran together in his mind.

Each day was one day farther away from the death, blood, and downright terror he had witnessed and participated in as a soldier — but those memories still stuck with him, and nothing more than a voice, an accent, could transport him back in time.

He had no choice but to relive those terrible memories all over again. It was like walking into a kitchen with the smell of baking bread permeating the whole house, and being reminded of his mother.

That was a comfort. This girl's voice was not a comfort. It made him even more leery, on edge.

"And that acquaintance would be?" Josiah asked.

"Fat Susie."

"The horse?" Scrap interjected. "Why in the heck would you be lookin' for news about Captain Fikes's old horse? I thought that horse was dead. You gave the Widow Fikes the ear after she told you to kill it."

"The woman the horse was named after. Not the horse."

"Oh," Scrap said. "The whore." He glanced over to the girl, whose face flushed red. "Sorry about that, ma'am. I didn't mean you no disrespect. Sometimes I don't think my brain is connected to my tongue."

"That makes two of us," Josiah said under his breath. He nodded at the girl. "You're right. I'm looking for a sign of Suzanne del Toro and another man, Juan Carlos. Juan Carlos Montegné. Do you know of him?"

"Can't say that I do," the girl answered. "Why don't you come up and sit, take a load off? Any friend of Fat Susie's has nothing to fear here. I got some Arbuckle's inside and a few biscuits I can share."

Scrap looked eagerly to Josiah.

"I suppose it wouldn't hurt," Josiah said.

"Good. Don't mind the mess. Things have been all amiss since that shack burned and those two men was killed the other night," the girl said, turning to walk up to the shack. "Ain't hardly had a chance to settle myself to what happened there's been so much coming and going around here."

"I have some questions about that," Josiah said.

"I figured you might." She made her way to the door of the shack.

Josiah and Scrap followed her up there, but Josiah stopped before stepping up on the small porch.

Scrap nearly ran into him, and the girl stopped, too, pulling open the curtain that acted as a door to her home, to her place of business.

"Just so you understand, we're not buying anything," Josiah said.

"Who said I was offerin' anything?"

A slight smile crossed Josiah's face. "My apologies."

"Not necessary. I know about you, Ranger Wolfe."

"You know our names, but we don't know yours."

"Maudie. Maudie Mae Johnson. Most people around here just call me Mae. Kids, bein' mean and all, call me Maddie 'cause I ain't got no use for their teasin'."

"Nice to meet you, Maudie Mae Johnson," Josiah said, following her inside the shack.

He hadn't thought about children living on the riverfront, and he didn't let his mind stay there, because it would surely lead him back to missing Lyle, wondering if leaving him was such a good thing.

"It sure is, Mae," Scrap said. His limp was almost gone, like he had drunk some kind of miracle tonic that made all the pain and tenderness in his ankle instantly disappear.

The shack itself was constructed out of pieces of wood that had more than likely been scavenged from the banks of the river and the surrounding area.

The corners were barely square, and the floor was nothing more than hard dirt. There were two rooms, if they could be called that, so the shack was separated in half. The sleeping quarter was walled off with a couple of patchwork quilts. The quilts themselves bore circular designs and looked like they had been hanging there since Lincoln was alive and well, sitting in the office of the president.

The mystery of what lay behind the quilts would have to remain one.

But the front room — again, if it could be called that — was sparse, as well. A high-backed chair with a cane-woven seat sat in the far corner, next to a stove and a small pit that was used for heat. A coffeepot sat on a grate, and the embers were dim, almost burned out. Two crates sat in front of the stove in a semicircle.

"It ain't much," Mae said. "But it's better than where I came from. Have a seat." She swept her hand outward, a generous offer considering she had little else but a place to sit and a place to lie.

"And where was that?" Josiah asked, sitting warily on the only chair.

"Arkansas, by way of Illinois, the southern part, near Olney, Richland County. You know of it?"

Scrap shook his head no, as he sat on the crate next to Josiah.

Mae stoked the fire with some twigs, saving the bigger logs for use if she had to. The smoke left the shack through an open chimney, a metal pipe exiting through the thin wall.

It was a wonder, Josiah thought, that more shacks didn't burn to the ground if they were constructed like this one.

"Can't say that I've been in those parts," Josiah said. "How'd you get here?"

"How'd anybody get here?" Mae said. "On the way to somewhere else. I took the long way, through Indian Territory. Thought California was the place where all my dreams would come true. We all did. I was ten when we left, just after the war ended. Lots of people thought it was time to start fresh — get away from the carpetbaggers and Negroes moving north. The war left all of our buildings standin', but there was a cost to the men who came back with ghosts in their eyes. Anyway, my pa was no good at farming, and those hills don't offer much in the first place. I hear it's a little like Kentucky, where I come from in Illinois, but I ain't never been there. We was close to the river. I guess that's why I like it here. In some ways, it reminds me of home. Memories is mostly all I have."

Josiah nodded unconsciously.

"What happened?" Scrap asked anxiously. "You run into Comanche, I bet, on the way to California. Or Kiowa. Lucky you didn't go farther north, there's some real savages thataway. I can't wait to get up there myself. I'll settle a score for you, if need be. I will, I truly will, Miss Mae. You ain't nothin' but a girl. Younger than me, aren't you? Not yet twenty?"

Mae looked to the ground, then back to Scrap. "It doesn't matter how old I am, or what we ran into. I'm here. This is my life. I've a roof over my head, food to eat. People who look out for me. Like I said, I've known worse. We can leave it at that. It's not important anyways."

Josiah was sure Mae was telling the truth. She surely had seen worse. The sparse mention of her family left that to be an easy assumption. He decided quickly that it was not his place to judge her, to accuse her of some certain sin, since he himself was not a churchgoer, or the sort who went around telling people what was right or wrong, as long as they were inside of civil law. He would have never ended up in Suzanne del Toro's bed if that was the case.

Judgment was better left to those in society who made the laws and thought they had some say in how the world should be run. It was Josiah's charge as a Texas Ranger to protect the population from Indians and cattle thieves — at the moment — and anything else the governor thought appropriate, and that was enough of a cause for him.

Whether a girl made her living by selling her body to those who would spend their time that way was not his concern. He did wonder about her folks, though, wonder what desperate situation had befallen her so she was left with no choice, and no wares, other than what she carried on her two feet.

"I'm sorry to hear that," Josiah said.

"Don't be." She dumped some Arbuckle's into the pot, and it only took a second for the aroma to fill the inside of the small shack. After settling the coffee on the grate, Mae took a tin from a shelf tacked to the wall and offered day-old biscuits to Scrap and Josiah.

"I'll wait, thanks," Josiah said.

"Me, too," Scrap said.

The coffee had yet to boil. "Suit yourselves," Mae said.

Josiah squirmed, a little uncomfortable in his seat, when Mae sat the tin on the grate. She'd leaned down, exposing her breasts in an innocent way. It was as if she was completely unaware of her body, and the effect it had on men. Most women were drawn up in fabric from head to toe, so to see a woman so unconcerned was like seeing a wild animal, free to run without the constraints of propriety or society's will strapped to her chest, or stuffing her sideways into a corset. She was like a big mountain cat, unaware of her power or beauty.

Mae glanced up and saw the uncomfortable expression carved on Josiah's face. "Oh," she looked down and saw how far the cut of her dress fell, "I'm sorry. I'm not used to having proper company. You probably don't think I know any manners at all."

"Doesn't matter," Scrap said. He could hardly restrain a boyish giggle that was brewing in his throat.

Mae quickly disappeared behind the quilt, leaving a hard silence between Josiah and Scrap in the front room. She returned almost immediately with a dingy white shawl thrown over her shoulders.

"How do you know of Suzanne del Toro?" Josiah asked.

Mae cocked her eyebrow. "Fat Susie?"

"Yes, you probably know her as that," Josiah said. He couldn't bring himself to call Suzanne by the nickname most people knew her by. She was hardly fat, but she was curvy. For whatever the reason, Captain Fikes had given her that name and it had stuck. "Do you know where she is?"

Mae shook her head no. "She was through here two days ago."

"Before the fire?" Josiah asked.

Scrap was watching Mae's every move as she poured a cup of Arbuckle's for Josiah, then him. He smiled when he took the coffee from her.

"Right before," Mae said.

"So she was gone before the shooting started, and the two men were killed?"

"I think so."

"Why was she here?" Josiah asked. "Do you know?"

"She takes a cut."

"I'm sorry?"

"She has a stake in the riverfront," Mae said. "Or, at least, she did. There's a new man, an overseer for most of us girls down here."

"So there's been a change?" Josiah asked. Mae nodded yes.

"What's the new man's name? Who is he?"

"I don't know his real name, but he's called *El Puño,* The Fist," Mae said. "He sends his boys to collect. They're new here, too. I hear he's a mean man. Most of 'em are — mean, you know — but this one will cut you if you don't pay. Or shoot you. The two men that were killed worked for Fat Susie. They looked after us. Collected, too. But were real nice about it. Susie never took much, and I think she was troubled by the competition up on the Reservation. Those girls are fancy. Sometimes one of us gets to move up there. But not now. We have no way out."

Josiah stiffened in his chair and took a long drink of coffee. "We passed the sheriff's men on the way down the trail. Have you talked to them?"

"They're not interested in talking," Mae said.

"I thought you might say that," Josiah answered. "Do you know where Suzanne was going, Mae?"

"No, I sure don't. But I sure wish she would come back. I'm afraid of what tomorrow might bring now that she's gone. The sheriff's new men think I know more than I'm sayin' about those killings."

"Do you?" Scrap asked.

Mae took a deep breath and lowered her eyes to the dirt floor. It suddenly became quiet inside the shack, the brewing Arbuckle's still as a pond in summer, and the embers of the little fire too exhausted to crackle.

When Mae looked back up, there were tears in her eyes, and Josiah knew right then that he couldn't just leave the girl to fend for herself.

CHAPTER 10

Dawn was yet to break on the horizon, but a robin had started singing in the distance. At first, the notes were short, a long gulf in between them, until the bird fully awoke and began to string together a full-fledged song. It wouldn't be long before the whole flock chimed in and the sun was rising happily into the cloudless sky, but as it was, the sky was black, full of silvery stars pulsing briefly, like they were ready to burn out.

The robin was an early bird, and Josiah didn't want to wake up. He was dreaming. The images in his fleeting dreams were as distant as the robin's song, and in his slumber, he couldn't make them out . . . only shapes, and a feeling that was comfortable and familiar.

In his dreamland, in his sleep, Josiah had come to rest in a place he didn't want to leave, and he was with people, or something of the sort, who made him feel welcome, and loved. It was a rare feeling, and he fought to keep his eyes closed, fought to hold on to the feeling as it slipped away, but he couldn't hold on to any of the images or feelings. They were just gone — suddenly out of his reach as his eyes flickered open, and he found himself alone, and his longings, his stomach and heart, empty, broken, and wanting.

He sat up and wiped the sleep from his eyes, anxious to rid himself of all of the jumbled feelings he had.

Scrap was nowhere to be seen.

They had decided to stay in Mae's shack. Mae slept alone on the cot in the back room, they on the dirt floor, their bedrolls retrieved from their horses at the livery. They'd kept the horses then, Missy and Clipper, tied up behind the shack.

Josiah hoped Scrap had woken and gone outside to relieve himself. He heard no sounds inside the shack, and presently he had the feeling that he was the only one in the shack. Alone. Something he should have been accustomed to but, in reality, hated thoroughly. It was not that long ago that he was cramped inside a small pine cabin with his wife and three little girls. There was no silence, no privacy, no aloneness. He missed those days more than he could say — and mostly he tried to force the memories away, but they kept coming back, taunting him in his dreams. He was sure of that now, sure that he had revisited the past in his sleep. Even now, he wished he could stay there. But he couldn't, knew that well enough to leave it alone.

He stood up quickly and strapped on his gun belt. He hesitated, then peered behind the quilt . . . and saw that Mae's cot was bare. No blankets, nothing . . . and as far as it went, there were very few belongings left in the tiny room. There was no sign of Scrap or Mae anywhere.

Concern started rising in the back of Josiah's mind. If it truly was Liam O'Reilly he had seen the night before, sporting a shiny silver star, then the color of power had edged toward black, toward dangerous and unpredictable, instead of safe and sure like it should be. Mae had good reason to be scared, and Josiah knew the best thing he and Scrap could do was get out of Waco as quickly as possible and let their commanders know what the situation there was and let them decide what to do, how to do it, and who to do it with.

No matter how he considered it, whether jurisdiction played into the decision to act or not, he knew that he was outmanned. He needed more Rangers than just Scrap Elliot at his back, and he was sure Scrap felt the same way. At least, he hoped he did.

Josiah peered out the front door cautiously, then stepped out of the shack.

The horses were packed and ready, and another horse, a smaller roan mare, was standing patiently next to Clipper. Scrap was cinching the saddle. He looked up at Josiah, nodded, then returned to the chore at hand.

The boy's ease with horses was obvious; he had shown himself to be a more than talented rider in the past, but even the exercise of saddling a horse looked easy in Scrap's hands.

He tied the latigo into a cinch knot like he had done a thousand times before . . . with his eyes closed. The mare was hardly irritable as Scrap made sure the saddle was perfectly set. Josiah had seen a lot of horses get cinchy, downright mad, about the way they were saddled.

Scrap whispered to the new horse constantly, reassuring it with a soft voice that all was well, and the horse believed him, trusted him, stood patiently, willing to let the boy do whatever needed to be done.

Mae stood back and watched, too, a look of interest on her face, almost like she had never seen anyone saddle a horse so competently before.

After expertly saddling the mare, Scrap looked back up to Josiah. He nodded again, but didn't make any effort to stop his preparation of the horse. He stepped easily to the animal's left side, dropped the nose piece of the halter off the nose, and refastened the crown strap around the neck. Scrap kept his head a good distance from the horse's head while he finished the bridling chore, and was extremely gentle about the ears, which the roan mare seemed to appreciate greatly.

Josiah didn't have to force a smile, though he fought not to let it show as big as it might have in better circumstances. A little confidence in Scrap's skills would go a long way when the time came and Scrap returned to being mouthy and rascally, when he got mad as a wet cat, or talked on and on about nonsense, or wouldn't shut up just to hear himself talk, like he was prone to do once they settled in on the long ride.

They were all aware that quietness was key, even though there was no particular reason to fear that they were being watched or sought out just now.

Josiah cast a glance to the other shacks, to where he had seen the man sleeping on the porch the night before, only to see that the man was gone and all of the shacks were dark — they were either empty, the business of the night done, or the occupants were still asleep, undisturbed by the early bird and the preparation to leave. Josiah was glad that the three of them were alone.

After Scrap was completely done readying Mae's horse, he made his way up to Josiah. Mae followed and stopped next to Scrap.

Josiah eyed the pair curiously, seeing if there was something between them other than Scrap's anxiousness about being near a woman. To his relief, he saw the same nervousness from Scrap, and Mae had prepared herself for a ride and dressed accordingly — to the best of her capability, that is. She had on a pair of scruffy boots, and a simple cotton dress.

"I thought you was going to sleep till noon," Scrap said.

"You should have woken me up."

"You was talking in your sleep. You do that a lot?"

"How would I know? What did I say?"

They were both talking at just above a whisper. Mae fidgeted next to Scrap, wringing her hands nervously, and shifting her weight like she was past ready to go.

"Nothin', really," Scrap said. He looked

away, averting his eyes to the ground so fast that Josiah didn't believe him — but he decided now was not the time to pursue any line of questioning that did not set them on the road out of Waco.

"Looks like we're ready," Josiah said.

"Where are we going?" Mae asked.

She and Scrap had decided to leave as they drank coffee, but hadn't discussed much of anything else.

"I got an aunt who lives up Fort Worth way," Scrap said. "We can take you there. She's got room to take you in for a little while."

"Fort Worth smells like cow shit," Mae said.

"They don't call it Cowtown for nothin'," Scrap said with a wry smile.

Josiah nodded in agreement. Fort Worth was a good destination. They could still follow the Chisholm Trail, get some supplies, then head on to the Red River and meet up with their Ranger company. For once, Scrap had a good idea, had thought through a solution to a problem.

Josiah was impressed.

He did have some concerns, though. He'd been through Fort Worth a few times in the past, and he knew the town well enough to know that it had its own disreputable district, its own Hell's Half Acre just like Austin's, which might be a lure to Mae. The entertainment area in Fort Worth was twice the size of the Reservation in Waco, just south of the courthouse. Fort Worth could be rowdy.

For some reason, Josiah hoped Mae would find a fresh start waiting for her in Fort Worth. Life had been hard for her, and he kind of liked her, in an uncle sort of way — she had a spark that he couldn't quite ignore. Physical restraint was not as hard for him as it seemed to be for Scrap. There was no question that Mae was a pretty girl, could be even prettier cleaned up and in proper circumstances, but she was too young for him to take notice of in an in-between-the-covers kind of way. Still, he was not immune to noticing female company.

"That sounds good, Scrap," Josiah said. "How long's it been since you've seen this aunt?"

"A few years."

"And you're on good terms with her? Good enough to ensure Mae's well-being until we get this all sorted out?"

Scrap nodded. "I think so. She's my ma's sister. About the only relation I got left that's livin'. She's always treated me right."

"I guess it's settled then," Josiah said.

"What if I don't want to go to Fort Worth?" Mae asked.

"You want to stay here?" Scrap snapped.

"No. But I don't like Fort Worth. And I don't want to stay with no natty old woman, neither."

"Aunt Callie isn't natty. She's a good woman. Likes a taste of whiskey every now and again, too."

"Really?" Mae said.

"Really. Not all respectable women are all buttoned up."

Mae sneered at Scrap, then looked away and spat on the ground. Scrap looked like he had just been slapped across the face.

Josiah had to restrain himself from laughing out loud. "I'm afraid we don't have much of a choice, then. Fort Worth it is. Let's go."

CHAPTER 11

Scrap led the way up the path, with Mae in the middle, looking uncomfortable on the roan mare, with Josiah bringing up the rear.

Light had just started to filter across the sky in the east, and they edged slowly, and as quietly as they could, up the ravine to Waco. It was the easiest way to get on the Chisholm Trail from the riverfront.

It looked and felt like it was going to be a scorcher of a day.

The birds along the river had come fully awake, and the chorus of songbirds was louder along the river than Josiah was accustomed to. There were plenty of places for life among the trees and shrubs that were thick across both sides of the river. Tall trees, including some pecan groves in the distance, stretched out in both directions, giving the birds, and other critters that found the waters of the Brazos bountiful, enough shelter and a multitude of ways to make a living — neither of which was easy in a lot of Texas that Josiah had seen.

Somewhere close a kingfisher chortled, and farther off in the distance, a cow bellowed, followed by another soon after. It would not be long before the rumble of cattle on the bridge across the Brazos drowned out all the other sounds, and the day would get on with itself — whether anyone was ready or not.

Josiah hoped to be long gone before that happened, before the herds, scattered as they were, started the next leg of their journey on the long trail north.

Mae had packed light, her keepsakes few, but even with that, the roan mare already looked haggard and worn out. Josiah was concerned about the trek to Fort Worth, certain that Mae's horse wouldn't make it alive, especially if they encountered any kind of hostilities along the way. They had no choice but to make do, though. There wasn't time to trade horses, and it was doubtful that any of them had the extra money to get a horse that was any better than the one Mae now called her own.

At present, the horse was without a name, and for that, Josiah was glad. He didn't want to get attached to something that would surely end up being an easy meal for the coyotes somewhere between Waco and Fort Worth.

But it was more than the horse that concerned Josiah. It was the hostilities that he was leery of, this man Mae called *El Puño,* The Fist.

He knew little about the commerce of flesh, but was certain it wasn't a business that he wanted to understand, or be a part of. Still, there was greed involved, and the abundance of customers passing through Waco surely made the business a prosperous one.

It came as no surprise to him that Suzanne was linked to districts outside of Austin. Suzanne del Toro appeared to be an enterprising woman at the very least. Still, regardless of his affection — if he dared call it that — or concern for her well-being, it was imperative that he keep his wits about him. This *El Puño* sounded like an unsavory character, a man willing to intimidate a poor girl like Mae for his share of her meager pie, and it was hard telling to what lengths he would go to protect what he just might consider to be *his* property.

With that thought in mind, Josiah looked ahead, past Mae, and up to Scrap, hoping that the boy was as aware of his surroundings as he needed to be.

Clipper was the first to set off the alarm that something was wrong about halfway up the ravine.

The tall Appaloosa's ears stiffened, and he let out a low snort at the same time, then jerked his head back in protest, even though Josiah had a light hold on the reins. Navigating up the ravine path wasn't real tricky, and he trusted Clipper to make the short journey without much direction from him. They'd been in tougher spots together, and the horse had always shown great sense when it came to riding the trail, especially when he was bringing up the rear.

Josiah immediately sat straight up in the saddle and gripped the Peacemaker, readying himself if need be. His hand had been only inches from the butt of the gun in the first place.

The Winchester was in the scabbard, but easily accessible, too — he could easily handle both weapons, and had done so in the past more than once. It wasn't that long ago that the Peacemaker had been new to him, an untrustworthy companion. But once he had grown used to it, understood its restrictions and finer points, he was glad to have it at his side. Same with the Winchester. He'd carried a Sharps carbine for many years. But the repeater, the '73, was something no Ranger wanted to be without these days, and it was easy to understand why.

"Whoa, boy. What's the matter, Clipper? Huh?" Josiah said.

His voice was just above a whisper, but Mae heard him and turned her head back to see what was the matter.

Before she could say anything, a man had jumped up out of the weeds, a thicket of tall nettle and touch-me-nots, and grabbed the tired roan mare's lead.

Mae's horse startled, let out a shrill whinny, and raised its two front hooves fearfully off the ground. Mae was surprised, but there was never any hint that she was in danger of falling off — the roan mare couldn't buck a fly if it had to — and she reacted quickly, pulling back on the reins and stopping the horse dead in its tracks.

Scrap reacted just as quickly and spun Missy around, his rifle aimed immediately at the stranger's head.

Josiah had cocked the hammer of the Peacemaker, a bullet certain in the chamber, his finger steady on the trigger.

The man did not have a gun in his hand

143

— so his intent was still uncertain. His long coat, black and tattered as it was, had drawn back when he jumped out onto the path, exposing a gun belt full of bullets, two Colt .45s in holsters, and a Bowie knife, secure on his hip. The man was well armed, and ready for anything that might come his way.

Josiah wasn't certain whether the man was friend or foe, though the element of surprise, the suddenness of his appearance, suggested he was not a savior of any kind — especially considering there was no need for Mae to be rescued — just the opposite in fact, particularly given Josiah's recent thoughts about *El Puño*. It was an oddity, an action that probably saved the man's life, that he did not use a gun or knife to slow Mae's progress, only his hands — and he went for the horse, not the girl.

"You best let go of the girl's horse there, friend. My partner's got an itchy trigger finger," Josiah said.

He stared at the man, unflinching, his voice strong and unwavering. He meant what he said — more than the man knew. Scrap might get a little too excited and put a bullet between the man's eyes before he could say squat and stop him.

Scrap glanced away from the man for just a second, made eye contact with Josiah, and nodded. A slight smile drew across his face at the mention of being a partner.

"I don't take to bein' startled, either," Scrap said. "You got about two seconds to state your business, or I'm gonna start asking questions after I shoot you."

The man had his hat pulled down over his eyes, but it was easy to tell he wasn't a youngster, probably about ten years older than Josiah, nearer to forty.

"Mae, tell 'em it's OK," the man said. "You know who I am."

"Clem Dawson, you're a fool. A doggone fool. You're lucky these fellas didn't just shoot you and leave you to die in the weeds. You damn near scared the life out of me," Mae said, her face hard as stone, her eyes even harder, if that were possible.

Fear was still stuck in the eyes of the roan mare, and the man, Clem Dawson, had to force some effort to keep the horse steady. The show of spirit from the mare surprised Josiah. Maybe the horse would make it to Fort Worth after all.

"Where you going, Mae?" Clem Dawson asked. His voice was almost weak and whiny, like a two-year-old's — even though he was a big, strapping fellow. It appeared that he was about to tear up and plead with Mae to stay.

The weakness puzzled Josiah, but only for a second. He eased the hammer off the Peacemaker. "You know this fella pretty well, I take it," he said, eyeing Scrap at the same time, making sure he backed off, too, but didn't totally relax.

"I know him once a week," Mae said.

Clem Dawson looked like he could be a handful of trouble if he didn't get his way. For a meek fellow, he was awfully well armed. Josiah didn't trust him. He could have been a skunk acting like a cat.

"Now, it ain't none of your business, Clem, where I'm going. What in the hell are you doin' out here anyways?" Mae asked, jerking the lead out of Clem's hands. "You should be home in bed with your wife, not down here covered in morning dew, traipsing after me."

The hardness fell from her face, and Mae let a slight smile flicker Clem's way — allowing Josiah to see his speculation was correct: Clem Dawson was a customer, and out of consideration for his own needs he didn't want to see Mae leave the confines of Waco.

If Dawson had known anything about Mae at all, he'd have known she might be in danger, and needed protection — from *El Puño*. But Josiah had known men like Clem Dawson before. Maudie Mae Johnson might as well have been a horse or something else that could be bought or sold to him, too. His pleasures were his king, her private whispers a vice he could not resist.

Clem glanced down to the ground and stepped away from the roan mare. He looked like he'd just been swatted on the knuckles with a ruler.

"I've kept a close eye on you," Clem said. " 'Cause I'm worried about you. Thought there might be trouble coming your way after the other night."

"That's sweet, Clem," Mae said. "But these two gentlemen are Texas Rangers. They're lookin' after me for a little while."

"So you are leaving?"

"For a little while. Go back to your house and to your own bed."

"Ain't allowed there. Every time I lie down next to Sally, she ends up pregnant with another child in her belly. Got enough mouths the way it is, can't afford no more," Clem Dawson said. "You know that, Mae. At least you don't ask for nothin' other than what I owe you for your time. What am I gonna do if you leave?"

Mae glared at Clem Dawson. She'd flinched at the word "pregnant." "You can find someone else, Clem. Ain't like I'm the only girl along here that'll take you inside her shack."

"You're the only one I like."

"I'm the only one you know. Now, go on home. Sally's probably waitin' on you. Probably knows you sneaked out in the middle of the night."

"She don't ask no questions."

Josiah tightened his grip on Clipper's reins. "We need to be moving on, Mr. Dawson," he said, easing up next to Mae. "You all right with that, ma'am?"

Mae nodded yes.

"You best say your good-byes then," Josiah said.

"Mae ain't goin' anywhere but back to her shack," Clem Dawson said. He stared at Josiah. Either the breeze or a swift unseen action had swept open the man's duster, making access to his weapons a little easier, a little quicker.

"You're making a big mistake, mister," Scrap said.

"I don't think so." Clem Dawson nodded, then looked up to the top of the ravine, drawing Josiah and Scrap's attention with him.

With the rising sunlight at their backs, three men stared down, silhouettes on horses, holding rifles, their aim sure, and there was no mistaking their intention.

Josiah and Scrap were in their gun sights. They had been tricked by Clem Dawson. They were outmanned and outgunned, with no way out.

Chapter 12

Josiah hoped Scrap was smart enough to follow his lead, because if he wasn't, he was about to become a dead man.

There was no way Josiah was going to let Mae go back to the shack, considering everything he'd learned since arriving there — and there was no way he was going to put his fate, and Scrap's, in the hands of Clem Dawson and the three men on the ridge. He was almost certain one of the men was Liam O'Reilly, and if he was correct, then all of their lives were hanging in the balance.

Josiah Wolfe lived by rules that were strict and mostly unbreakable. One of his main rules, a credo he'd sworn to long ago when he wore a soldier's uniform, was to never kill a man . . . unless he absolutely had to.

At the moment, he didn't see any way out of the situation he was in but with a gun.

He knew he was risking Mae's life as well

as Scrap's, but he didn't figure she'd have much of a chance if he surrendered — he didn't figure she had much of a life anyway, when you got right down to it.

If this overseer, *El Puño,* thought Mae knew something more about the killings on the riverfront than she was telling, then she was a threat to his power — and the easiest way to deal with her would be to kill her and toss her in the river. Who would miss a whore? Or care in the first place? Even the newspaper put news about the "deadly row" all the way at the bottom of the page.

He hoped that little roan mare had some life left in it.

Clem Dawson solidified Josiah's decision to shoot his way out of his current troubles when a knife appeared out of his right sleeve and he jerked Mae off the roan mare in one swift motion. It was more like the strapping man lifted Mae up off the horse and plopped her down on the ground feet-first — without any apparent effort at all.

The point of Dawson's glistening Bowie knife quickly came to a rest against Mae's throat, barely poking into her skin, but enough to make his intention certain.

Mae cried out in protest, momentarily drawing Dawson's attention away from Josiah, whom he had held a fixed gaze on

— but before Josiah could swing the Peace-maker up to shoot from the swivel rig, Scrap fired off a round from his rifle.

The shot echoed across the river and up the ravine as the bullet cut through Clem Dawson's right temple, exploding out the other side of his head in a gush of blood and bone. Clem Dawson didn't have time to swat away the bullet, or object to the sting like it was an unexpected insect bite. He just collapsed.

The one shot was thorough and on target. Dawson's knife fell away from Mae's throat and landed on the ground in a thud, next to the man's lifeless body.

Maudie Mae Johnson staggered a bit to the right of the body and screamed at the top of her lungs. "What the hell have you done?" She scowled at Scrap, then teared up as she rushed back to Clem Dawson and leaned to his chest, trying to find a heart-beat. "You killed him. You killed him. You didn't have to go and kill him."

Scrap looked shocked at the outburst and froze in his saddle, lowering his rifle only after taking a deep breath.

Josiah spun Clipper around, swiftly pull-ing his Winchester out of the scabbard. The three men on the ridge had disappeared. All he could see was a cloud of dust heading their way.

After finding no sign of life in Clem Dawson, Mae stood up with rage carved on her face and hate set in her eyes like it would stay there forever. "You didn't have to kill him," she said, her fists clenched, as she strutted toward Scrap. "Clem Dawson never hurt a fly. He's got children to raise, you idiot."

"He was going to kill you," Scrap yelled.

"No, he wasn't. He wouldn't have hurt me. You're a fool. A damned fool. Look at what you've done."

Josiah had no intention of saving Scrap from Mae's wrath. But whatever her quarrel with him was, it would have to wait — they needed to get out of there, and they needed to get out of there now.

Josiah spun Clipper around again, sliding the Winchester back in its scabbard.

His movement had caught her attention, and she stopped her angry march toward Scrap. Mae still looked mad — mad as a thousand hornets who'd just had their nest destroyed, but her anger was fading away to curiosity, or maybe it was fear — as Josiah aimed Clipper right for her.

He heard the first report of a rifle shot as he leaned down and caught hold of Mae's arm. He yanked her up, using the horse's motion to catapult her up onto the saddle in front of him. Mae didn't have time to scream. It looked like the breath had been knocked out of her. Her rage had been replaced by shock.

There'd be time for explanations later.

Another shot came from behind them, barely missing them.

"Let's go," Josiah yelled over his shoulder, pressing Clipper to ride harder and faster than he'd been asked to in a long time. The Appaloosa stallion responded knowingly, and the wind rose in Josiah's face.

Scrap had pushed Missy to run hard, too, and was neck and neck with Josiah and Clipper. The boy had his rifle out, firing back at the charging horsemen — who were about a hundred yards behind them, and gaining.

"He didn't have to kill him," Mae snarled out of the side of her mouth, situating herself in the saddle, leaning forward, her body as far away from Josiah as possible.

Josiah had no answer for Mae. He ignored her. As far as he was concerned, Scrap had acted as close to heroically as he'd ever seen him, deciding on his own to step up and end a situation that was quickly going from bad to worse. If Scrap hadn't shot Clem Dawson, Josiah would have.

They passed her shack, and from there Josiah was not sure of where to ride.

He just kept riding, pushing Clipper to ride harder and faster. He figured the best thing to do was ride as fast as they could along the riverfront and hope to find a spot somewhere where the water was low and running easy and they could cross. Not knowing much about the Brazos or Waco had left him at a severe disadvantage. He was ignorant about this part of Texas in general. Most of his time had been spent east in pine forests around Tyler, and south down San Antonio way and beyond, down to the border. He had a feel for that land, how it rose and dipped, what the inside of a canyon felt like, where to watch the trail for snake holes and ambushes — but he was lost in central Texas, lost along the river. He'd have to rely on his senses and nothing else.

"What's the best way across the river from here?" he asked Mae.

The force of Clipper's run had pushed her back, and he felt her stiffen against him, but she remained silent. After a few seconds, after looking over his shoulder to see the three men gaining ground on them, he nudged her elbow. "Come on, Mae. These men aren't going to ask any questions, and you know it. They catch up to us, we're all three dead."

"It would serve him right," Mae said, glaring over at Scrap.

"What about you? Do you want to stay here? Face whatever is waiting for you back there?" Josiah asked, meaning the shack and the three horsemen.

"I've dealt with worse."

"I want to help you, Mae."

"For what? For what in return? You think you're gonna have free rights to me in the middle of the night, too?"

"No. I just want to help you, Mae. It's what I do."

"You're not going to come to me expectin' payment of some sort or another for your kindness? I don't believe you."

"I don't imagine you do, but a thank-you and way out of Waco is all that I'm asking for, Mae. My life is in your hands." He hesitated for a second, then said, "I promise, I don't want anything from you other than a way out of here."

Mae exhaled loudly, loud enough for Josiah to hear — and feel — over the wind washing their faces.

The river was coming up fast on the path. There were three or four shacks left before a thin line of neck-high scrub trees growing in between boulders, rocks, and mud skirted the river for who knows how far. There was no way the horses could navigate among the boulders, since there wasn't an open path visible, at least one that could be run on as fast as they needed to. Josiah was sure there was a path worn by a generation or two of girls making their way to the water for bathing and clothes-washing purposes.

"There." Mae pointed to the next to last shack. "Go there, then past three more shacks, it'll circle back. If you go right, you'll come out by my place. And if you go left you can ride up the ridge, but . . ."

"But those men know the way in and out," Josiah said, finishing her sentence.

Mae nodded. "You can edge along the river, but it ain't gonna be easy."

"Where'll it take us?"

"To the other side of the bridge. If you make it there, we could mix in with some of the herds. Maybe get a few cowboys' notice, and get their help."

"All right." Josiah had two choices: go his own way, or trust that Mae was telling him the truth, giving him the right directions and not leading him into a trap.

For all he knew, she might have some currency with the men that were chasing them and be able to buy her way out of trouble

Josiah jerked Clipper to the right, and they cut up between the two shacks Mae had pointed to.

Scrap followed, not questioning Josiah's lead. Not that there was time or the chance. The three riders were gaining ground, their bullets coming closer and closer. A splinter of wood flipped off the corner of one of the shacks, the report from the rifle and the slice into the shack behind the bullet's target certain, but short of coming up successful.

Josiah urged Clipper to run faster, then turned after the third shack like Mae had told him. He looked to the ridge to see if they had put a man there to cut them off, but it looked clear. Scrap was still neck and neck with him, and Josiah nodded upward, not wanting to shout out his intentions for the world to hear.

Scrap surprised Josiah and shook his head

no, then suddenly pulled back on Missy's reins. He didn't brake her to a stop, but he slowed the mare, putting himself in closer range of the three riders' aim than Josiah was comfortable with.

"What are you doing?" Josiah yelled over his shoulder.

Scrap pointed up the ridge. "I'll catch up before you get to Fort Worth. Go on," he yelled back, bringing his rifle up to his shoulder, firing at the horsemen without saying another word.

One shot took the man in the middle clean off his horse. The rider screamed in agony, setting off a morning alarm of fear and violence on the riverfront. No one came outside to see what was happening, to offer help or another gun.

Josiah was sure that no one wanted to be involved in the latest shooting, the latest threat to what was surely a dangerous place to live and do business in the first place. Death was a frequent visitor to the riverfront, a common foe, always lurking at the corner, whether at night, or at the dawn of a new day. You were as likely to step in a puddle of blood as you were to step in a pile of horse shit.

Even in the speed of flight, Josiah was gratified to be whisking Mae away from such a place. She hadn't asked to be rescued, and he was not one to offer — or seek — salvation on a regular basis, but it did give him reason to ride harder, to push Clipper to his limit.

They needed to be free of Waco.

Mae needed to be in the presence of a respectful influence, and Josiah and Scrap needed to be in the midst of the other Rangers, learning the new ways, the new restraints and disciplines instituted by Major Jones and Governor Coke.

As much as Josiah was concerned about the fates of his friends Juan Carlos and Suzanne del Toro, he was losing confidence that his excuse to be as late to camp as he was would hold water with Captain Feders. It wasn't like he was malingering, or fleeing from his duty — being a Texas Ranger was the second most important responsibility in his life, his son, Lyle, being first and foremost.

While outrunning a gang of unknown men whose sole purpose was to bring even more death and fear to the riverfront did not seem like the most appropriate time to lose focus, to be concerned about his son or his duty, but if Josiah Wolfe knew anything, it was how precarious life was, how easily death came to those just in the midst of living every day.

If he were to get shot in the back of the head and die a nearly instant death, then he would want his last thought to be of Lyle, of his squealing little dark-haired boy playing pat-a-cake with Ofelia.

Mae leaned back into him. "Once you get to the top, there's a trail that edges over the river. There's not much protection there. You'll be out in the open, at least until you get close to the bridge, then there'll be herds backed up to pay the toll."

"Lean forward," Josiah ordered.

Clipper was starting to struggle up the steep ravine.

Mae did as she was told. "I hope they kill him," she said, under her breath.

Josiah ignored the remark; he knew she felt nothing but rage toward Scrap, and he found it odd that she would hold so much remorse for a man like Clem Dawson. Not that he knew the man well enough to judge him, but Dawson didn't come across as an upstanding member of society.

Maybe Josiah himself wasn't an upstanding citizen either, now that he thought about it, but he wasn't a man like Dawson. He'd never use a weapon to make a woman do something she didn't want to. Ever.

He glanced over his shoulder again.

Scrap had edged himself along the last shack and was firing as rapidly as he could, holding the two remaining men at bay.

In the dim light and through the lingering smoke, Josiah could see the two remaining riders react to Scrap's decision to face them. They slowed down, then slid off their saddles, almost in unison, using their horses as shields as they returned fire at Scrap.

Scrap Elliot would never shoot a horse on purpose, so he started shooting at the feet of both men. He hit one square in the toe. It was the last thing Josiah saw before navigating the trail up the ravine took his full attention.

He hoped Scrap would be all right. The boy had created a problem for himself, but solved one for Josiah and Mae, giving them time and plenty of room to escape. There was a lot to be said about Scrap's forward-thinking act — and there would be plenty said, a thank-you all around, when the time came.

If it came at all.

Ahead there was a sea of longhorns pushing to and fro, nervously, for as far as the eye could see.

Clattering horns rose above the gunshots from the riverfront below, like a chorus of voices, like trumpets that had all been stepped on at once. And then there was the smell, always the smell of wet fur, hot, baking leather, and fresh prairie coal underfoot, that accompanied the herds on the Chisholm Trail. Never mind the flies in July. It could be an unbearable situation if you weren't a cowboy unaccustomed to the ways of cows, and unpaid for the trouble. But when you were being chased and shot at by a couple of unknown gunmen, well, there could be mountains of shit to climb and swarms of insects to swallow, and it wouldn't matter.

Mostly, Josiah thought, the herd would help them far more than it would hurt them, and he was more than grateful for the presence of the longhorns once they reached the top of the ridge.

The suspension bridge was about a hundred yards to the north, and there was a herd waiting to cross it, but they had to pay the toll first — five cents a head for the cows and steers, ten cents for each cowboy.

They were backed up, head to butt, cowhands riding up and down, back and forth, trying to keep the cows calm while the head count was conducted. The hands were obviously concerned and angered by the goings-on between Scrap and the two remaining riders. The shots were fewer, more calculated, but still rising from the distance, loud enough to make even one cow skittish, much less a thousand.

The sun was rising quickly into the sky, breaking free of the gray horizon, casting soft morning light on the Brazos River and everything beyond. The suspension bridge itself reflected in the water, a marvel of engineering and pure human sweat.

Josiah had never seen anything like it — nor had anyone else who came upon it for the first time. The bridge was less than five years old, put in use in January of 1870. At nearly 475 feet, it was said to be the longest bridge of its kind in the world. A stone tower was ensconced on each bank, a grand entrance and exit.

The bridge was wide enough for two stagecoaches to pass each other, or a herd of longhorns to pass on one side and townsfolk to walk on the other side. The use of the bridge had been almost constant since its opening.

Josiah was not planning on crossing the bridge — there was not time to wait and pay the toll, and he didn't want to jump his place and risk being chased down by more locals. But he was glad for the distraction, for the crowd to get lost in.

Two cowhands rode toward him, serious

looks on their faces, both angling for the six-shooters at their side.

"Looks like more trouble," Mae said.

"Let me handle it."

The cowhands did not slow down; they rode right past Josiah, heading for the ravine.

He was tempted to double back, uncertain if they were friend or foe, but he hoped Scrap could fend for himself, that the cowhands were more concerned with stopping the shooting and keeping the longhorns calm than jumping into the middle of a gunfight.

For all he knew the men were enforcers for *El Puño* — but if that were the case, they would have surely stopped and taken possession of Mae any way they saw fit.

Josiah was certain then that they were cowhands, sent out by the trail boss to quell the nerve-wracking gunfire.

He slowed Clipper, then swung right into the thick of the waiting cows, easing cautiously through them, his eyes focused on the horns, avoiding them entirely if that was possible, keeping Clipper as safe as he could. One stab could hobble his trusted Appaloosa, and just the chance he was taking matched his nerves with the longhorns.

In the distance, he heard a new volley of

shots and then silence. At least from the guns. The cows responded in a deeper, guttural chorus, pushing a little harder toward the bridge.

The swing and the flank riders joined together, two dust-covered cowboys who looked like they had been on the trail all of their lives — or at least since they'd joined up, probably in San Antonio. There were no wanderers, no cows for the flank rider to cut back into the herd, but this herd needed calming immediately. And both of the riders knew it.

They were two snorts away from a stampede.

Luckily the day was clear, no thunderclouds on the horizon or lightning to spook the herd any more than they already were.

"You're crazy," Mae said. "You're gonna get us killed."

"Be quiet."

Josiah didn't snap at her, but there was a force of seriousness in his voice that made her stiffen and pull forward as far away from him as the saddle would allow.

He ignored her, glad to be able to concentrate on the task at hand. One false move and he could hobble his horse or send the herd into a frenzy, and that would be a miserable death, being stabbed and stomped on by an angry mob of longhorns. He'd rather die quickly, by that unknown gunshot in the back of the head he'd been thinking about earlier.

They were in the middle of the herd before Mae relaxed. "You know what you're doing, don't you?"

"I'm just lucky Clipper knows what to do."

They were talking at just above a whisper.

"You've had him a long time?" Mae asked.

He nodded yes, then turned his attention to his right side. A big red steer had pushed its way next to Clipper, the point of its horn swinging precariously under the horse's long throat as it tried to keep pace with the rest of the herd.

Josiah pushed the side of the cow gently with his boot, tapped it really, then brought Clipper to a full stop. They were only about four cows away from reaching the other side of the herd and escaping the danger of puncture or stampedes.

The steer protested at first, then moved off, taking its sharp horns with it.

"That was close," Josiah said.

"Too close."

"I can't imagine anything happening to this horse. He's about the only family I have left."

Mae cocked her head around and looked

at Josiah curiously out of the corner of her blue eyes. "You don't have family, either?"

"I have a son, Lyle. He's a little over two years old."

Another steer headed toward Clipper, but Josiah saw a way out of the herd, and eased through the maze to the edge.

"Where's he at?" Mae asked.

"What? Who?"

"Your son."

"Sorry, I was trying to miss that other steer." Josiah took a deep breath as they pushed out of the herd, unscathed. "He's in Austin. A family friend is looking after him till I get back."

"Must be hard," Mae said. "Bein' away as much as you are, I expect, bein' a Ranger and all. Doesn't seem like it would be healthy for a little boy not havin' his pa around all the time to tell him the difference between right and wrong."

Josiah looked back over his shoulder, saw the flank and swing riders pushing the herd across the bridge.

The gunshots along the riverfront had gone silent, but there was no sign of Scrap.

He couldn't stand there waiting for him; at least, Josiah didn't think it was a good idea anyway. He wanted to get as far away from Waco as he could, as quickly as he could.

Scrap would just have to catch up. He knew they were heading to Fort Worth, knew the route and the destination. He'd found Josiah once before, and he could do it again . . . if he was able.

That was the worry.

"It isn't healthy to be away from Lyle as much as I am," Josiah finally said. "But right now, I don't have much of a choice about how things are."

"That makes two of us."

Josiah pressed his legs firmly against Clipper, pulled the reins back a bit, then gave the horse full permission to run full-out.

Clipper obliged, just as happy to leave the cows and Waco behind as Josiah was.

CHAPTER 14

By the time Josiah allowed Clipper to rest, the sun had reached its apex, hovering in the sky like an unrelenting overseer, its heat and oppressiveness growing by the second. He had swung away from the Brazos and stuck close to the Chisholm but avoided it, and the herds easing out of Waco, as much as he could. The outside route was faster, less noticeable.

The land north of Waco was hilly, grassy in a lot of the flatter places, a perfect run north for the thousands of cattle that had passed through the area, and would continue to.

There were scatterings of trees here and there, and in some places a copse, or motte, as most Texans called them, of live oaks that stood like a thick plot of weeds that had sprouted up out of nowhere.

The air was thick with the promise of growing hotter as the day pushed on, and after a hearty and continuous run, Josiah thought it best to find some suitable shade, take a rest, eat some food, and wait a bit to see if Scrap was able to make tracks and catch up.

There was no lack of concern for Scrap's welfare, at least on Josiah's part. He was more than a little worried about the boy's safety and well-being.

Plain and simple, Scrap Elliot had set himself up as the bait so Josiah and Mae could flee safely out of Waco. Regardless of whether or not it was the smart thing to do or the right thing to do. It was a selfless act that nearly finalized Josiah's glad feeling that Scrap took his Ranger responsibilities as seriously as he did. In the last day or two, the boy had shown himself to have some sense, some nerve, and not just a dose of immaturity that looked more like a show of frail manliness than calm confidence.

Mae, on the other hand, had not mentioned Scrap once since they had broken free of the cow herds at the suspension bridge and bolted out of Waco. She remained stoic, offering no manner of reasonable company, and had been glad, it seemed, when Josiah had stopped and put her behind him on the saddle.

She held on to him loosely, accustomed to

showing little fear, or surely confident in Josiah's riding skills, he wasn't sure which.

There was little sound between the two of them as they rode away from Waco in a rush. Nothing but the wind in their faces, a few muttered commands to Clipper, and a check of comfort — if such a thing were even possible.

The Appaloosa's back was no Butterfield stagecoach, and riding double from Waco to Fort Worth was not an enviable proposition, no matter how much Josiah missed the company of a woman. The feel of her against his back, the smell of her sweet sweat — neither offended him nor excited him.

Maudie Mae Johnson was his charge now, a responsibility to see to safety — and would be nothing other than that. After depositing her in Fort Worth, then it would be on to the Red River, on to his own Ranger duties as a sergeant.

He finally brought Clipper to a stop in a thick motte of live oaks, in the middle of a vast expanse of grasses. A stream feeding to the Brazos cut to the right, the sandy bank eroded, exposing a massive system of gangly roots with tangles of dried grass dangling in the wind, remnants of a spring flood that was just a memory now.

The stream ran slowly and was about a third of its original width until it met a crop of fallen trees. A pool formed from the natural dam, offering a deep respite for some larger fish to find a home, or other creatures who found salvation in the motte.

The trunks of the oaks were massive. Josiah guessed he could curl around one of the trees and just touch his head to the soles of his boots. The biggest tree would have been at least six feet around, and they all looked to reach up past seventy feet in the air. Broad canopies mixed about, but one tree looked to cover about a hundred and fifty feet, and they all created a perfect ceiling, holding out most of the light from above. Inside the motte, it was gray and overcast, like there was a storm coming even though there wasn't a cloud in the sky. A slight breeze wound its way through, moving about the smell of decay, not allowing it to settle on any one thing for too long.

"Watch yourself, now," Josiah said to Mae. He'd dismounted and offered her his hand. "Critters are bound to be drawn to this place as much as we were."

"You think I'm a-scared of critters?"

Josiah shrugged his shoulders, pulled the saddlebag off Clipper's back, then led the horse to the stream.

The stream was healthy, full of shiners, their silver sides flashing in the muted sunlight that had managed to poke through the tall ceiling of leaves. Scattered spots on the ground had circles of light shining directly on them, and dirt particles floated in the air, the sun bouncing off them like they were jewels dropped from the trees as gifts, or insects floating freely about because they had nothing better to do, or worry about, than enjoying the peaceful ride to the ground.

Somewhere close, a raven croaked as if it were annoyed by the presence of Josiah and Mae. It sounded like it was saying, "ronk, ronk, ronk," whatever that meant. Probably "go away, go away." But it didn't matter, Josiah decided quickly, they weren't going anywhere until they'd rested up and given Scrap some time to find them.

Josiah left Clipper to enjoy the stream.

When he turned to go back to the girl, to make temporary camp, Mae was about twenty feet off to his right, facing him, her dress pulled up to her knees as she squatted to pee. He immediately spun around, and stood with his back to the girl.

He could hear the tinkle spraying on the ground, and Mae laughed out loud. "Ain't you never seen a woman pee, Ranger Wolfe?"

"Sure I have." He crossed his arms.

"Well, what are you gettin' all red-faced about?"

"I don't know you. And besides, a woman ought to have some sense of privacy about certain matters."

The tinkle on dried leaves came to a stop, and Mae rustled herself back together.

"Are you decent?" Josiah asked.

"Does it matter?"

"Of course it matters."

Before he could say anything else, Mae was standing next to him, staring up at him. "I'm gonna get rid of all of this dust. Are you coming?"

Josiah looked at Mae confused, until he saw her intent, saw her reach down and pull her light cotton dress over her head.

In the blink of an eye she was standing before him, naked.

There was no mistaking the desire in her eyes — that she wanted him to join her — but as long as it had been since he'd been with a woman, especially one as young and firm as Mae, he couldn't bring himself to face the kind of desire she offered.

He still couldn't find the burning heat deep inside himself, the heat that drew him to a woman in need and want — at least under these circumstances.

He still dreamed of waking up in his marriage bed, with Lily breathing softly, still sleeping next to him. But it was not to be — ever again — it was just a dream, a desire that would forever go unfulfilled.

Just because the offer of sex was there didn't mean it should be taken up, no matter how much he longed to feel a woman's body against his.

"You're sure not shy, are you?" Josiah said.

Mae reached up to the top button of his shirt, an impish look in her eyes. She licked her lips and smiled coyly.

Josiah grabbed her hand, shook his head no, and stopped her before the button popped out of the hole.

A flash of anger crossed Mae's face.

He saw the same hardness in her face he had seen when she condemned Scrap, hoping out loud for his killing. There was a coldness that existed deep inside of Mae Johnson, and that didn't surprise him, all things considered. He understood her anger, at least at that moment — he had rejected her. But the look also reminded him of something else. It reminded him not to get too comfortable, not to trust her any more than he would any other stranger.

"I ain't gonna ask for no money. You probably saved my life," Mae said. "Clem Dawson wouldn't have hurt me, but those other fellas, well, I just don't know them good enough to guess what they would have done, given the chance. I ain't got much to offer in thanks for takin' me off the river. You're my man, now."

"There's no need to repay me, and I'm not your man. I'm taking you to Fort Worth. After that you're on your own." Josiah stepped back away from her. "Go on, rinse off if that's your need. But you're going to do it alone."

He understood then that it wasn't him, but his role as a man that she was after. She had taken charge of him, just as he had of her . . . but in a different way. Mae needed to pay her way, acknowledge the man in her life with her body.

He could only imagine how that transaction had come about in the first place in her young life, and chose not to think about it any further. She saddened him the way it was. Her past was an unknown country — one where he knew nothing of the language, currency, or history — and he planned on keeping it that way.

"You sure you don't want to come in with me?" Mae asked, a pout growing on her face, rejection settling firmly in her heart and mind.

"I'm positive. You go on. There looks to be a pool a few feet off to Clipper's right. Just watch yourself near the fallen trees; there might be some water snakes or snapping turtles lurking about."

Mae didn't move. A bead of sweat trickled down her throat, cascading between her upturned breasts. Josiah watched the sweat pass down to her belly button, then looked away quickly.

"You don't think I'm pretty enough, do you?"

"It's not that."

"What? Then you ain't been with a whore before? Been with a woman who gives herself to one man after the next for a dollar or less?"

"You really don't want me to answer that question."

The raven had stopped calling and flew overhead. The movement and shadow pulled Josiah's attention fully away from Mae.

"Yes, I do," she said. "Answer me."

Josiah watched the raven fly out of the motte and disappear over a hill to the north.

The bright sun made the black bird seem even blacker, like a hard shadow flying into the sky. If Josiah had been an Indian or a man of superstition, he might have known what the bird's movement meant, if anything. But as it was, he was not a believer in much of anything otherworldly, religious or otherwise, so he was unaware of the sign, good or bad.

There was a feeling in the air, though, a real bad feeling.

He turned back to Mae, who was still staring at him expectantly.

"It's none of your business what women I've been with," he said. "Now go rinse off. I'm going to go see if I can find us a meal."

With that, Josiah pushed past Mae, hustled over to Clipper, and pulled the Winchester out of the scabbard.

Mae had not moved. She stood frozen, her eyes full of mature hate, her feet planted solidly, as if she were prepared to make her final stand in life right then and there.

"I hope you die," she sneered.

Josiah marched past her, not acknowledging her presence for one second, following the raven out of the motte and into the sunlight, as quickly as he could.

The rabbit had no idea that the blade of grass it was chewing on was going to be its last. Josiah took a deep breath and pulled back firmly on the trigger.

The shot from the Winchester echoed across the grassy rise and off into the distance, rolling like thunder into the silence that had surrounded the live oak motte. Several ravens lit to the air from the high canopies, a circling rise of feathers that looked like smoke and called out after the echo in a panic, checking to see, perhaps, if all their brethren were accounted for.

The bullet caught the rabbit in the neck, almost decapitating it. Death was instant. At least, Josiah thought, the meat would not taste of struggle and suffering.

It had been many a year since Josiah had injured his prey instead of killing it outright with the first or second shot. He was confident in his shooting ability, and had been certain of the shot and the outcome before he took it. There was no stomaching the thought of a wounded animal crawling off somewhere to die a slow, miserable death at his hand. That had happened when he was a young boy and inexperienced, but he would not stand for such an error now.

He hurried to the rabbit and made sure it was dead.

Its back legs kicked once before he picked it up, and he slit what was left of its throat in one quick swipe, just to make sure.

Josiah set about quickly skinning and

dressing the meaty buck, but suddenly slowed his actions. He decided he was in no mood to make haste, that there was no need to hurry back to the motte.

He wanted nothing more, at that moment, than to revive his strength and refresh himself after fleeing Waco. Then he could get on to Fort Worth as quickly as possible and be done with Maudie Mae Johnson once and for all. Wipe her from his memory as soon as he could.

If he never saw another yellow-haired whore again in his life, it would be too soon.

He could understand her anger, her shock, at Scrap, but to wish death on *him* when he had done nothing more than turn away from an intimate encounter, was not just unacceptable — it was beyond rude. It was the most hateful thing anyone had said to him in a long time.

It was Mae's good fortune, though, that he was not the kind of man who held a grudge, who would take a curse so personally that he would leave her alongside the trail to fend for herself.

He had scooped her up and brought her this far, but he did not have to be concerned about much else other than keeping her safe until his part of the bargain, as unspoken as that bargain was, was finished and he was rid of her from his saddle. That was that. The decision made.

Every ounce of rage he felt toward Mae was executed in the angry rip of rabbit skin and the lopping off of the head. He had never dressed a rabbit so thoroughly. It almost made him hesitate and go after another one, since he still could feel the blood coursing through the throbbing veins in his forehead.

One rabbit was plenty, and besides, the shot and the ravens calling about had probably set off the alarm for the rest of the critters around the motte that there was danger afoot. A human in the midst.

No matter what, the presence of a man always seemed to signal danger to the animal kind.

Josiah had tossed his small game satchel over his shoulder, and he stuffed the fresh red meat inside.

Normally he would bury the guts and the pelt — if he had no use for it — but he didn't take the time. He just walked away, leaving a gift to the coyotes, an apology for the ruckus.

He was halfway back to the motte before he realized that the stillness of the land had not returned to normal.

There is an usual quiet passage after rifle

fire, after an animal falls to the will of a man. Birds flutter deeper into the shrubs. Rabbits drop into their holes. Badgers freeze, standing so rigid they look like a small rock in the distance. But it doesn't take long before life, especially around a motte, returns to normal.

Something was wrong.

Josiah quickened his pace, searching in the shadows of the trees for any movement, for any sign of Mae.

It wasn't until he heard a bloodcurdling scream — a bloodcurdling woman's scream — that he broke into a full run, cocking his rifle as he went and flipping his Peacemaker up out of the swivel rig, certain that he was going to need it.

CHAPTER 15

He didn't see Mae when he ran into the motte, but Clipper had moved away from the stream and was standing unconcerned next to the trunk of one of the larger live oaks.

Glad that his horse was not alarmed, Josiah searched for the girl. The light was dim, dimmer than when he had gone off to hunt, but it only took a second before he saw Mae standing at the far end of the motte, her back to him, filtered light dappling over her like she had stepped directly into it so she could be seen.

She had dressed, and somehow produced a gun, her dainty little stingy gun, and was aiming it at the silhouette of a man. He looked to have fallen to his knees before her and was in the process of begging for his life or, at least, praying that she wasn't a good shot or as crazy as she seemed.

Josiah knew immediately that the man was

not Scrap Elliot.

He could hear the whispers of the man's voice, hear lyrical pleading in Spanish. Urgent whispers that almost had a religious flavor to them. He knew the voice then, knew the man, and was immediately concerned that Mae could be impetuous and fearful, that she could, with little provocation, shoot the man square between the eyes and not think twice about it. Especially if she felt threatened or weak. It was hard telling what Mae Johnson would do if she was chased into a corner or threatened by an unknown man.

"Stop," he yelled at the top of his lungs. "Leave him be. He isn't going to hurt you."

Mae jerked her head to the side, Josiah's demand instantly drawing her attention away from the man kneeling on the ground.

Her action — or distraction — gave the man a brief opportunity to save himself, and being the sly survivor he was, he took full advantage of Mae's blind side. The man jumped up from the kneeling position as swiftly as a jack-rabbit and grabbed Mae's wrist, easily gaining control of the hand that held the little gun.

Mae screamed again. Only this one held no fear or surprise, but was full of anger. The outside world was silent, the echo of her scream escaping the motte and riding over the grassy hills, announcing her rage to the world one more time. If Josiah's shot at the rabbit had drawn a peaceful visitor to them, it was hard telling what Mae's screams would bring.

The man twisted her wrist, not too forcibly, just enough to let her know he meant business. After a deep, reticent breath, the gun fell safely into his open palm from Mae's outstretched hand.

As soon as the man had control of the gun, he released Mae from his grasp, a mistake known only to Josiah, for the moment.

Knowing the girl a bit better, Josiah broke into a run across the motte, watching his step as best as he could, trying not to take his eyes off the two. He put his Peacemaker away. There would be no need for it after all.

Mae challenged the man, swatting at him like he was a swarm of flies, cussing the entire time.

To his credit, the man did not point the gun at Mae and make her stop. He just kept stepping back away from her.

"Give me my damn gun," Mae screamed.

She squatted one second, bounced to the right the next, then to the left, searching, it seemed, for a way to tackle the man. There was no end to her anger.

"Give me my damn gun, you stinkin' bastard," Mae screamed again.

A broad smile grew on the man's deep brown, leathery face. His stark white hair seemed to glow, even in the shadowy light of the motte, and there was absolutely no mistaking who the man was now.

It seemed that Juan Carlos had found Josiah and Mae.

Whether it was the rabbit shots that drew the old Mexican to them was yet to be known, but it was a great surprise to see Juan Carlos. And a happy one. Happy surprises were rare on the trail. Very rare indeed.

"I want my gun, you fool." Mae slapped at Juan Carlos, and he jumped back even farther now, laughing fully, like he was playing a game of keep-away with a two-year-old.

Juan Carlos was in his mid-sixties, and his arms were skinny, but what meat was there was still muscle. He was dust-covered, like he had been on the trail for days, and there was not a weapon showing on his belt or anywhere else. Juan Carlos always traveled light, but it looked like he was traveling even lighter than normal. There was not a horse to be seen. Still, Josiah knew the man was armed, that he didn't travel unprepared unless there was cause.

Josiah stopped his run and walked up to Juan Carlos's side, grabbing his shoulder warmly and smiling for the first time all day.

"She is a wild one, this girl, Señor Wolfe?" Juan Carlos said.

Mae stopped bouncing. She was panting. "You know this Mexican?"

Josiah nodded his head. "One of the few men I trust without question. He is my friend."

"You trust a Mexican?"

"Why wouldn't I?"

"You don't look the type. You don't look like you trust anybody."

"Neither do you," Josiah said, doing his best not to show any emotion on his face for Mae to misconstrue in any way. His tone had changed, though. As glad as he was to see Juan Carlos, the air still had not been cleared between him and Mae. He stared at her coldly.

Juan Carlos looked down and examined Mae's little gun, trying to ignore the two of them. "Have I interrupted something, *mis amigos?*"

"No," Josiah said. "Not at all."

"Can I have my gun, please?" Mae said,

standing stiffly, her ankles together, with her hand out to Juan Carlos. Her voice was softer, and so was her expression. She had transformed herself in a matter of seconds into a needy schoolgirl.

Juan Carlos shook his head no. "Maybe once I get to know you. Know that I can trust you with a gun."

"What makes you think you'll be around that long?" Mae asked, her normal demeanor returning once she realized her ploy wasn't going to work.

"He's welcome in my camp for as long he wants to stay," Josiah said. "Come on, friend, let's get this meat on the fire and catch up. It has been a long time since we shared a meal."

Juan Carlos smiled broadly and nodded. "*Sí,* it will be nice to be somewhere safe and familiar. *Tengo la suerte de encontrarle.*"

Josiah glanced over at Juan Carlos, a question forming, but he held back, figured there'd be plenty of time to catch up once they got settled.

Juan Carlos read the look as a misunderstanding, and he would have been correct, but not because Josiah did not speak fluent Spanish, but rather because he wondered what had happened in Austin and how and why Juan Carlos had come to be this far north. But even more than that, Josiah wanted to know if Juan Carlos knew anything of Suzanne del Toro . . . but it could all wait. Wait until they were comfortable. There didn't seem to be a rush, and the old Mexican certainly didn't look to be in a panic, like he was being pursued, and that made Josiah even happier. The last thing he needed at the moment was the worry of another pack of men on their trail, set on doing them as much harm as possible.

"I am fortunate to find you," Juan Carlos said.

Josiah continued to smile, but it was a smile of curiosity now, as he headed back toward Clipper.

Mae had not fallen in behind them, had not joined them. She was standing her ground, her hands firmly planted on her hips. "What about me?"

Josiah dug his boots into the sandy soil, stopped, and said, "Suit yourself. There's plenty for everybody . . . as long as you can be civil."

Mae stuck her tongue out at Josiah, and for some reason, he and Juan Carlos both broke into belly laughs.

It was mid-afternoon and the air under the canopy was still hot, but a breeze was snaking its way through the trees, making the environment much more comfortable than it would have been without the shade.

There was little left of the rabbit. Mae sat off by herself, on a rock overlooking the stream. Josiah and Juan Carlos were sitting easily at the edge of the motte, both of their backs propped against towering oaks, looking to the south, toward Waco.

Josiah was in hopes that Scrap would breach the horizon and join them for the rest of the journey north — but so far the only thing Josiah had sighted was a few ravens soaring off in the distance.

"You are losing daylight, then," Juan Carlos said.

"We have time," Josiah answered. "Our lateness will not be translated into desertion, so there is no need to worry about severe consequences, not that the Rangers employ such stringent military bindings, but it may provoke objections to future advancement for the remainder of our employ, for both Scrap and me," Josiah said.

"You have reasons for these consequences . . . and this girl?"

Josiah stared at Juan Carlos. "I went looking for you."

"For me?"

"Yes, in Austin. I wanted you to keep an

eye on Ofelia and Lyle while I was away. I went to the livery to find you . . ."

"But I was gone. I was already gone. I had left a few days ago."

"I didn't know that. While I was at the livery, it caught fire. I think it was purposely set on fire, but it may or may not matter now that I have found you. After the fire was put out, there was a charred body found inside. I thought it might be you, so I went to look for you. I went to see Pearl, and she told me that you had been there, and if she needed you then she'd be able to contact you at the Paradise Hotel — so I went to Little Mexico in hopes that you were there, alive, and not dead."

"That is true, amigo, I did tell Pearl that."

"I went there, but alas, as you know, I did not find out anything. Even more disturbing was the news that Suzanne del Toro had left about the same time as you and had not been heard from, either. Did you leave together?"

"No, amigo, I went looking for her," Juan Carlos said. "I feared for her safety."

"Why?"

"She is in a weak position. There are those who want what she controls."

"*El Puño,* The Fist?" Josiah said.

Juan Carlos nodded. "*Sí,* how did you know?"

"Mae told me. I had to get onto the trail, but I stopped in Waco. It seems *El Puño* has business there, too."

"He is everywhere."

"I think the sheriff there, at least his deputies, have fallen under his sway. Scrap and I couldn't stand against them all. I was going to alert the Rangers once I saw Mae to safety in Fort Worth. She saw some killings. I thought you and Suzanne del Toro might have been involved, since the paper mentioned a Mexican man and woman fleeing the riverfront."

Juan Carlos shook his head no. "It was not me. I have not been able to find Suzanne. I fear for her life. *El Puño* is serious about overtaking her properties."

"Who, exactly, is this *El Puño?*"

"You do not know?"

"How could I?"

"Who did you talk with at the Paraiso?"

"Her brother, Emilio."

Juan Carlos took a deep breath. "Then you stared *El Puño* in the eyes, Señor Wolfe, you most certainly did."

CHAPTER 16

A cloud of dust appeared on the horizon, promptly ending the conversation about Suzanne del Toro. The shock of *El Puño*'s real identity hung in the air, and Josiah had a lot of questions forming in his mind — primarily, why a brother would be threatened by or do harm to his sister. But money was the cause of many a conflict, and Josiah was certain that it, and power, were at the core of the troubles.

But that would have to wait.

Upon seeing the movement of dust heading toward them, both Josiah and Juan Carlos stood and eased back into the shadows of the motte, not taking their eyes off the coming rider or riders.

It was too far away to see anything that would give Josiah a clue as to who or what was causing the dust, but there was no question it was at least one rider — how many and their intent were entirely speculation.

Erring on the side of caution was his normal tack, so Josiah wasn't necessarily going to overreact, but he intended to be ready for whatever was coming his way. Most likely it was bad news. All his good luck had probably been used up with the arrival of Juan Carlos.

"Looks like we're about to have company," Josiah said.

"*Sí*. It does."

"Expecting anybody?"

"I am always expecting somebody, señor."

"I suppose we both are."

"*Sí, somos.* Yes we are. Always. *Siempre.*"

Josiah stood stiffly, eyeing the rising dust, disconcerted about everything that was happening.

Dust was a nearly universal warning in Texas that life was about to change. "Emilio played me for a fool," he said.

"You are lucky he didn't kill you. He takes his reputation very seriously. He is not called *El Puño* for nothing."

"I gave him no cause to kill me."

"You are an acquaintance of Fat Susie; that is reason enough. She is extremely fond of you, Señor Wolfe."

Josiah sighed heavily. He was even more worried about Suzanne del Toro now than when he'd left Austin. Juan Carlos had not brought him good news at all. "You are on foot?" he asked, pushing the thought of the woman from his mind as quickly as possible.

But no matter how much he tried, he could not rid himself of worrying about her. Suzanne was so different from his Lily, from the wife he'd buried a little more than two years ago, and he was not sure what he felt for her. All he knew was that he felt something, and that was news to him — good or bad was hard to say. Regardless, anything more than a gentle concern was all that was possible. Their lives were far too different for anything respectable to bloom.

Juan Carlos nodded. "*Sí.* I have no horse, señor."

"I was afraid of that." Josiah gripped his Peacemaker. "Do you have a gun?"

Juan Carlos waved the stingy gun he had taken from Mae. "This is all that I have."

"You made your way here without a gun?" An incredulous look flashed across Josiah's face. Juan Carlos was withholding information from him, not offering a full explanation why he was north of Waco, how he got there, or how he expected to survive without a gun.

It was no surprise, though.

Juan Carlos was more like a shadow than

a fully formed man made of flesh and bone anyway. He was there one minute and gone the next, had always been that way. The last time Josiah had seen Juan Carlos was when he'd disappeared into a large crowd just outside the jail in Austin, a day before his brother's funeral.

Perhaps it was being half-Mexican and half-Anglo, never fitting in one place or the other, that gave the Mexican the skills of a lizard, the face of a chameleon.

Captain Fikes had never openly acknowledged Juan Carlos as his brother, but the two were usually never far apart. Josiah was certain Fikes had used Juan Carlos as a spy, gaining information about cattle rustlers and other criminal escapades through his brother's efforts. A large part of Fikes's success and heroics was probably due to Juan Carlos.

And then there was Fikes's relationship with Suzanne del Toro, the same Fat Susie that Josiah had fallen into bed with in a weak moment. But it was a hidden affair for the captain; an affair with a Mexican whore would not have played well in the upper Anglo society of Austin, and as far as Josiah knew, that relationship was still a secret — buried six feet under, now that Captain Fikes was dead. The captain had lived a double life, existing as the owner of a large estate and a Texas Ranger, but more comfortable on the trail and in the arms of a whore than anywhere else.

Josiah had the same conflict the captain had, not having the ability to avoid Suzanne del Toro's bed but knowing he should walk completely away from her embrace. It was difficult. One of the most difficult things Josiah had ever had to do.

The fact that Juan Carlos was the captain's brother, of the same blood, only made him a more mysterious man than he already was. Josiah could only hope that his friend had not put them in a more precarious situation than they were already in by showing up at the motte like a straggling stranger, begging for water and salvation.

"I've got a Winchester in the saddle," Josiah said. "And plenty of bullets. But we're in a bad spot if there's a posse of men looking for you . . . or us. We best get ready."

The dust on the horizon drew closer. It was still difficult to tell how many riders there were . . . but there was one thing for certain — whoever it was was heading right for them.

"I have a knife, too. If it comes to that," Juan Carlos said, tapping his leg.

Josiah grinned, glad the man had a weapon

hidden somewhere. "Stay here and keep an eye out. I'll get the rifle, then see Mae to safety."

"No, you won't," Mae said.

Josiah stopped dead in his tracks. Mae had retrieved the Winchester from the scabbard and had it squarely aimed at Josiah's chest.

Juan Carlos clicked his tongue and shook his head. *"Vergüenza, vergüenza, señorita."*

"Don't talk to me like that. You say what you mean or I'll just shoot the Ranger right here and now. Shoulda killed him already."

"I said, 'shame, shame.' Now," Juan Carlos said in a very calm voice, "lower the rifle. We are your friends. *Entiendo, mi amiga?*"

"I won't," Mae yelled. "They killed Clem Dawson. He was my friend." Tears had welled up in Mae's eyes, and she was biting her lip. Her finger quivered on the trigger.

Josiah was growing more nervous by the second.

He didn't dare take his eyes off of Mae, but he was concerned about the approaching rider or riders, too. If they were the men from Waco — Liam O'Reilly and his fellow deputies — then they just might take sides with Mae and not ask any questions. Killing Clem Dawson could label him and Scrap as outlaws even though they were Rangers. It had happened before, rightfully, but that was not the case now, at least not to Josiah's way of thinking. Scrap Elliot had been well within his rights to shoot the man.

Juan Carlos cleared his throat. "I am sure Señor Wolfe and Señor Elliot had a good reason for any harm they may have caused. These are very fine men. The best Texas Rangers this side of the Brazos."

Juan Carlos did not break eye contact with Mae, nor did his voice waver. It was like he was trying to make friends with a snake — the whole time planning on attacking it, before it had a chance to attack him.

Josiah knew the ploy, had seen Juan Carlos use it before, but he didn't think it would work this time. Not with Maudie Mae Johnson. As it was, Josiah had had about enough of her unpredictability and rage. She made him nervous. But even more than that, she made him mad. Mad as a damn hornet.

"Shut up. Just shut up, Juan Carlos," Josiah said.

Mae drew back. So did Juan Carlos. He froze up like he'd been hit with a sudden, unforeseen blizzard.

Josiah stepped forward, stepped right up to Mae, pressing his chest against the barrel without one blink of his eye. "I did my best to see you to safety, girl. I meant you no harm. Not then, not now. So if you're going to shoot me, do it now. Just shoot me right now and get it the hell over with."

"Señor Josiah," Juan Carlos whispered.

"No. I mean it. Shoot me right now. I am doggone tired of this girl waving a gun in somebody's face every time she gets a chance." Josiah paused, his eyes still focused on Mae, boring into her, daring her, demanding she do . . . something. "There's somebody coming. A posse or a friend? I don't know. The possibility of a real threat to our lives, and here we stand, one more time, faced down by somebody that I've tried to help on to a better life. If I can't do any better than that, then shoot me, damn it."

Josiah pushed against the barrel with his chest again. Mae staggered back a few feet, a horrified look on her face.

"But you have a son," Mae said.

Josiah shook his head, and in one swift motion reached up and swept the Winchester out of Mae's quivering hand. He stepped forward so he was nearly nose to nose with her. He could smell her foul breath. "Don't ever do that again, do you understand? Never again."

Mae cowered, pulling back quickly, like she was about to be beat.

"And stop that, too," Josiah yelled, clutching the rifle as tightly as he could. If the Winchester had been made of weak wood, he would have snapped it in half. "If I haven't hit you by now, I'm not going to."

"Señor," Juan Carlos said, grabbing Josiah's shoulder gently from behind.

He didn't turn around. "What?"

"The horseman approaches."

For a second, Josiah didn't move, didn't break eye contact with Mae. He stared at her, certain she was going to come at him, claws open, like a wild animal. But she didn't. She stood, exhaled, and let a tear drain onto her cheek.

"I've made myself clear, then?"

Mae nodded yes, not bothering to wipe away the tear.

"Good. Don't make me repeat myself," Josiah said, flipping up the rifle into a comfortable position and chambering a round as he made his way to the edge of the motte, each step heavy and full of intent.

Juan Carlos was close on his heels.

Mae held back, an odd, indeterminable look molded on her face. It was like she didn't know what else to say . . . or do, after Josiah's outburst.

Juan Carlos was correct. It was only one rider heading their way, riding full-out,

"We ain't got much time," Scrap said, dismounting from his blue roan mare, Missy. "There's a posse of six men coming out of Waco, hot after me like I'm some kind of outlaw. Boy, that was a mess I'd just as soon not have to revisit."

He quickly led Missy and the other horse, a young black stallion sporting a well-worn California rig, to the stream. Both horses took to the water gladly. It looked to have been a hard ride.

Scrap kneeled on the bank of the stream, cupping water for himself, then washing the dust off of his face.

Josiah looked over his shoulder, to the horizon. It was calm, free of the predicted coming storm . . . for the moment.

Juan Carlos waited patiently, offering nothing but a serious, thoughtful look on his face. The Mexican showed no outward emotion that indicated he was happy to see

Scrap Elliot.

Mae had marched off upon seeing Scrap ride in, positioning herself on the other side of Clipper, so she would not have to face the young Ranger. Josiah had given her a stern glare, silently reminding her of his promise, before she'd disappeared from his sight.

He didn't trust her, but there were no weapons within her reach that he knew of, so he was reasonably comfortable she wouldn't try to shoot Scrap.

Scrap stood up from the stream, water trailing easily off his bare chin. He glanced over at Juan Carlos with disdain, then said, "Where'd he come from?"

As far as Josiah could tell, there was an unstated feud going on between Scrap and Juan Carlos, at least from Scrap's point of view.

After Captain Fikes had been killed in the spring, Josiah and Scrap had been charged with taking his body back to Austin for burial and the proper accolades due to a true Texas hero like the captain. Juan Carlos had joined them about halfway in, in Neu-Bronfels, and stayed until they parted company outside the jail in Austin. Juan Carlos was wanted for the murder of a man in San Antonio, a man that had tried to kill

Josiah, but it was a bogus charge as far as everyone involved was concerned — everyone but the law in San Antonio, that is. As far as Josiah knew, the matter had been cleared up. But all of that had little to do with Scrap's attitude toward Juan Carlos. As far as Josiah could tell, Scrap had a streak in him that couldn't abide Mexican blood mixed with Anglo blood. He knew that Juan Carlos was the captain's half brother, but that, unmistakably, didn't earn any immediate respect from Scrap Elliot.

"I followed the señor here," Juan Carlos said. "I was outside of the shack the night you both arrived on the riverfront. I followed you down from the Reservation, just in case you encountered trouble. I knew what was there, waiting."

Josiah thought back, and he remembered seeing a man sitting, covered with a blanket and sombrero, on the porch of one of the shacks that night. "Why didn't you say anything to us?"

"I was glad to see you, but Emilio's men had just left. I was afraid to show myself, and I could do more for you hidden than out in the open if it came to that. It is usually best if I stay hidden."

"Who is Emilio?" Scrap asked.

"*El Puño,*" Josiah answered.

Scrap shrugged his shoulders but continued to glare at Juan Carlos.

"All right," Josiah said. "It doesn't matter anyway. He's with us now. It doesn't matter where he came from or why he's here. We need to make some plans, fast, if there's a posse from Waco coming after us. I don't think our being Texas Rangers will cool their trigger fingers."

Josiah was still angry from his outburst at Mae, and the last thing he wanted to deal with was any animosity that existed between Juan Carlos and Scrap. Mae already had a chip on her shoulder when it came to Scrap, which, if added to the mix, could really make things uncomfortable inside the motte. Getting out of there as quick as possible made more sense to him than anything else he could think of.

So he knew the best thing he could do was assume the presence and practice of his rank as sergeant. It wouldn't necessarily carry any weight with Mae, or Juan Carlos for that matter, but it would with Scrap. Or at least, it'd better.

"We're still a good ways from Fort Worth," Scrap said. "But we got some daylight left, and I think Missy still has some gumption in her to run. The stallion I took looks to be a damn fine steed full-out. Probably the most beautiful creature I've seen since I was fixin' to buy Missy. And before you say anything, I ain't no horse thief. One of them men that was chasin' after me fell off in the middle of the herd. I wasn't gonna leave the horse there to die, to be flayed by one of those darn steers. He's too good a horse to be useless and all, and besides, Mae needs somethin' to ride since her horse was lost back at the river."

"That old shaggy horse would have never made it this far," Josiah said.

"Probably not," Scrap agreed. "I think we ought to make out for Fort Worth then; get as far away from here as we can. I know the land up this way a bit better than I did south of Waco, and there's plenty of places to run full-out, then pull back, especially after we get past Fort Graham. That's just a piece up the trail; we might be able to safely spend the night there."

Juan Carlos stepped forward. "There's a little village there now. That fort's been closed for years. Not much there but a saloon and maybe a smithy. Probably less than two hundred people around in the hills, if that. We might be able to replenish ourselves, but I doubt there's much there that'll help us."

"Do I look stupid?" Scrap said.

"You look young," Juan Carlos replied, without missing a beat.

"And you look like —"

Josiah forced himself quickly between the two of them. "I'm not going to tolerate this kind of behavior from you any more than I am from that girl. Now, we can stand here and argue while that posse of men bears down on us, or we can cover our tracks and get a move on. What's it going to be? Stand here and fight to the death, outnumbered? Or head north as quick as we can where we have a better chance?"

"You're in charge," Scrap said, kicking his boot into the sandy soil.

"I'm glad you noticed." Josiah headed toward Clipper, but stopped just short of reaching the horse.

Mae was standing on the other side of the Appaloosa, watching everything that went on.

"I think we ought to split up, just to even things out," Josiah said.

Juan Carlos nodded. "That is a good idea, señor. If I head west, maybe I can draw one or two of the riders away. That will leave you and Señor Elliot to face three or four of them, if it comes to that. I will need the black stallion, though."

"No way," Scrap protested. "I didn't go

into that herd of longhorns and risk my neck so I could hand off a fine horse like that to a Mexican. Especially that Mexican. I meant to give that horse to Miss Mae as a token of my sorrow for shooting her, um, friend."

Mae came out from around Clipper. "It'll take more than a horse for me to take any kind of shine to you." She spit at the ground, then looked sheepishly toward Josiah.

"He has no horse of his own," Josiah said, ignoring Mae.

"He can walk then," Scrap answered.

"He'll take the horse and return it when we meet up in Fort Worth. Is that agreeable to you both?" Josiah said.

Juan Carlos nodded. "*Sí*. I think it would be very wise of me to search Hell's Half Acre in Fort Worth for Fat Susie. Emilio could very well be holding her there against her will."

Scrap was staring down at the ground, still nudging a deep, frustrated trench with his boot.

"Elliot?"

"That's fine. I guess I don't have no choice."

Josiah pushed the last bit of sandy soil over

211

the charred embers of the fire he'd built to cook the rabbit. All three of the horses were on the edge of the motte now, packed and ready to go, while the three men smoothed the hoofprints and footprints and covered up as much of their existence under the trees as possible.

Mae stood by the black stallion, stroking its neck. She had remained remarkably quiet and compliant while they prepared to leave the motte.

Josiah watched her closely and tried to manage Juan Carlos and Scrap as best he could. He thought splitting them up was a really good idea. It would be less for Josiah to be concerned with, and Juan Carlos was right, it might split up the posse. He and Scrap were armed well enough to take on three or four men under the right circumstances. They had done it before.

"All right, that looks good to me," Josiah said.

"If they have a good tracker with them, it won't matter anyway," Juan Carlos said. "They will know how many of us there are. They will know we have the *niña* with us."

"Better to try and throw them off the trail than point a sign toward our intentions," Josiah said.

"*Sí*, I agree, señor. Where shall I meet you

in Fort Worth?"

"Scrap?" Josiah asked.

"My aunt Callie owns a boardin' house two blocks from the Tarrant County Courthouse. A two-storey affair, a big sign out front says, 'Melhaven's Boardin' House.' At least it did the last time I was there."

Juan Carlos nodded. "I will meet you there then, in a day or so."

Josiah offered his hand, and the Mexican shook it firmly. "Be safe, my friend."

"*Sí, mis amigos,* you, too," Juan Carlos said, glaring at Scrap, and not offering his hand to the boy — who had not offered his hand, either. "I will not allow anything to happen to the horse."

"See that you don't," Scrap said. "It belongs to Miss Mae."

Juan Carlos nodded, mounted the black stallion, said good-bye to Mae, and rode off into the west.

Josiah watched the Mexican disappear, then got Clipper ready to go. Mae walked up to him, stopped, and looked at him expectantly. After a long silence, Josiah said, "You're not riding with me, if that's what you're thinking."

"I'm not gonna ride with him," Mae said, flipping her head back at Scrap, who was settling himself into Missy's saddle.

"I'm afraid you are," Josiah said. It was clear to both Mae and Scrap that it was an order, not a request.

Mae kicked the dirt, turned her lip up, and started to say something, but Josiah stopped her. "Get up there with Ranger Elliot, now. I'm not telling you again."

Scrap eased Missy over to Mae and offered his hand down to her. She stared up at Josiah, her lips still twisted, but said nothing, then went over and reached up to take Scrap's hand, allowing him to pull her up on the saddle behind him.

Josiah didn't breathe easy until they were out of the motte, running full speed toward Fort Worth.

CHAPTER 18

It was almost dusk when Josiah finally slowed Clipper to a trot.

Scrap and Mae were not far behind, and Mae had been unusually quiet since they'd left the motte. They had either outrun the posse of men from Waco, or there was another reason they had made it this far without any trouble. Josiah hoped that the men had chosen to track Juan Carlos instead of them. It looked like splitting up had been fruitful — the Mexican was far better at eluding capture and confrontation than Josiah was.

The sky was clear, not a cloud to be seen, the blue streaked with silver and a bit of pink on the horizon. It was going to be a bright night since the moon was just past full, waning, just a sliver of it cut off in a dim shadow. The evening star was pulsing below the moon, a lone star at the moment, dotting the sky confidently.

For the most part, Josiah was glad to have an uneventful night of weather to contend with. There was a storm sitting behind Scrap in the form of a blond-haired whore, and it was hard telling what she would try next. As it was, Josiah knew he'd be sleeping with one eye open.

They had eased past Fort Graham, or what was left of it. The fort had been built in the late 1840s, not long after the war with the Mexicans, when Josiah was barely starting to walk, by the 2nd U.S. Dragoons. But the fort was closed less than ten years later, and now there was little in the way of a settlement around it, since there was no protection offered against roaming Indians, thieves, or whatever. The fort itself had been set upon by scavengers. A few of the barracks stood, and a livery where a smithy plied his trade to those in the area. It didn't look like he got much business.

There were plenty of groves of pecan trees about, and some hearty oaks that could have gone a long way in building cabins, but they stood untouched.

Josiah wasn't too concerned about finding a place to bed down for the night, but he wanted to stay out away from any population that might exist around Fort Graham. They were now well past any cabins and ranch houses and continued to ride north.

He was more than a little leery about how far Emilio's — *El Puño's* — reach extended north.

There was not enough time to face another circumstance like they'd had in Waco, and Mae was more than a wild card, so it was best just to find a place close to the Brazos so they could have some privacy, keep an eye out, and get some rest.

Scrap eased up alongside Josiah. "About near time to stop off for the night, ain't it?"

Josiah nodded. "Just looking for a place where a watch'll be easy."

"I think we lost them fellas from Waco," Scrap said.

"I hope so."

"They won't give up until they find me," Mae said.

Before Josiah could say anything, Scrap said, "What makes you think that?"

"I'm worth more than that horse you stole, you fool boy."

"You talk like you're a slave. Ain't no such thing as a human ownin' another human anymore. Especially not a Mexican ownin' a white girl."

"Then you're dumber than I thought you was," Mae snipped from behind, pulling back in the saddle as far as she could.

217

"Both of you hush up," Josiah said. "There looks to be a spot on a ridge overlooking the river. We can stop there for the night."

"Good," Scrap said. "I'm starved."

"I got some rabbit and jerky in my saddle-bag. We can cook up some johnnycakes and have some Arbuckle's. That'd suit me just fine this evening. How about you, Mae? Does that sound good?" Josiah asked.

Mae glared at him, refusing to answer. According to the look in her eyes, if she would've had a knife, Josiah was sure he would have been a dead man before he could draw another breath.

The fire crackled comfortably in the clearing of oaks on the ridge.

They were about fifty feet up from the river, and the ridge stretched down an easy roll of land, not as severe and steep as it was in some places along the Brazos, like Waco. Every direction was reasonably open, any riders coming were sure to be seen in the light of the moon that beamed down from overhead.

The moonlight was a blessing and a curse, as far as Josiah was concerned. It made the camp just as visible from a distance as it did any threat, but it was a chance he was willing to take. A Texas Ranger going into hiding just didn't seem right . . . it wasn't Josiah's way. Especially considering they had done nothing wrong.

Regardless, Josiah was glad for the rest and for a decent meal.

At first, Mae had refused to eat, but the smell of warming meat proved too much for her to resist, and she eventually joined Scrap and Josiah for a meal, creeping up next to Josiah like a wounded animal too weak to do anything but beg silently.

Mae ate ravenously, and any manners that may have been bestowed on her in her young life were not evident. It was doubtful that she had ever experienced any proper training with concern to eating — and it really didn't matter, other than Josiah noticing that the girl was just this side of wild.

Josiah emptied the rest of the Arbuckle's from the pot into his cup, and Mae stood up and walked right past him, like he didn't even exist.

She brushed by him so close he could smell her; a heavy mix of sweat, trail dirt, camp smoke, and a hint, just a hint, of womanhood. There was nothing sweet about her smell, nothing that would draw him to her like a bee to a flower, and that made him even sadder for Maudie Mae Johnson.

Scrap had settled down, after eating as much food as was available, and was leaning back on a boulder, smoking a quirley, a hand-rolled cigarette. His eyes were glued to Mae, but he had taken the hint and stayed as far away from her as he could, eating on the other side of Josiah, ignoring her as best he could.

Mae stopped just past Josiah and looked over her shoulder. "I want to wash off."

"At night?" Josiah peered over the rim of his cup as he took a deep swig of coffee. He had made it really strong, knowing that he was going to sit watch the first round, letting Scrap catch some sleep. The bitterness of the coffee settled directly on his tongue, and he nearly spit it out.

Scrap straightened up. "Ain't you afraid of snakes, Mae? You can't see them swimming so much in the dark. You could get bit and die, pulled into a nest of water moccasins, and we wouldn't be able to save you."

"I can see a snake coming from a mile away," Mae said.

Scrap drew hard on the quirley and exhaled a big puff of blue smoke. He started to answer her back but obviously thought better of it. He clamped his mouth shut, stubbing out what was left of the cigarette with far more force than he needed to.

"Suit yourself," Josiah said. "I expect you'll be fine."

If there was anybody that knew the ways of a river in the darkness of night, it was probably Mae Johnson. He wasn't certain how long Mae had lived in the shack in Waco, but he got the impression that she'd been there for some time. A nighttime rinse was probably a regular occurrence.

The muscles in Mae's face didn't move. She didn't flinch or show one ounce of emotion. "I was gonna go anyway." And just like back at the motte, she reached down and swept her loose dress over her head.

Scrap gulped loudly.

Mae turned, leaving her dress in a bundle on the ground, and walked away slowly, naked as the day she was born.

Neither the swiftness of her action nor the sight of her bare bottom shocked Josiah this time around. He had come to expect the unexpected from Mae — she surely wasn't modest about her body.

No man enjoyed seeing a beautiful woman naked more than Josiah, but there was something that troubled him immediately as he watched Mae ease down the ridge to the riverbank.

In the brightness of the moonlight, he

could see what looked to be a series of scars on her back. Some were healed up pretty good, but others looked recent, more like little wounds than scars. He hadn't noticed them back at the motte, but then she'd had her back to the stream, and the shock of her nakedness had embarrassed Josiah to a certain degree the first time around. He didn't gawk at her then, or drool over her like a piece of fresh meat, like he thought Scrap was probably doing now.

There was no question Mae had been living in an environment where she could have been beaten, lashed, or even worse. Some men used their fists more for currency than attitude, what the Mexicans called *machismo*. And on one hand — even though he hated to think it — Josiah hoped, in an odd way, that that was exactly what had happened to Mae — because another explanation wouldn't be so easy to cure. Or live with.

It was entirely possible that the scars and wounds were not scars and wounds at all — but sores. Sores from the sickness that comes from her line of work. Cupid's disease. Syphilis.

There might be more to Mae's erratic behavior than just anger and a hard life. Depending on how long she'd had the disease, if that were the case, it could be affecting her demeanor and her sanity.

Josiah had seen the madness of men who returned home from the War Between the States infected from when they'd been away from home, taking advantage of the opportunity to be with any woman they could pay for. Josiah had seen the sadness of a disease eating away at the brain, day by day, until it was too much, and the men ended their own lives, or went off in the woods to die a lonely death on their own.

Josiah hoped he was wrong about the sores. He hoped like hell that Mae had been beaten, and that he and Scrap had saved her from facing anything worse.

Scrap had made his way next to Josiah, unheard . . . or else Josiah was lost in deep thought, and regret, and hadn't noticed the boy.

"Damn," Scrap whispered. "She's pretty. It's a shame she's ticked all the time."

"Well, maybe she's got reason," Josiah said.

He hadn't taken his eyes off Mae. "I think I might take me a swim."

Scrap started to walk toward the river, but Josiah stuck his arm out, putting up a gate, bringing the young Ranger to a dead stop.

"Leave her be, boy," Josiah said.

"That's not for you to say, Wolfe." Scrap was incredulous. He was stiff, balling his fists like he had just been called the worst name he could have been called.

Josiah spun, putting his leg in between Scrap's, grabbing him by the shirt collar with both hands, and pulling him so they were nearly nose to nose. "If you touch her, you could die."

Scrap, of course, misunderstood what Josiah meant, and, Scrap being Scrap, he reared back, pulling Josiah with him, and threw a weak, ill-timed punch at Josiah's face.

Josiah ducked, stepped forward, then pushed Scrap back, tripping him and guiding him to the ground, where his knee immediately landed in the boy's chest, his hand sliding up, gripping his throat. "Don't ever try that again, you fool."

"You ain't got rights to her, Wolfe," Scrap yelled, his arms flaying, trying to strike Josiah, trying to break free.

"Stop it. I have no interest in her. Stop it. She might be sick. If you go be with her, you could get sick, too."

Scrap heaved his chest and relaxed after a second or two. "What do you mean?"

Josiah leaned to Scrap, just in case the wind caught his voice; he didn't want Mae to hear him. "She's got sores. Or they look like sores."

"Like . . . ?"

Josiah nodded. "Like the kind of sores a girl who does what she does might have. Syphilis sores. She could infect you, cause you a lot of grief."

"Damn. Are you sure?"

"No. But I've seen sores like that before." Josiah took his hand off Scrap's throat. "I'm going to let you up. If you're thinking of throwing another punch, I'm here to tell you, you'll live to regret it."

"I'm not stupid."

Josiah didn't say anything. He stood up off Scrap's chest and extended his hand. Scrap hesitated for a second, then allowed himself to be pulled up.

"I'd apologize," Josiah said, "but . . ."

"There's no need." Scrap dusted himself off, cocked his head toward Josiah, then walked off, shaking his head, not bothering to look down at Mae.

Josiah stood there for a second, taking everything in, catching his breath. It was times like this that he wished he smoked. He needed to calm down. Instead, he walked away from the camp, out of the glare of the fire, and looked down to the river.

Mae was standing up on the bank, facing

him, looking up at him, her naked body washed in silvery, alluring light. She motioned for him to come down and join her.

Under other circumstances, he would have welcomed her invitation, and found it difficult to turn his back on a willing, beautiful girl, standing in the moonlight. But that's exactly what he did. He turned and walked away, back to the camp, sad that they both were going to spend the night alone.

CHAPTER 19

Fort Worth didn't seem as populated as Austin, or at least it wasn't near as strung out. The courthouse that Scrap had spoken of was still under construction, and there was a bunch of hubbub going on in town, because the first westbound stagecoach had set up a stop along a route that would take a person to Yuma and beyond. A ride had just left the stop, a crowd cheering at a cloud of dust.

The morning ride for Josiah, Scrap, and Mae had been an easy one, and it had stretched into afternoon without hardly any notice.

The thought of the men in the posse out of Waco, perhaps on their trail, perhaps not, was never far from Josiah's mind. Nor was Juan Carlos. He was concerned about his friend, but he also knew there was nothing more he could do than worry about his well-being — that, and acknowledge that the

Mexican had probably saved him a lot of trouble, once again.

Mae sat comfortably behind Josiah on Clipper.

Scrap had refused to take her onto Missy, had refused to get near her, or even speak to her. There had been more tension in the air when Josiah cooked up some breakfast, but Mae seemed to be glad of Scrap's sudden distance, even though she didn't know the why of the boy's actions.

Josiah felt a little regret about that, about Scrap's obvious fear of contamination or infection, but who would knowingly choose madness for a moment's pleasure? No one that Josiah knew, and he couldn't blame Scrap for his fear, but Mae had probably been treated less than human most all of her life. If she was sick, the last thing she needed now was to be treated like she didn't exist. But Josiah had decided at some point through the night, as he sat watch, that he wasn't even going to broach the subject of her sickness with Mae, or anybody else for that matter.

Once they'd ridden into the outskirts of Fort Worth, if it could be called that, Josiah hung back and let Scrap take the lead since he knew where his aunt's boardinghouse stood. Besides, it had been a while since

Josiah had been to Fort Worth, and it was almost unrecognizable. He wouldn't have known Main Street from First Street if it wasn't marked.

Of course, everybody called Forth Worth, Cowtown, because of its proximity to the Chisholm and the array of opportunities for a cowboy to rest up and raise a little ruckus in Hell's Half Acre on the way north to Abilene. A lot of the northern cattle buyers had established their headquarters in town, and that, of course, drew other businesses to Fort Worth.

"I always heard a girl could make a good livin' in Fort Worth," Mae said. "I shoulda run off from that riverfront a long time ago."

Josiah ignored her. As they passed by several businesses — B. C. Evans Dry Goods, and Martin B. Lloyd's Exchange Office, a few proper women glanced up their way, spied Mae, then looked to the ground quickly. The women were dressed in the latest fineries: a plum velvet basque jacket on one, a gray paletot on the other. Both wore tall, fancy hats with large bird feathers poking out the tops. Their hair was pulled into curls, almost identical to each other, and held in place with expensive bone combs. The layers of clothing hid most of their skin, and Josiah thought — as he always did when he saw a woman all put together — that it must be very warm and very uncomfortable to be so proper.

Yet there was envy in Mae's eyes when he glanced back at her to see if she had seen the women looking at her like they had. He wasn't sure if her envy was for the clothes or the women's lack of worry and the lives they led. She probably could not imagine what it was like not to have to forage for a decent meal with few or no prospects for a decent life, and not to have to wonder if the next man who walked into her bedroom brought her a fist or a disease that would show the edge of madness.

After spending a little time with Mae, even Josiah thought he could come to envy a fancy banker's wife's easy way of life.

Josiah urged Clipper on. "Don't pay any attention to those women, Mae."

She didn't say anything, but he felt her press a little closer to him.

He had the same fearful inclination that Scrap had to pull away, but he refused to shun the girl, especially when he wasn't entirely certain if she had the syphilis or not.

If Fort Worth had changed since the last time Josiah had been through there, it was poised to change even more in the coming days. The railroad had yet to come through, but there was word that construction was about to start again in the near future. A delay had been caused by the Panic of '73.

There were a lot of things Josiah didn't understand, and high finance, gold buyers, the stock markets in New York City, and whether coins were based on silver prices or something else were all part of a bigger picture that was well out of his grasp or daily concern.

All he knew was that times were hard everywhere, and money was scarce. People were scared, including the wealthy fellas who built railroads. Nearly a hundred railroad lines had gone bankrupt since the start of the Panic out east.

Progress and new construction had slowed to a trickle after Reconstruction, but if there was one thing Josiah was certain of, sooner or later the fear would subside, and progress would return to the expansion of the railroad, bringing new life and even more change to Fort Worth and beyond, whether it was welcome or not.

Still, there was optimism in the streets of Cowtown, the economy more dependent on the cattle drives than anything else — and it seemed there was one thing that Texas had plenty of that the rest of the country wanted and needed, and that was the meat and hide of the longhorns, the Herefords, all of the different types of cows that prospered all the way down to the Rio Grande and up to the stockyards in Kansas.

Josiah could only hope that some of the prosperity in Fort Worth would find its way to Mae and that she would not find her way to Hell's Half Acre. But in the end, he knew there was nothing he could do for her once they left her behind. The thought made him swallow hard. Leaving her was going to be much harder than he'd ever thought it would be.

Scrap stopped Missy in the middle of a cross street. Josiah pulled up next to him.

"What's the matter?" he asked.

"I'm not sure this is gonna be a good idea," Scrap said.

"What's not a good idea?"

Mae remained quiet. She seemed overwhelmed by the goings-on around her, by Fort Worth as a whole, and didn't appear to know — or care — what Scrap was talking about. Josiah figured it out quickly. Scrap was looking past Josiah, staring directly at Mae.

"What else do you think we should do?" Josiah asked, knowing now that Scrap was having second thoughts about leaving Mae in Fort Worth with his aunt.

Scrap shrugged his shoulders. "I don't know. My aunt, she's a proper kind of lady. Runs a respectable boardinghouse. I'm just not so sure . . ."

"You go to hell," Mae shouted.

"Mae," Josiah said, his voice soft and even. "Don't pay him any mind."

"I ain't dirt."

Josiah shifted himself around, so he could turn and look at Mae. "Nobody said you were."

"He just did."

"Tell her you're sorry, Elliot."

"I didn't ask to be brought here." Mae started to push herself off Clipper's saddle.

"Don't." Josiah grabbed Mae's wrist, not hard, but firmly enough to let her know he didn't want her to go anywhere. "If Elliot's aunt is as decent a woman as he says she is, then we'll let her decide if she's got room to take you in. Don't worry, I'll speak on your behalf."

"What happens when you're gone? What happens to me then?"

Josiah didn't have an answer for Mae. He honestly didn't know. He just hoped that something good would come to her. But he knew, considering her situation, that the chance of Mae encountering a dose of heartfelt charity was about as likely as the street being free of shit.

"Did I make myself clear, Elliot? We'll let your aunt make the choice. If she says no, then we'll figure something else out. We can't take her up north to the camp, and we can't just leave her here in the streets."

"What's the difference between here and Waco?"

"I'm not asking you, Elliot."

Scrap exhaled deeply, nodded reluctantly, then spun Missy around, pressed her firmly, and said, "Heeyaw."

Josiah had no choice but to follow after him.

Melhaven's Boardinghouse was a two-storey Victorian affair with a wraparound porch, two opposing turrets, the shingle siding painted dark green, with shiny glass windows that were as clean as a baby's bottom and trimmed in a rust color. A black wrought iron fence surrounded the house. Tea roses lined the walk, all red and dainty and perfectly pruned. Cotoneasters edged along the front of the house, and a single chinkapin oak stood facing the street at the corner, casting a healthy dose of shade down onto the porch. An empty slat swing sat waiting for a cool evening.

A simple sign was attached to the gate, announcing the availability of a room, and that the house was, in fact, a boardinghouse.

By the time Scrap was tying Missy to a post, a tall, elegant-looking woman with long brown hair draped over her shoulders appeared on the porch, easing out the front door, drying her hands on a bright white apron, and looking down curiously on the trio.

"Is that you, Robert Earl Elliot?" There was a slight drawl to the woman's voice, not Southern and twangy, but deep, certain, and pure Texan.

"It sure is, Aunt Callie." Scrap pronounced "aunt" just like he said "ain't." "I hope you don't mind me intrudin' on you. I know it's been a long stretch since you've heard from me."

Callie Melhaven stepped down off the porch and made her way to the front gate. "Don't be silly, Robert Earl. You're welcome here anytime. You and your sister both. You know that." She looked past Scrap to Josiah and Mae. "Now, who do you have with you?"

Scrap had a younger sister, Myra Lynn, that lived with the Ursuline nuns in Dallas, and Scrap hardly ever mentioned her. They both had survived the Comanche attack on their farm and had chosen different paths afterward. "That there," Scrap said, pointing to Josiah, "is Ranger Wolfe. Josiah Wolfe. He hails out of Austin now, but his folks come from around Tyler."

Just as Callie opened the gate, Josiah stepped forward and doffed his hat. "A pleasure to meet you, ma'am."

"I don't know any Wolfes. Do you all have kin in Fort Worth?"

"Not that I'm aware of."

"What a shame. A Ranger you say? A Texas Ranger? One of the new Frontier Battalion Rangers?"

"Yes, ma'am. Me and Scrap, um, your nephew, Robert Earl, both," Josiah said, a slight smile crossing his face as he spoke Scrap's proper name.

"Oh, Robert Earl, that's wonderful news. A Ranger. My, I would have never thought you'd do something like that. That just makes me so happy. Your mother would be so proud if she were here. God rest her soul."

Scrap lowered his head. "Yes, ma'am, I think she would be."

"You can call me Callie," the woman said to Josiah, with a smile. "Will you all be staying long?"

They looked to be near the same age,

Josiah and Callie Melhaven, and the woman comported herself perfectly. She was an attractive woman, and Josiah certainly didn't want to give her the wrong impression, but an attraction of any kind was the last thing on his mind at the moment. It was an odd feeling for him, though, allowing himself to notice a woman's beauty.

He had mourned Lily for so long that every time he saw a woman, he compared them, and no woman could ever compete with a ghost, especially one that had borne a man four children.

Callie Melhaven was fully alive, and there was no comparing her to anyone, living or dead. Plain and simple, she was a pretty woman, nearly as pretty as Pearl Fikes and Suzanne del Toro and as open and welcoming as she appeared. Josiah respected boundaries, and he imagined an unmarried woman running a boardinghouse had to have her rules known far and wide.

"That's awful kind of you, Miss Melhaven, but we're in a bit of a hurry," Josiah said. "We can't stay too long."

A flash of disappointment crossed Callie's face, then disappeared instantly. "Well, then, that's just the way it will be. And who is this fine young thing?" she said, walking over to Mae.

CHAPTER 20

The inside of Callie Melhaven's boarding-house was just as well kept, orderly, fancy, and impressive as the outside.

Shiny walnut floors were covered sparsely with heavy wool rugs. The rugs bore intricate designs that oddly reminded Josiah of the floor in the Menger Hotel in San Antonio. It had been only months since he'd been in that hotel, but it seemed like years.

The house was quiet, except for the tick-tock of a perfectly wound clock hanging on the wall just inside the door — every minute, it seemed, accounted for. All of the boarders must have been gone for the day or obeying some unspoken rule of silence. It was as quiet as Sunday morning in a church.

All of the furniture looked to be in exceptional shape and well cared for, too. There were a lot of furniture makers where Josiah had grown up in the Piney Woods of East

Texas, so he knew good craftsmanship when he saw it. His father had had a foot-powered turning lathe in a small shed just behind the barn and had crafted most of the furniture in the house Josiah grew up in. Unfortunately, the skill of chair-making did not fall to Josiah. He could shingle a roof if he had to, but assembling a usable piece of furniture was beyond his reach — or desire, much to his father's disappointment.

An upholstered daybed sat in a room just off the main entry, not quite a parlor, and Josiah imagined that in busier times the room was rented out just like all of the others in the big house. The daybed was probably stuffed with horsehair and Spanish moss, and was reasonably comfortable when Josiah sat down on it to wait.

A painting faced him, hanging squarely on the opposite wall, a gold-framed picture of a blond-haired little girl picking daisies on the rise of a summer hill.

He looked away from the picture quickly, a flash of memory poured through his mind, so vibrant with smells and colors it was like he was standing in the field himself, wondering where his three daughters had gotten off to. His stomach rolled, and he felt a sharp pain in the pit of it that he tried to avoid as much as possible.

The grief of losing his girls never, ever went away; it was always just under his skin. No matter how much he tried to force the memories away, they would always exist. Most days, of late, he knew how to live with them, but Mae had poked his heart in a way he hadn't known was possible anymore. He had never lusted after the girl, not for one minute. Maybe it was because he saw the wounds in her eyes long before he saw them on her back. But it was even more than that. Maudie Mae Johnson was some man's daughter, and whatever the story was, that man had lost her to the world. Maybe her own father was dead, or maybe he'd done unspeakable things to her, setting her on the path that Josiah had found her on, but Josiah would never know, had no desire to know. All he could do was care for her and hope the road of life would rise up and meet her with some grace and good fortune.

His girls would never have the chance at happiness — they were taken too young — and he was silently surprised that he was starting to care about Mae's long-term happiness at all.

Josiah sat in the room alone, stiffly, not looking at the picture then, trying not to make a single noise, not venturing to places unknown where he was not allowed with his eyes or feet. For more reasons than he could admit, he was nervous inside the house, ready to get back on the trail, ready to be free of the self-imposed responsibility he was feeling for Mae.

Mae herself was off getting a bath, and Scrap had disappeared at Callie Melhaven's beckoning — after receiving a harsh look and after an immediate apology to Mae for his lack of manners.

Much to Josiah's relief, Callie Melhaven had agreed to let Mae stay with her in the house until she was able to get her feet under her in a new town.

The thought of a bath sounded pleasurable to Josiah, but he had declined when Callie offered her facilities to him. He had decided that once Scrap had had a moment or two to spend with his aunt, they would leave straightaway. He knew he and Scrap both needed to get to camp, but more importantly, he didn't want to lead the posse of men to Mae and Callie.

There would be no one to protect the women after they were gone, and Callie didn't look the type to be able to hold her own against the likes of Liam O'Reilly and the other men he was riding with.

Footsteps made their way to Josiah from the back of the house.

Callie appeared in the doorway seconds later. "There you are, Ranger Wolfe," she said, an odd smile on her face.

Josiah stood up. "Josiah will be fine, ma'am."

"Then Callie will be, too." Her smile grew broader.

Josiah returned the smile and nodded happily. "I don't want it to seem like we're rushing off and leaving Mae here with you out of turn. It's just that . . ."

"It's not an issue, Josiah, really." Her voice was calm and her eyes warm.

"Well, Mae, is . . . can be a handful."

Callie and Josiah stood about a foot apart, both unmoving. Josiah could smell a hint of lavender in the air since Callie had walked into the room.

"I believe I can handle Miss Johnson properly," Callie said. "I have work that will keep her occupied, if she is up to it, and I have the ability and means to show her another way of life different than the one she has obviously been subject to. If she chooses to stay here, she is welcome as long as she wants. But if she chooses to find her way to the section of town that is as familiar as the one she came from, then there is nothing I can do about that. I will not chase her down, Josiah, nor will I force her to do anything against her will. Even a fool could see she has had a lifetime of that, and I guarantee you, I am no fool."

"No, I don't imagine you are," Josiah said. "Thank you."

"For what?"

"For taking in Mae. For your hospitality."

"It is what I do, Josiah. And, I think, what you must do, too," Callie Melhaven said, the smile fading from her face. "Come, let's get you some supplies for your journey."

She turned and walked out of the room, and it was then that Josiah realized the little girl in the picture had just been standing before him, all grown up into a woman who still believed in the possibility of hope and summer.

Scrap walked out onto the porch and said, "Where in the heck did that come from?"

Josiah was standing at the gate, looking up and down the street. "I don't know. It was just here when I walked out," he said, glancing back to the black stallion that was tied up to the post next to Clipper and Missy.

"That Mexican's got to be around here somewhere," Scrap said.

"Well, yes, he has to be. Or was while we were inside."

Scrap walked to the gate and stopped next to Josiah. "That's a damn fine horse."

"You're planning on leaving it here for Mae, aren't you?"

"What else would I do with it?"

Josiah shrugged his shoulders. "I thought you might be opposed to it."

"I could take it on up to the camp. I'm sure I could sell it for a fair price, but it's not mine to sell."

"I'm glad you see it that way."

"I still ain't happy about her stayin' here with Aunt Callie. She could spread her sickness to anyone, but . . ."

"I'm sorry I told you that. It's just speculation on my part. You realize that, don't you?" Josiah said. "I didn't want you getting into something that you might have paid for a long ride down the trail, just in case I was right in my thinking."

Scrap started to say something, then obviously thought better of it. "I appreciate that, Wolfe. Besides, it ain't like Mae's a dog. We can't just take her out back and shoot her if she's sick. Aunt Callie is gonna see to it that the doc takes a look at her."

"She's a good woman, your aunt."

Scrap agreed silently with a slow nod. "Where do you think the Mexican went?"

"Who knows," Josiah said. "I quit trying

to figure out Juan Carlos's actions a long time ago. He meant to let us know he's here, at least around, and that's enough. I'm sure he had his reasons for not coming up and ringing the buzzer."

"Sometimes I think that man is a ghost," Scrap said.

"Me, too," Josiah answered, glancing over his shoulder when he heard someone walk out onto the porch.

He turned fully around when he saw Mae, all cleaned up, dressed in a comfortable cotton dress suitable for a proper July day, her straw-colored hair combed and pinned back. There was a glow about the girl, albeit a shy glow.

Callie was standing back in the doorway watching.

"I figured you was gonna go ahead and leave while I was cleanin' myself up," Mae said. She grabbed the sides of the dress with each hand, pulled up slightly, like she was about to curtsy — though Josiah wasn't sure that she wasn't going to pull it up over her head, and was glad when she didn't, when she spun around like a girl half her age. "This is the purtiest dress I have ever wore. And Miss Callie says I can keep it for myself."

"So, you like Miss Callie?" Josiah asked.

246

Mae stopped spinning. "I think she was nice enough to help me get cleaned up, and she gave me this here dress, and Lord Almighty, I ain't never seen a house so grand as this one. I can't imagine sleepin' on one of those fine feather mattresses. Did you jump on one of them things? Goodness. I could have done that all day long."

Josiah smiled. "I'll be happy to know you're going to stay here, then." He pointed to the black stallion. "This horse here is yours to do with as you please, if Miss Callie has a place for it."

Callie Melhaven eased out of the door. "There's an empty stall. But she'll have to tend to the horse herself. I have plenty to take care of on my own, as do the helpers that come along to tend to the house."

The smile retreated from Mae's face, like a dark cloud had crossed in front of the sun. She hung her head down then ran to Josiah, throwing her arms around him. "You're really gonna leave me, aren't you?"

Josiah's first inclination was to unwrap her arms from around him. He could feel her heartbeat, smell the same subtle hint of lavender on her skin that he'd smelled when Callie Melhaven walked into the front room. But instead he allowed her to hug him, to touch him — and himself to hug her back.

"We have to go, Mae. Miss Callie will look after you."

Her eyes were growing glassy. "But," she stuttered, "I could love you."

"Scrap and I will be back through here. You'll see us again," Josiah said.

"I don't care nothin' about him. He killed Clem Dawson in cold blood. They'll hang him for that, you wait and see."

Josiah tipped up Mae's chin, so they were looking eye to eye. "You remember this if you don't care to remember anything else. Robert Earl Elliot most likely saved your life. He doesn't expect anything in return. Not now, not then. But every breath you take in this fine house from this day forward will be because of him and no one else. You remember that, and get rid of that hate inside of you. It's not doing you a bit of good."

Josiah stepped back then, pulling himself out of her clutch.

Somehow, Callie, who was a head taller than Mae, had made her way to Mae's side, and she pulled the girl to her, kept her from melting to the ground right then and there. Mae buried her head in Callie's chest and started to sob.

"Thank you, Aunt Callie," Scrap said,

pushing out of the gate. "Thank you for everything."

"You boys best be getting on now. Don't worry about us. We'll be fine," Callie said.

Josiah took a deep breath, backed away, then made his way to Clipper.

Their saddlebags were full, replenished with fresh jerky, some dried sausage, crumb cakes, and enough pickled onions and beets to last until the first hint of cold air blew down from the north.

Scrap had cleaned himself up some and had briefly mentioned that he needed to refresh his tobacco supply, to which Callie had told him she had none of the vile substance in her house — and never would — so he would have to stop on the way out of town, if that was his need.

They mounted their respective horses and made their way, nose to nose, down the street, slowly riding away from the boarding-house.

Josiah was willing himself not to look back, not to wave good-bye, but his will was not that strong, not when he heard Mae break away from Callie and run out into the road behind them.

He stopped Clipper and looked back.

Mae shouted, "I could have loved you, Josiah Wolfe. I could have loved you," then fell to her knees, dirtying her new dress in the road, crying as she did, like a girl seeing her lover off to war, or breaking off with a beau who'd rejected her, he wasn't sure which, other than that her cries were painful to listen to.

Josiah turned away from Mae then, as fast as he could, and urged Clipper to a run, even though he was in the midst of the city.

His heart felt like it was breaking all over again. There was nothing worse than burying a daughter, much less three, but leaving a girl like Mae to a stranger, even one as upstanding as Callie Melhaven, well, it was nearly the hardest thing he had done in a long, long time.

CHAPTER 21

Fort Worth disappeared quickly behind Scrap and Josiah. At no time did Scrap mention trotting off to Dallas to see Myra Lynn, so Josiah didn't bring it up either.

Their route north continued to skirt the Brazos River — the plan being to head up toward Fort Belknap and hopefully catch up on any communication about the Frontier Battalion along the way: if the Ranger camp had moved or remained stable since Scrap had left, if there had been any skirmishes with the Comanche or other troubles. So far as they knew, the camp was still intact.

The troubles Scrap mentioned when they'd first met up were farther north. They were far enough to stay out of the way of any major Indian troubles — at the moment, to not have to worry too much about their safety on the trail. But, still, there was a dangerous storm brewing with almost all the tribes since the second battle at Adobe Walls had ended a few weeks earlier, toward the end of June and into the beginning of July.

It would be foolish not to remain alert, certain of every movement in the shadows. If Josiah knew anything about Indians, it was that they could be anywhere, anytime, there one second, and gone the next.

Juan Carlos had probably learned a lot from the Indians. He acted just like them sometimes, Josiah thought, trying not to question why the Mexican had left the black stallion for Mae and then disappeared. It was easy enough to accept the act — it was purely within character for Juan Carlos — but there were two distinct messages his friend could have meant to send. Either he had lost the posse and felt safe, or the posse had followed him to Fort Worth, and Juan Carlos was throwing them off his trail. Either notion was speculation on Josiah's part, so all he could do was hope that the posse had been lost and had stayed as far away from Fort Worth as possible.

Josiah knew he needed to turn his attention and concern back to the Indians. The newspapers in Waco and Fort Worth were still ripe with the tales from up near Indian Territory, from the attack on Adobe Walls, and on the other side of the Red River.

Adobe Walls had been a buffalo camp, and reports were that nearly seven hundred Indians attacked the camp at dawn. The Indians, mostly Cheyenne, Comanche, and Kiowa, fought under the charge of two well-known Comanche leaders, Quanah Parker and Isa-tai — invoker of the Sun Dance, a ceremony that would supposedly make the white man's bullets fall harmlessly to the ground when they struck Indian skin.

At the time of the attack, there were twenty-nine defenders in Adobe Walls, and all but one were men who'd gathered at the saloon. The role of the single woman had not been reported in the newspapers, but four men were killed, and on the second day, a man on his own, Billy Dixon, pretty much ended the attack when he shot an Indian off a mesa, seven-eighths of a mile away, killing him. Isa-tai and his Sun Dance had obviously not protected that Indian from the power of the white man's bullet. The newspaper in Fort Worth called it the "long shot heard across Texas."

Hunters sent out word of the attack, and now there was a huge movement among the army to confront the renegade tribes and move them permanently to a location farther north, completely out of Texas, onto a reservation in Indian Territory.

It would certainly be a war. The Indians weren't going to go without a fight, and Josiah was sure the Texas Rangers, the Frontier Battalion, would be right in the thick of things.

The trek out of Fort Worth was Josiah's first venture this far north. He had not been out of Texas since he'd returned home from the war, nearly ten years before, so the landscape and way along the river were foreign to him. He was glad Scrap had earned some of his confidence, since he would have to rely on him heavily to see them safely to the Ranger camp.

Josiah and Scrap had ridden at a full run out of Fort Worth, speaking little.

It was the quietest and most distant that Josiah could ever remember Scrap being, and maybe he should have been concerned, but honestly, after leaving Mae, after seeing their way clear north, Josiah was glad for the peace and quiet. He needed to digest everything that had happened since he'd left Austin, and consider what he — they — were riding toward.

Removing Mae from danger had seemed the right thing to do, and in the end, it had only slowed their journey by a day at the most — but it had changed his relationship with Scrap, some for the better and some for worse. Most certainly, one more than the other. Josiah just wasn't sure which would win out in the end between him and Scrap, but there was no question that he saw Scrap — Robert Earl Elliot — in a different light than he had in the previous months.

Scrap was more dependable and definitely more trustworthy, but still rash and immature. Josiah wasn't sure that behavior was going to change anytime soon.

Either way, he knew he was going to have to leave his feelings and concerns about Mae and that part of the journey north behind him, just like he had the fire in Austin. It would be easier knowing Mae was under Callie Melhaven's influence, but there was no protecting her from herself, or those who would see her harm.

Josiah still had plenty of other concerns to weigh him down, since there was no forgetting about the posse out of Waco, Liam O'Reilly, the whereabouts and welfare of Suzanne del Toro, her brother Emilio — *El Puño* — and his intentions and influence, as well as what kind of reception Josiah would face when he arrived at the Ranger camp. It remained to be seen how his captain, Pete Feders, would receive his justifications for being errant and late to camp.

Josiah had no choice but to keep riding north, riding toward a coming Indian war and everything that it brought with it. He didn't savor the idea of war, of facing off with an enemy that consisted of multiple tribes. One war in one man's lifetime was enough as far as he was concerned — but he was certainly going to fight. That's exactly what he'd signed up to be a Ranger for.

After thinking it all through, he decided that there was no other place he'd rather be than where he was at that moment — except one place, sitting on his front porch in Austin, watching over Lyle as he discovered a safe and sure world.

The blue sky was falling rapidly into the gray western horizon as dusk reached up to bring the day to a close, but Josiah and Scrap kept pushing their horses to ride harder and farther than they probably should have. Clipper offered no argument. Not that he would. Scrap's mare was just as enthusiastic as Josiah's Appaloosa, her broad shoulders shining with blue sweat in the fading light.

Scrap remained intent, focused on the trail ahead, never once looking over for instruction or permission to slow. The boy seemed lost in his own thoughts, seemed almost angry and tense, but Josiah wasn't certain about that. He could have been misinterpreting Scrap's mood.

As it was, Josiah wanted to be as far from Fort Worth as possible before settling in for the night — and after another hour of riding full-out, it looked like they had just about pushed the horses as far and fast as they could.

The blue sky was fully black now, the color of the day drained from it so nothing was left but a few wispy gray clouds and some faraway stars starting to pulse. The moon, still waning, cast a fair amount of light to the ground, but it was not as bright as it had been on previous nights.

The breeze had exhausted itself, and the air was still, cooling off a bit after trying to outrun the hot sun all day. The river was close, running shallow and slow, pushing over rocks thinly, almost quietly — trickling just enough so Josiah knew it was there. Oddly, he found no comfort in the consistent run of water. They had followed the river for nearly the entire journey, and it was a contrary companion — offering refreshment, an occasional bath and meal, but also a few memories featuring Mae that he would just as soon have been without.

They finally stopped, making camp along the riverbank in a broad clearing. The trees were thinning out the farther north they went, flat open land with distant, open hills and a few mesas casting dark shadows away from them toward the north.

As Josiah eased off Clipper, a coyote yip sounded in the distance. He stopped and scanned the area, uncertain if it was a lone animal or an Indian announcing his presence. It was difficult to tell the difference, especially for Josiah. He had avoided Indian encounters as much as possible in his life, so he was unaccustomed to their ways — only knowing not to trust anything that he saw or heard when he was on grass that they walked on, too.

"Ain't nothin'," Scrap said, tying Missy to a tree that wasn't any bigger around than a healthy man's arm.

"You sound pretty sure," Josiah said.

"And you sound like a greenhorn."

"I never said I knew everything."

"You sure act like it."

Josiah followed suit, tying Clipper up to a similar tree a few feet from Missy. "You got a burr in your butt, or what, Elliot? You've been disagreeable since before we got to Fort Worth. I told you I was sorry for put-

258

ting you on the ground about Mae."

"It ain't that."

"What is it, then?"

Scrap, who was wandering around Missy, picking up some kindling, stopped and crossed his arms heavily. "Why can't you just leave it alone, Wolfe?"

Josiah put up both hands. He was standing about ten feet from Scrap. "I can do that. I just figured you might need to get something off your chest."

"Maybe I could have loved her?"

"Mae?"

"Yup, Mae. She was pretty enough."

"Scrap, she was not the kind of girl that . . ."

"But she loved you."

"You're jealous?" Josiah laughed out loud. He hadn't meant to, the laugh just slipped out of his throat before he could catch it.

"It ain't funny."

"I know. I'm sorry," Josiah said. He laughed again. This time, the laugh came from deep in his belly, and there was absolutely no stopping it. He felt bad for Scrap, he really did — but he found his need to be jealous completely and utterly ridiculous.

"You're makin' me mad, Wolfe."

"Well, you best just get over it, unless you're aiming to fight me and end up in the dirt again."

"I'm serious."

"I can see that." He'd stopped laughing and was trying to catch his breath. "You need to get over that line of thinking. The last thing you got to be jealous of is me and any other woman. I've got enough troubles without considering that."

"Women like you," Scrap said. "Mae, Pearl Fikes, even my aunt Callie acted different around you."

"It's not something I encourage."

"Well, I want my turn, damn it," Scrap said.

Josiah laughed again, but this time it was not a belly laugh but an uncomfortable laugh. If there was one thing that Josiah knew a little about, it was loneliness, not women. And Scrap was expressing more than jealousy. "You'll have your time, Scrap. Don't worry."

"How can you say that? We're headin' back to camp, where we're most certain to join up with the army and go after the Comanche. I lost my family to those savages. I'll lose my head, I just know it. Once I see my way to revenge, I just won't be able to help myself. I know it. I just know I'll do something stupid and die."

"What's that got to do with Mae?"

"You're gonna make me say it, ain't you?"

"What?"

"I want to be with a woman before I die, Wolfe. I want to know what love feels like. Is that too much for a man to ask out of life?" Scrap said, stalking off into the darkness, leaving Josiah alone in the clearing to consider the silence, and the words that hung in the air like vapors from some stinging tonic.

CHAPTER 22

The rest of the ride to the Ranger camp was uneventful.

Josiah and Scrap left the comforting flow of the Brazos River behind. The river was nothing more than a series of springs as they neared the headwaters, and once they veered northwest, toward what was left of Fort Belknap, the water disappeared altogether.

The fort had been abandoned a few years after the close of the War Between the States — a set of barracks and a cemetery sat square on the flat land, amid a grassy and barren landscape. Most folks avoided the crumbled stone encampment, fearing ghosts or supernatural retribution for trespassing.

Josiah didn't subscribe to a belief in ghosts or revenge cast upon a person by the wind or ethereal spirits, but he did respect the past, the hallowed ground of battle, where death had occurred and men had died valiantly for what they believed in. Regardless, there was something that could be felt in those places where blood had been spilled. He had no desire to visit the shell of the fort to see if those feelings existed there or not.

The trail was starting to become rocky, and the oak mottes were far behind them, mesquite being the most prevalent set of trees to be seen anywhere on the horizon. The broad sky loomed high over them, stretching out in every direction as if it were a fragile blue bedsheet falling to the earth. With the land so flat, so still on the other side of midday, the sky looked much bigger than Josiah could ever remember seeing it. He wasn't certain about what lay ahead, but one thing was for sure, it would all be new to him, keeping him occupied and curious.

Clipper eased along the trail, following closely behind Missy and Scrap, just off to the side and a little to the rear.

They rode silently for the most part, the companionship between Josiah and Scrap becoming easier, more akin to a partnership than Josiah had ever imagined it could be, and he was, to some degree, not looking forward to parting company with Scrap. It was a good feeling to have at your side a marksman and rider that you felt you could trust.

Once past the empty fort, it was easy enough to find the Ranger camp, set up in a shallow valley. About a mile out, they encountered the first man sitting watch.

The man, who identified himself as Fredric Overmeyer, was dressed in a buckskin shirt that covered a belly that overhung his belt. He was probably nearing fifty years old, wore a long beard, and hearkened back to the days of mountain men and the beaver trade. He had thick red hair that flowed over his shoulders, and was fully armed, albeit with a carbine. A full complement of bullets sat waiting on his belt, and a Bowie knife sat firmly on his hip, in a hand-tooled leather scabbard that looked old and worn from plenty of use.

It was not uncommon for Rangers to dress in the fashion in which they were comfortable, since there was no required uniform — one of the appeals of signing up for Josiah was the lack of regimentation. He'd had enough tight military control in his younger life; he didn't care much for the strictness now.

Some men wore corduroy suits, while most were comfortable in heavy woolen clothes and a simple felt hat, more like

Josiah and Scrap. And most of the Rangers Josiah had encountered of late wore high-heeled boots and spurs. The heels prevented the foot from slipping through the stirrups, since the Rangers — who saw the same reasons for high-heeled boots as the cowboys — rode the stirrup in the middle of the foot. They didn't use leather-hooded stirrups like the army, where the sole of the foot bore most of the weight. The Ranger method was far more comfortable for long-distance riding.

Overmeyer didn't wear a badge to identify himself as a Ranger. But there was no question that the man in buckskin was a Ranger, once he acknowledged the secret word to allow entry into the camp perimeter after Scrap had spoken it, the word being "salt."

"It is good to see you again, Elliot," Overmeyer said, reaching up to shake Scrap's hand.

Overmeyer spoke in a halting kind of way, his German accent not real heavy but evident to anyone, like Josiah, who had been in and around German communities, such as Neu-Bronfels.

"Good to see you, too, Red. This here's Josiah Wolfe."

Red Overmeyer walked over to Clipper, reached up, and offered Josiah his meaty hand in friendship. Josiah leaned down and responded in kind. "Good to meet you," he said.

Red was chewing a plug of tobacco and spit a dark stream of spit to the ground, making a spewing sound with his lips. "I best be warnin' you, Captain Feders is in a foul mood."

"Why's that?" Scrap asked.

"Major Jones is headin' up this way for an inspection of some sort. The captain doesn't think we're ready."

"Looks like we're just in time, Wolfe," Scrap said.

"Looks that way."

"Yeah, well you haven't missed much," Red said. "A lot of card playin', huntin' and fishin', yarns at the fire. But you would have surely liked the horse racin', Elliot, that's been takin' place."

"I bet Sam Clooney's been takin' everybody's money with that white stallion of his," Scrap said.

"How'd you know?" Red asked. "I lost a week's wages, 'bout ten dollars, on that horse. I wished you would have told me before you went out after Wolfe, here."

"I knew that horse was a runner the second I laid eyes on it. Sorry about that. I figured you were a good bettor, so I didn't think to tell you. That stallion would probably leave little Missy here in the dust." Scrap leaned forward and patted his blue roan mare affectionately. "She's a good one, that's for sure. Just not a race winner. I wouldn't trade her though, I sure wouldn't."

"Wilson's about a half mile up. Best start whistling as soon as you get close. He's got an itchy finger, that one," Red said.

Scrap nodded. "Will do. Thanks."

"Well, we best be getting on," Josiah said.

"Welcome to camp, Wolfe," Red Overmeyer said. "Scrap's been tellin' everybody about your trials and tribulations the last couple of months, the trip up from San Antonio and all. It's good to finally meet you."

Josiah nodded, his facial expression null of any emotion, frozen hard like granite. He sure hoped Scrap hadn't pumped up or torn down his reputation with his notions about heroics, or lack thereof, that had happened in the past. He was certain there would be some embellishments to be dealt with.

Just when he was starting to get comfortable with Scrap, he was almost immediately reminded not too trust in him too fully.

They passed through the next watch, the Ranger, Wilson, waving them through, as

Scrap had called out ahead, alerting the man that they were coming. He leaned down and said the password, not slowing Missy one step. Neither of them wanted to chew the fat with a man whose finger sat ready on the trigger. Besides, the day was falling away, and they wanted to get settled down in camp as soon as they could.

It didn't take long for the camp to come into sight.

A line of canvas tents sat at the base of a slight hill that angled upward to the north. The top of the hill was flat enough for a corral to be built there, and at least a dozen horses mingled about, obviously content and well cared for. Josiah was glad to see the camp so well appointed. Once they got everything squared away, it would be nice to give their horses a good rest.

Early evening was setting in, and several campfires crackled and popped, and the smell of mesquite filled the air. A chuck wagon sat at the end of the line of tents, its contents strewn about in some order only the grub cook could understand, but of everything he saw, riding into the shallow valley, Josiah was elated to see the potential for a meal cooked by knowing hands.

The thought of beefsteak and potatoes, stewed just right, made his stomach roar to life. Trail food was never his favorite, at least when he rode alone, and Scrap Elliot had not proven to be a knowledgeable cook. Now that he thought of it, Scrap had not offered to cook one meal. Probably didn't know how, Josiah thought to himself.

Riding easily next to him, Scrap laughed out loud. "Lord, Wolfe, ain't you ate today?"

"Just reacting to the smells, I guess. Don't know about you, but I think I've had my fill of rabbit and jerky."

"A decent meal and a hot tub of water sure will be nice, I agree with that. You ain't too gifted when it comes to cookin'."

"Funny, I was just thinking the same thing about you."

Scrap ignored the comment by not responding, which suited Josiah just fine. He was more interested in trying to get his bearings and figure out where the captain's tent was and what was going on.

There was a bit of nervous energy flowing about the camp. A few men walked in front of Josiah and Scrap, apologizing, then hurrying by, their purpose unknown as they went from one tent to the next. More than one man was sitting on a canvas seat in front of his tent, cleaning his rifle. Another man was standing outside the tent that was obviously set up as a bathhouse, trying to finish up a shave in the fading evening light.

The nervousness was certainly due to the impending visit from Major Jones.

"Feders is in the last tent," Scrap said.

"We best get this over with as soon as we can," Josiah said.

"He knows we're here."

"How do you figure?"

Scrap nodded down to the end of the tents. Josiah followed his nod and made eye contact with Captain Pete Feders, who was standing outside the open flap of his tent, his hands on both hips, eyes as hard as stone, looking like he had just found two likely candidates to scream at.

CHAPTER 23

Captain Pete Feders was a lanky man, nearly as tall as Josiah. He was built lean and tough, though, the kind of man you'd want at your side when it came time to fight hand to hand. That had happened more than once in Josiah's presence, and the captain was a fierce fighter.

Feders and Josiah were nearly the same age, both veterans of the War Between the States, though Feders had not fought with the Texas Brigade — for some reason he'd fought early on with the 2nd Alabama Cavalry Regiment and had spent time in Florida and Mississippi.

As far as Josiah knew, Feders and his family came from one of the counties in West Texas where Feders had fought the Comanche and the Kiowa more times than he liked to talk about. Why Pete Feders had served with the 2nd Alabama was a mystery, one they'd never discussed, because, in the end, the past was over for both Josiah and Feders. The war still waged on behind both men's eyes, in the unspoken dreams and nightmares that all veterans of that war shared but usually kept to themselves.

Soldier's Heart was an affliction that could never be cured.

The only remarkable or notable feature Feders bore was a thin scar that ran from the corner of his right eye to his ear. Josiah always tried not to stare at the scar or wonder if it came from an Indian fight. It was another part of his life that Feders never spoke of, and no one, as far as Josiah knew, had ever had the courage to ask about the scar's origin. Including Josiah.

One thing was certain, though, Pete Feders, who had served with Captain Hiram Fikes as a Texas Ranger in the previous incarnation as well as briefly in the State Police, took his new position as captain extremely seriously.

"Where in the hell have you two been?" Feders yelled as Josiah and Scrap brought their horses to a stop in front of the captain's tent.

Feders was wearing gray wool trousers, high-heeled black riding boots that were clean and buffed, a thin undershirt, and a pair of suspenders that looked like they were about to wear through.

A .45 Peacemaker, similar to Josiah's own gun but bearing a carved pearl white handle, hung comfortably on his hip. Feders's face was flushed red, his scar pulsing as he set his jaw hard and stood glaring at both men.

"We ran into a little bit of trouble," Josiah said, his voice calm and confident as he eased off the saddle. He was glad to have his feet firmly planted on the ground as he faced Pete Feders for the first time in a long time.

Scrap sat stiffly on his blue roan mare, looking more like a frightened boy than a Texas Ranger reporting to duty.

"You going to sit up there all day, Elliot?" Feders demanded.

"No. No, sir. Not at all."

"Get off that damn horse and get inside here. We got company coming first thing in the morning, and you've got an evening's worth of explaining to do."

Pete Feders didn't wait for Josiah or Scrap to join him. He spun around and stalked inside the tent, kicking up a good amount of dust as he went, not saying another word. His order hung in the air like the scream that comes from a bee sting — sudden, short, and loud, echoing off the ridge behind the row of tents.

Josiah had experienced the shouts of frustration from a commanding officer before, but it didn't look like Scrap had the ability to take the outburst any way but personally. It was him that was bee-stung, or hornet-stung — or just stung — which was too bad. Scrap would have to learn to hold his head up on his own. Josiah was certain he couldn't teach the boy how to do that.

Scrap jumped down off Missy and trailed after Feders, his head hung down, not looking at Josiah, not saying anything that was intelligible, only muttering to himself, chastising himself, it seemed, for some fool act that in the end he probably wasn't responsible for in the first place.

At least that's how Josiah saw it.

As for himself, Josiah drew a deep breath, shook off the day's ride as best he could, and followed both men inside the tent.

There was not a sheepish bone in Josiah's body — but if there was, now was sure not the time to let it show, and he knew that — knew better than Elliot, and most men, how to deal with Captain Pete Feders.

"I sent you after Wolfe, not to go out on an adventure of your own," Feders said, sitting down stiffly behind a rough-hewn desk that was a rat's nest of maps, journals, and writing papers. An ink tank was knocked over on its side, the ink still dripping onto the hard, dried ground — echoing inside the canvas tent like a distant and weak heartbeat.

A hurricane lamp lit the inside brightly, and it smelled strongly of coal oil and wet blankets. The captain's bedroll was tossed sloppily in the corner.

Josiah was surprised by the lack of order inside of Feders's lair.

"I wasn't on no adventure of my own, Captain Feders," Scrap offered. "I found Wolfe here like you sent me for, and as we was makin' our way through Waco . . ."

Josiah stepped forward and put his hand on Scrap's chest, stopping him mid-sentence. "You don't have to grovel, Elliot. If anyone's going to get their hide tanned, it'll be me and not you. Not this time. Pete . . . um, Captain, if you don't mind, can we speak alone?"

Feders sat back in his chair, clasped his hands, then nodded. "That'd probably be best, Wolfe. Elliot, go wait outside. But don't go thinking I'm done with you yet, because I'm not. Not by a mare's tail. You understand?"

"Yes, sir." Scrap nodded as he glanced up at Josiah, his expression uncertain and curious, then he scurried out of the tent as fast as he could.

Josiah waited until Scrap was all of the way out of the tent before he spoke. "You ought to go a little easier on Elliot, Pete."

Feders stood up and leaned forward on the desk. "Don't tell me how to do my job, Wolfe, and you better get used to the idea of calling me Captain."

Josiah shrugged his shoulders. "I'd rather it be you that took Fikes's place than anybody else, Pete, but I've known you way too long to start treating you any different than I did before. I'll be glad to follow your lead, if you offer it, but I'm not going to be ass-whipped and shamed like a new recruit. You can save that tone for somebody else who doesn't know any better."

Pete Feders glared at Josiah, his jaw clenched in place, his eyes fixed in anger.

Josiah took a deep breath, though he tried not to let it show. He'd said what he had to say, now it was best to shut up.

Besides, there was a new, recent, unspoken rub that had grown between the two men. A rub that had become evident and apparent after the murder of Hiram Fikes. It wasn't a lack of respect, or envy, or even jealousy, that had put an extra dose of feelings in the air. The rub existed in a physical form — in the form of a woman. A woman that Pete Feders had a shine for and ached to call his wife, though she had rejected his on-the-knee marriage proposal . . . to which Josiah had been a secret witness.

The woman in question was Pearl Fikes, daughter of the late, great son of Texas, Captain Hiram Fikes himself.

When Josiah had seen Pearl for the first time, standing on the balcony of the fine, grand mansion in Austin, clueless and unaware that the wagon pulling onto the lane was carting her dead father home . . . he thought she was the most beautiful woman he had ever seen. The most beautiful living woman, that is.

Pearl Fikes could never compare to Lily, no woman ever could, but at that moment, at that time, seeing Pearl stirred something awake inside of Josiah that had been asleep for a long time. Desire. Most definitely desire, and the ability to acknowledge life and beauty when he saw it.

Pearl had rejected Pete Feders, and though Josiah didn't know the reason, he was certain that there was something — an attraction, an acknowledgment of desire — something, between him and Pearl, something he chose to run away from after a stolen, almost accidental kiss.

He wasn't sure if Pete Feders knew of the kiss or of the attraction that existed between Josiah and Pearl, and Josiah surely wasn't going to broach the subject.

Pete Feders was his captain now, and that most certainly complicated things between Josiah and Pearl . . . another reason to stay as far away from her, and her world, as possible.

It was after the kiss that Josiah had ended up in the bed of Suzanne del Toro, complicating things even further for him.

Feders still glared at Josiah, an expression of rage holding firm on his scarred face. "I know better than anybody in this camp what you're capable of, Josiah Wolfe, what your skills are, and trust me, I'm glad for your presence in the company. That's why I sent Elliot off to look for you. I was certain you had fallen into trouble somewhere along the trail."

"I appreciate that, Pete." Josiah nodded, catching himself. "Captain."

"Well?"

"There's little explanation, though I have some concerns. I was not errant out of lack of desire to be here, honoring my obligation and duties."

"You're planning on staying?" Feders asked.

Josiah was surprised by the question. "Why wouldn't I?"

"Fikes had to ask you the same question, if I remember right. I know your situation better than most, and I wouldn't blame you for taking the position of deputy in Austin to be closer to home, off the trail more."

"I'm not much of a big-city fella. It'll take a long time to adjust, just living there," Josiah said. "That, and Rory Farnsworth is quite sure of himself. An educated sheriff seems a dangerous combination to me. Can't see nothing but trouble lying in wait. Might be anyway. In Austin and Waco."

"You're speaking of the reason that held you up?"

"That and a reluctance to leave my son. To answer your first question, Pete, I'll answer it the same way I answered Captain Fikes. I don't mean to be anything else other than a Ranger. I'm not sure I know how to be anything else. I have made suitable arrangements — at least, for the moment — for my son's care. There's no question that he suffers because of the lack of my influence, but I will cross that bridge when I come to it. He is safe and well cared for, for now. Let's just leave it at that."

"As you wish," Feders said. "I'll take you at your word and be pleased that you have accepted your rank as sergeant under my command. I'm still angry, though. I would suggest that you don't make the same mistake again."

"I understand that. I would be angry, too, if I were in your situation. But I hope you'll hear me out."

"I'm listening."

Josiah told Feders about the fire in Austin, that he hadn't thought it was a major concern until he and Scrap arrived in Waco and encountered a similar incident and learned of Emilio — *El Puño* — and his reach from Austin to profit from the result of the whore businesses far and wide. He touched briefly on the rescue of Mae and leaving her in Fort Worth but didn't dwell on that story for his own benefit and Scrap's.

"You are certain it was Liam O'Reilly you saw riding with the lawmen?" Feders asked. "He sure didn't take long to find another gang to ride with after they hung Charlie Langdon this spring."

"A man like that usually doesn't have much trouble meeting up with his own ilk. But O'Reilly's a beast, a vicious killer. He'll be leading his own gang soon, if he isn't already," Josiah said. "If he lives long enough," he added.

"That would sure save a lot of trouble for a lot of folks."

"It would."

"You're sure that it was O'Reilly riding with the posse?"

"Not entirely, but I'm pretty much assured that the sheriff's office in Waco has been subverted by men who mean to use the power in a selfish and profitable way. That in itself should be enough for some concern beyond the city limits. The bridge there is a gateway north, and there's a lot that could go wrong if the entire city falls under bad circumstances."

"The cattle bosses may very well rub out the problem on their own," Feders said.

"Or they're paying the salaries of O'Reilly and his men already."

"I'll discuss this with Major Jones when he arrives. I think the Rangers have their hands full at the moment. Whether the situation in Waco warrants any attention will have to come out of Austin and Waco itself."

"The incident at Adobe Walls was a spark to a bigger flame," Josiah said in agreement, knowing instinctively that the situation in Waco concerning the sheriff's office and the fate of the whores there was of little consequence compared to the recent activities of the Comanche and Kiowa.

"Indians draw far more hatred than a lawman, or lawmen, turned bad," Feders said.
"Most folks have seen that once or twice,
especially in a city the size of Waco — a bad
apple in the barrel. If the residents of Waco
ask for the Texas Rangers to come in and
help them rid the town of corrupt lawmen,
I'm sure Major Jones and Governor Coke
will be glad to oblige them. But the threat
of a savage war stirs deep inside the minds
of many more people in the state, leaches
fear like you've never seen. My guess is
Jones wants to see some Indian action on
his own — assure the governor that the
Frontier Battalion is worth the recent
investments made in it. You up to going
along on that journey if it comes to that,
Wolfe?"

"North?"

Feders nodded.

"As long as Elliot comes along," Josiah
said.

"You're sure about that?"

"Yup. I think if we leave him behind, it'd
be a mistake. Besides, the boy's a heck of a
shot."

"I know, I saw his work in Seerville. Too
bad Liam O'Reilly escaped to live another
day."

Josiah nodded. "You cut the head off a

roach and it can live long enough to procreate. We haven't heard the last of Liam O'Reilly — especially if he's in cahoots with Emilio del Toro."

"Let's keep our minds on the moment, Wolfe."

Josiah turned then and headed to the closed tent flap that served as a door. He saw a shadow scurry away and knew full well Scrap had been standing outside, listening to every word spoken between him and Feders.

"Wolfe," Feders said, stepping out from behind the messy desk. "Did you happen to see Pearl Fikes before you left Austin?"

Josiah stopped just as he reached for the flap to exit. He took a deep breath and knew he only had a split second to decide whether to lie or tell the truth. "Yes, I did see Pearl. I went to the estate looking for Juan Carlos."

The truth, it seemed, had never failed Josiah in the past. But when it came to a matter of the heart, of a woman's affection, he was surprised that he thought of lying. Regardless, Josiah respected Feders, and the last thing he wanted to do was get in the middle of a relationship that, at that moment, Josiah wasn't sure existed or not. If Pearl Fikes didn't want to marry Pete Feders, it had nothing to do with Josiah, he was certain of that. Well, almost certain.

"And?" Feders asked.

"And what?"

"Did she send a letter, any correspondence at all?"

Josiah took a deep breath. "No, Captain, she didn't. I have no news for you from Austin. No news at all. I'm sorry."

CHAPTER 24

The camp was reasonably familiar to Josiah — navigating it would be like walking through a curtain of memories, back to the days of the war. He was different now, older, more accustomed to the ways of men who depended on guns and artillery and, most importantly, each other, for their very lives. Camp should have been like returning home, he'd spent so much time in camps, but it wasn't, it couldn't be. The smell of fear and death should never be associated with home — at least, that's how Josiah saw it. He was certain Scrap Elliot had a completely different take on that matter than he did.

The Frontier Battalion was still a young entity, untested and lacking lore and legend like the Texas Brigade or the 2nd Alabama had, but those times would surely come. But at the moment, heroic feats and holding the touch of death at bay and facing down an enemy who sought to do nothing but destroy you were the last things on Josiah's mind. He was curious where Scrap had gotten off to.

It didn't take long for him to figure it out.

The camp was small, and Scrap was a creature of habit — he would see to his horse before he saw to his own comfort — so Josiah made his way up the hill to the top of the ridge, and as he'd thought, the horses, Missy and Clipper, were standing comfortably in the corral. Their saddles were off, and there was a full trough of water next to a mound of freshly thrown straw.

Scrap had found a spot for keeping to himself after completing his chores, moping, sitting with his back propped against a big granite boulder, overlooking the camp. He was smoking a quirley, one puff after another, and didn't look near as comfortable as Clipper and Missy.

"I figured I'd find you here," Josiah said.

"You didn't have to go and do that," Scrap answered.

"Do what?"

"Treat me like a child."

There was just enough dim light left from the proceeding day to allow Josiah to see the discomfort on Scrap's face.

Below, in the camp, several fires burned brightly, and a small crowd of men had gathered around the chuck wagon. The first notes from a harmonica reached up into the cool night air, rising into a comfortable dance with the mesquite smoke. There was, at the moment, the prospect of a peaceful evening, a respite from the trail, from the ride out of Austin and to the camp. At least it seemed that way in comparison to Scrap's mood, but the camp wasn't nearly as relaxed as Josiah had hoped it would be when they'd arrived.

"I thought I was saving face for you," Josiah said.

"I appreciate everythin' you said to Captain Feders about me, Wolfe, but I'd just as soon speak for myself in the future. Ain't nobody gonna take me serious if I can't take the heat for the things I do myself."

Words started to form in Josiah's mind, but he held back, didn't let them slip from his mouth.

Scrap was right, of course, but Josiah knew Pete Feders, knew he was looking for someone to lay his nervousness on, and all Scrap would have had to do was open his mouth in protest, and Feders would have gone off on an angry tangent for ten minutes. It would have served no purpose. But explaining that to Scrap was pointless, and besides, something else had quickly drawn Josiah's attention away.

All of the horses in the corral perked up in unison, stiffened, as the direction of the breeze changed.

Clipper snorted, his ears twitching as a few other horses trotted away from the fence and began to run nervously in a circle. Snorts and nays were soft but growing louder. Something had stirred the horses out of their laziness.

Scrap stood up, sensing the same thing Josiah did. "What's the matter?"

"Don't know," Josiah said. "I guess they could have gotten the scent of something when the wind changed. I don't hear anything. You?"

Scrap shook his head no. "It'd have to be somethin' awful bold to try sneakin' into camp with all this noise around. Comanche might be scouting us."

"They'd have to have gotten by the watch."

"Slittin' a man's throat can be done real quick-like."

Josiah agreed, then saw something heading for them in the final gasp of daylight on the horizon. A rider on a horse, running full-out, was coming down the ridge, from the direction opposite to where Josiah and Scrap had entered, directly toward the camp. The rider would have had to have gotten past a lookout, too.

"Looks like trouble's coming." Josiah unconsciously let his hand slide down next to his Peacemaker.

"Can't be anythin' good this time of day."

"At least it's not a Comanche scout," Josiah said.

They headed down the ridge and stood in wait for the rider in between the tents, a path wide enough for two wagons to pass. There was still grass trying to stand up, still struggling to live. The path, like everything else around them, was new and not yet completely worn down.

A few other men had gathered in the makeshift street, including Red Overmeyer, his watch duty obviously over. The buckskin-dressed man had seen the rider, too, his curiosity, like most everyone else's in the camp, was more than piqued.

With Major Jones due to arrive in the morning, there was an unspoken nervousness among a lot of the men — most of whom were near Scrap's age and lacked any kind of military-style experience at all. The harmonica had never fully engaged in a full blown sing-along, its player probably too distracted to string together more than a few notes.

Josiah had met Jones before, and his immediate judgment about the man's ability to lead was ambiguous. On a personal basis, Josiah thought the major to be a cad, a single man who was rumored to keep more than one woman, each in a separate town. Josiah didn't abide by gossip of any kind, but still, Jones was very particular about his attire and manners, and it would take an idiot not to see that the man had a weakness for beautiful women.

Jones had made overtures to Pearl Fikes at the funeral of her father — an egregious error even to those unfamiliar with the manners of mourning. "Cad" might not be a strong enough word for Jones, but Josiah knew he would have to cleave the human frailties of man from Jones's title and ability to lead the Texas Rangers if he was going to be a successful sergeant himself.

The coming visit from Jones did not pose a serious concern for him. Majors come and majors go. They leave behind orders and rarely face the consequences of their decisions.

At least, that had been Josiah's experience in the past.

There were a few officers he had come to

know, had had the pleasure to serve under, who'd had that special knack — the knack to see the present, the immediate needs of their men, and the effects of the leadership they offered.

Captain Fikes had had that gift. He could command a regiment without saying a word. And there was no question among those who imposed and lived by a moral law, a Christian law, that Fikes was just as much a sinner as Major Jones. It seemed to Josiah that one trait was not necessarily dependent on the other.

Pete Feders had a lot to learn and was most obviously overwhelmed. The inside of his tent was a testament to that thought, which explained, more than anything, why there was a palatable, nervous flavor in the air surrounding the camp.

Regardless, Josiah was just glad to be off the trail and in the camp at all. Most of the men didn't know who he was or what his rank was, but that was exactly how he wanted it to be . . . at the moment.

The rider stopped in front of the crowd of men. The man was nearly out of breath, his face caked with dust and sweat, and a trickle of blood had dried at his temple. He wore no hat, and his clothes were tattered like he'd run through a wall of brambles. His horse looked beat down and rode out.

"Comanche attacked the Loving ranch, killed one of the hands," the man said, leaning forward in his saddle. "You got some water?" He wasn't talking to anyone directly, but Scrap nodded and tore out after a cup.

"Was they raiders or a full party, friend?" Red Overmeyer asked, stepping forward.

Josiah stood back, though Red was only a few feet in front of him, and remained silent for a moment. The man on the horse was almost immediately surrounded by young Rangers, anxious to hear about any confrontation with the Comanche. They were all standing shoulder to shoulder, at least two men deep, their eyes wide open and fixed on the rider.

"How far away is this ranch?" one of the Rangers on the other side of the horse asked.

"I've been ridin' full-out for about three, three-and-a-half hours now. Comanche hit us straight-up at noon, aggressive-like, not makin' a sneak attack out of it. Just came straight at us out of nowhere, changed their ways to surprise us. That they did."

Scrap hurried back and offered the man a tin cup full of cool water. "Here you go," he said. "Looks like your horse could use some tendin', too. I'll be glad to take care of him for ya."

The man stared down at Scrap. "You a Ranger?"

Josiah stepped forward and took hold of the mecate, the long rein that dangled off the horse's sweaty nose. It was an old horse, probably couldn't take a bit, its teeth soft or gone completely, and the rider was using a hackamore.

"He is a Ranger, friend," Josiah said. "And he'll take good care of your horse. Now, I think we best go see Captain Feders so you can tell him your news."

Feders had not exited his tent or showed his face since Josiah and Scrap left him. Whether or not he had heard the commotion and the rider coming in was questionable.

The rider nodded, and dismounted. "Name's Zeb Gill. I've been a hand for Oliver Loving for nigh on three years now. The feller them savages shot was a good man and a fine friend of mine. We heard tell Major John B. Jones himself was heading up this way, and I was sent to set him, and the Texas Rangers, on the trail of those murderers."

"You heard right, Zeb. Major Jones is due in camp tomorrow," Josiah said as he handed Scrap the mecate. "Ranger Elliot will care for your horse, rest him up and get him some water. Then we'll get you some grub. You aren't going anywhere till morning."

"Jones ain't here then?" Gill asked. "I sure hope those Comanche don't hit the ranch at night."

Scrap led Zeb Gill's horse away without saying a word to Josiah, but he looked glad to see to the animal.

"We all understand that the major and his escort party are due in tomorrow. If they are close, they might already be aware of the troubles at the Loving ranch. That might change his plans, but if there's a need to get after the raiders, he'll surely want to pick some fresh men to take along with him."

"I sure hope he ain't too late. We've been hearin' 'bout a gatherin' of savages for a time now. Looks like the tea leaves were right," Zeb Gill said, wiping his brow.

Josiah put his hand on Gill's shoulder and led him toward Feders's tent. "There's no need to worry, friend. We're all here to see to it the Comanche and the others don't threaten this part of the country anymore. Let's go see Captain Feders so you can tell him your tale yourself."

CHAPTER 25

A scattering of sparrows were singing at the top of their ability not far from the tent. A new day had dawned over the camp, and there was nothing like the smell of coffee brewing over a well-tended fire, and a batch of gravy simmering in an iron skillet, to pull a man out of a dreamless night and square into the bright day.

The edge of the day, Jones's impending visit, and Zeb Gill's tale of a Comanche raid were not too deep in Josiah's mind but rather just under the surface of his skin as he made his way out of the tent.

Still, first things first — a fresh shave and the wash of a face could wait — he'd woken up famished.

The major had not arrived in camp yet, and Zeb Gill was still stuffed in the corner of the four-man tent, snoring like he was up to competing with the newest, fanciest, most powerful steam engine set on raging across all of Texas.

If Josiah hadn't been so trail-rugged and flat-out exhausted, he would've stuffed a sock into Zeb Gill's mouth to shut him up, but as it was, he'd slept like a newborn.

There were no clouds in the sky, and the morning sun cast a hard glare of yellow light over the top of the ridge. A few other Rangers were milling about, angling down toward the chuck wagon themselves, easing into a day that promised to be long, and trying for those uninitiated in the ways of an inspection.

There was no sign of Scrap. He had chosen to spend the night on his bedroll next to the corral.

That didn't surprise Josiah at all.

There was no sign of any activity when Josiah passed by Feders's tent. The captain had been more than a little concerned about Gill's tale of the attack on the Loving ranch, and like Josiah had expected he would, Pete had sent out six more men to keep watch at the perimeter of the camp.

Josiah had volunteered to sit watch, but his offer had been declined by Feders. There was no argument from Josiah. He hardly had any fight left in him at that point.

Somewhere in the interim, between the time when Josiah and Scrap had arrived in camp and when Josiah had escorted Zeb Gill to see the captain, Feders had focused on getting his tent in order.

The messy desk had been organized, and the whole of the tent, including the sleeping area, which had now been cordoned off with two clean orange-and-brown striped horse blankets, was neat and tidy. Everything was ready for a visit and inspection from Major Jones.

Josiah hesitated at the captain's tent flap. After the good night's sleep, he wondered briefly if he should opt to bring Feders his breakfast, then quickly dispensed with the thought. It was not his way to act like a servant, especially to a man he'd known as long as he had known Feders. He wasn't about to start kowtowing to the man now, just because he was a captain.

Josiah headed straightaway then to the chuck wagon and found his place in a line that was already forming. To his good fortune, Josiah found himself behind Red Overmeyer.

"Morning there, Red."

The hefty man, dressed in the same buckskin shirt as he'd worn the day before, turned and smiled. "Oh, Wolfe. Morning to you. Now, why is it you didn't tell none of us you was our sergeant?"

The man's German accent was pronounced on the end of each word, but unlike most Germans, Red didn't add a Z or put an extended S to his words. It was almost like the burly man had been born in Texas but surrounded, maybe, by parents or kin who spoke fluent German. The thought made Josiah wonder about Lyle — wonder if his son would have a Spanish flavor to his voice because of spending so much time around Ofelia. Mornings were the hardest, thinking about and missing Lyle.

Josiah shrugged at Red's question. "Didn't seem to matter. I wasn't about to start spewing out orders to a bunch of strangers before I even set down my bedroll. Besides, that's Captain Feders's place, not mine."

"Well," Red said, stepping forward a bit, close enough for Josiah to get a good whiff of his week-old stink. "Somebody needs to start telling these young boys which way is up. I got the patience of a saint, myself, but I'm a telling you, there's been no sort of legion here in the camp unless you want to count horse racin', gamblin', and shooting contests. Isn't a one of them that knows how to defend themselves from an Indian attack — with a gun, or a fist for that matter."

Josiah eased back a step and nodded. "I'm

sure Captain Feders just needs some time to get his footing."

"He best get it soon or he's going to wake up and find a Comanche or Kiowa standing over him with a bloody tomahawk in one hand and a handful of scalp in the other."

"Those are pretty strong words, Red."

"I've spent too much time in Indian Territory to serve under a man who hardly comes out of his tent. You need to take a firm hand here or you're risking every man's life, not just your own."

"Thanks, Red," Josiah said, "I'll sure keep that in mind."

There was time after breakfast for Josiah to shave, wash up, and put on a fresh shirt. Since this was not a full-blown military inspection, he didn't worry like he had at one time in his life, when he had worn a true uniform.

Scrap had shown up at the chuck wagon, gotten himself some breakfast, biscuits and coffee, then gone off to see to himself, at least that was what Josiah thought. He wasn't too concerned about the boy at the moment — but he was keeping a keen eye on Feders's tent.

As the sun rose high into the sky, not quite reaching the apex, there had not been one sign of the captain outside.

Josiah was starting to question Pete Feders's state of mind, wondering why the man who was so fierce and in charge on the trail was so visibly . . . absent . . . from taking command of the Ranger camp.

There had been a few times when Josiah had been tempted to go to the tent and see if Feders was all right, but he'd resisted. Whatever the problem was, it would have to work itself out . . . and fast.

A cloud of dust broke over the top of the ridge, bringing with it the immediate sound of thundering hooves — horses advancing toward the camp at a good speed and, from the sound of it, quite a few of them.

It had to be Jones.

If not, it was a huge Indian raiding party — another bold run by the Comanche, attacking a Ranger camp in the pure light of day.

There had been no sign of warning from the watch, and there was a redundant setting of men, ring upon outer ring of sentries, so someone would have surely posted an alert by now and fired three rounds into the air. Josiah doubted that the coming riders were Indians.

He turned his attention away from Feders's tent for the time being and walked to the edge of the camp to await a sign of the advancing party.

Major John B. Jones wielded a huge amount of power and popularity in Texas at the moment, and his arrival would be nothing short of myth taking human form and stepping onto the earth as a welcomed savior.

Jones had been a member of Terry's Texas Rangers in the War Between the States, had been put in charge of the Frontier Battalion by Governor Coke, and had, as Josiah had learned from the late, great Captain Fikes, little tolerance for disorder or showmanship, other than his own.

There was a great amount of lore attached to Jones, and that seemed to be what everyone, including the greenhorns in camp, wanted and needed most at the moment — a larger-than-life figure to take charge.

Even the Indians were curious and showing some discomfort in response to Jones's appointment to the Frontier Battalion. The attack on the Loving ranch was probably a test to see what Jones would do, how he would react. The Comanche knew the major was on the hoof, probably knew where he was at every moment. How he would react would precipitate their next move.

Josiah tried to remember as much as he

could about Jones. He knew that Hiram Fikes had served under Major Jones in the 8th Infantry — Terry's Texas Rangers — and the two men had fought together until the last engagement at Bentonville, North Carolina; hence the quick appointment of Fikes to the rank of captain in the Frontier Battalion. It was a shame the captain had barely lived to see the day when there was a fully funded establishment of Rangers.

Jones had attended Fikes's funeral, and it was there that Josiah had met him for the first time and judged the officer a cad. Josiah had to wonder, if the major had put his charms on another woman besides Pearl Fikes, would it have mattered to him all that much?

It was then that Josiah stumbled on a possible cause for Pete Feders's odd behavior. Feders knew about Jones's play for Pearl — he had been there and had most likely taken great offense at the pass, maybe even considered it a reason that Pearl had declined his offer of marriage.

Because Josiah had himself felt something for Pearl, had enjoyed her presence one-on-one, and had kissed her, as odd and ironic as it was, he understood how Feders could feel uneasy serving under the command of John B. Jones. He just wished he'd thought of the cause earlier, maybe spoken with Feders about Jones and calmed the new captain down a bit.

There was a lot of space in Texas for all three men to roam. They could all be Rangers and serve the greater good and leave Pearl Fikes to her own devices in Austin.

But there was more to Jones than his reputation with beautiful women, and Josiah knew it, so he couldn't be certain that Pearl was the sole cause of Feders's sullen mood.

Major John B. Jones was another Ranger who didn't hail from Texas. Some men bore a prejudice about such things. Rangers should be true Texans, but Jones was born in South Carolina, and the evidence of his place of birth could easily be detected when he spoke. His voice had the tone of an aristocrat, a fancy man with fancy manners. His drawl seemed to be a testament to a judgmental attitude in itself.

Somehow, Major Jones had earned the respect of Governor Coke and was, at the very least now, an honorary Texan, after briefly serving in the state legislature. Governor Coke had appointed him the head of the Frontier Battalion in the early spring, assured that the man was as trustworthy as he was demanding.

Josiah didn't necessarily disagree. Since

the Texas Rangers weren't regimented on a strict military foundation, it would take a strong man to maintain honor and exert his leadership over all of the companies that had been formed, and he would be expected to police the state in the most efficient way possible.

It was rumored that Jones was intentionally on the trail and conducting the inspection near Indian Territory with high hopes of seeing conflict himself with the Comanche or Kiowa, so he could prove his worth to the ranks of new Rangers and, more importantly, to Governor Coke and the purse string holders back in Austin.

The cloud of dust broke over the horizon, and as Josiah had thought, the coming riders were Jones and his escorts. Not a band of renegade Comanche. He was relieved. But only briefly.

They rode into the center of camp, coming to a halting stop after Jones raised up his arm and yelled back a ringing command to the fifteen or so men who rode in behind him. There was no question about who was in charge of this outfit.

The major quickly jumped off his horse — a tall, black stallion with a perfect white diamond centered on its long, glossy nose.

Jones was about a head shorter than Josiah and was dressed impeccably, even though it was obvious that he'd been on the trail for a good while. The major's long black riding coat matched his solid black, thick hair. His hair still held a pomade shine, though there was a touch of dust above his ears. Facial hair on Rangers was as acceptable as any other way of dress for a man — it was a Ranger's own personal choice. Jones's mustache was as thick as Red Overmeyer's meaty thumb, a perfect V drooping over his lips, trimmed to perfection. He did not wear a hat, at least not on this day, and the sun had burned his forehead and nose; they were bright red but had not blistered yet.

At forty years old, Jones remained unmarried, and the reputation he carried for appreciating a beautiful woman in one town, and then a new one in the next, was most certainly based on his profile, grooming habits, and the hearty dose of self-esteem he carried with every step he took.

All of which mattered little to Josiah at that exact moment.

Pete Feders had exited his tent upon hearing the commotion of the arriving company, his six-shooter securely in his right hand, and a hard glare chiseled on his face, his

CHAPTER 26

Major Jones stalked over to Pete Feders, never looking away, his jaw clenched, and his hand inches away from his gun, a Dance .44 revolver. The gun was modeled on the Colt Dragoon, had an eight-inch barrel and an iron back strap. Josiah had never seen a Dance before, but he sure knew one when he saw it.

It was the same kind of weapon the outlaw Wild Bill Longley used. The previous governor, E. J. Davis, had used freed slaves as policemen in the State Police, and Longley, still bitter about the outcome of the War Between the States, wore his prejudices openly. He killed a Negro state policeman with a Dance revolver — reportedly the first person ever murdered with that kind of gun — and started to gain a reputation as a fast-draw gunman. Josiah found it ironic that the head of the new battalion of Texas Rangers wore the same kind of revolver at his side as an outlaw. It made him start to question his previous assumptions about the major.

"Feders, what the hell are you doing?" Jones asked, drawing to a quick stop not six inches from the captain.

Pete Feders stood stiffly, not moving a muscle, still glaring at Jones. For a second, Josiah considered interfering, rushing to Pete's aid, but he decided just as quickly to stay out of the way. Feders was acting unpredictably. Jones was a leader who was unknown and untested, as far as Josiah was concerned. And every man in camp was on edge because of his arrival and the news of the attack at the Loving ranch.

"Waiting for you." The scar on Feders's face pulsed; then he tapped his fingers on his holster, bit his lip, turned, and stalked inside the tent.

A surprised look flashed in Major Jones's eyes — like he had just given an order that had been rejected, like Feders had acted in an unsuitable, insubordinate manner. He started to trail after the captain but stopped and spoke to Josiah.

"Get these men ready, Sergeant. We got word that the Comanche that raided the Loving ranch were heading southeast, down Salt Creek. I need fresh men and fresh horses. We will be on that trail within the hour. Do I make myself clear?" Jones said.

Josiah nodded. "Captain Feders riding with us?"

"He'll remain here. I want you with me, Wolfe. You and the finest men you have to face these savages. Any man with experience fighting Comanche or Kiowa had better saddle up."

Jones started to say something else, then thought better of it, and rushed into the tent, hard on Feders's heels.

The air was sucked out of the moment. Silence settled in around the tent. Even the birds had the sense to keep their beaks closed.

Josiah was certain that whatever ill will existed between the captain and the major should be worked out between the two men — but the obvious anger between them wasn't good for anybody in the camp.

"All right, men, show's over. You heard the major. Let's get ourselves ready to ride. Elliot," Josiah said to Scrap, "I want you to make sure we've got the best horses on this ride. My guess is we're heading toward Lost Valley, and from what I understand that terrain can be difficult to traverse. Loose, rocky trails on the side of the mountains that rim the valley. It's not a meadow ride, so we won't need speed, we'll need strength and stamina to get around the rim."

Most of the men hurried off, including Scrap, heading for the corral. Red Overmeyer hung back, easing next to Josiah.

Raised voices from inside Feders's tent added to the stir and rush to get ready to depart, and Josiah headed for his tent at the end of the row. Red walked with him, keeping pace with his stride — which wasn't hurried, but it wasn't easy, either. Josiah didn't want to hear the argument between Feders and Jones. If he was right and Pearl Fikes was square in the middle of their quarrel, the best thing he could do was get as far away from them as possible.

"You know what that's about, don't you, Wolfe?" Red asked.

Josiah slowed his pace. "What's it matter?"

"Doesn't really, except if I'm riding with a man, or servin' with him, I like to know what subjects to duck."

"And if you can trust his judgment?"

"I'm a-startin' to wonder about Feders. He seems unstable."

"Give him time. I trust him with my life."

"Do you now?"

"You think I'd just say that?"

"No, Wolfe, I don't imagine you would,

now that you ask straight out."

Josiah stopped at his tent. "Thanks, then, Red. I want you to round up the best Indian fighters in camp. You'd know better than me."

Overmeyer nodded. "There's a few of us who have traveled together into Indian Territory. Saw some skirmishes, survived a hard fight or two. What about you?"

Josiah hesitated, a flash of memory rising in his mind. His hand trembled for a second as he remembered the encounter he'd had when he was twelve. Thankfully that day had not gotten any worse. He had run back home, fearing that he would find his mother and sick father dead . . . scalped, and the farm burned to the ground, but it was just as he had left it. The only thing that was worse was explaining the loss of the gun to his father.

"I've had my run-ins with an Indian or two."

"But not a full-fledged fight?"

"I've seen plenty of battle, if that's what's worrying you," Josiah said.

"Ain't so much worried about you fightin' as I am about takin' orders from a man who don't know much about the ways of the redskins."

"Me or Jones?"

311

Red shrugged his shoulders and said nothing.

Josiah grabbed the tent flap. "You heard Major Jones. We've got an hour to ready ourselves. If that's not enough time, Red, then I'll be glad to rely on somebody else."

"I've been ready since I rose this morning."

"Me, too. I'm always ready."

Red Overmeyer looked past Josiah, into the tent, and nodded. "I suppose you are. Sorry, I didn't mean to insult you."

"No worry," Josiah said. "You've got your rights to wonder about who's got your hide covered."

The man stuck his hand out, his frayed buckskin shirtsleeve swinging wildly from the suddenness of the movement. Josiah responded in kind, his hand immediately swallowed up in Red's. It hurt when he pulled away, but he tried not to show his discomfort.

"I got your back, Josiah Wolfe, don't you worry about that."

At the end of the path, Josiah had assembled the troop of men he meant to take on the trail. They all stood waiting in a small clearing just opposite the chuck wagon. Including Major Jones, who was still inside Pete

Feders's tent, there would be thirty-three men in the outfit.

The wagon was to be left behind, the need for urgency too strong to cart along a chuck wagon and all that went with it. The troop of Rangers had been ordered to store up on rations, but each was pretty much left on his own to decide what the right amount was. There were some skilled hunters mixed in among the men, so hopefully, if the need and opportunity arose, fresh meat would not be a concern on the journey to Lost Valley.

Scrap had been assigned to bring up the tail of the riders, keeping an eye out mostly for horse trouble, but also for anything else, as far as that went. He seemed happy that Josiah had given him so much responsibility, and he kept pretty much to himself, going about his chores without question. He interacted with the new Rangers with ease and unquestionable purpose. A smile was quick to come to his face when he had the opportunity to educate a man on a more efficient way to saddle his horse — if it seemed welcome — or make friends with the horse itself.

There was a giddiness among the men readying for departure, too. After all, fighting the Comanche and Kiowa was one of the main reasons the Frontier Battalion had been formed. Most men had signed up to fight the Indians, and now they were about to get exactly what they had come to camp for.

Josiah watched the tent for a sign of Major Jones but was more taken with the cloud banks forming on the western horizon. Big, puffy clouds, tall as mountains and just as gray, were starting to roil and bluster toward them. The wind had shifted, and the smell of rain was fresh, as a distant clap of thunder echoed toward Josiah. He sighed. Riding out in the rain was not something he looked forward to.

He walked over to Clipper and made sure his slicker was tucked into the saddlebag. It was, but he was glad to make sure.

Scrap walked up to Josiah, an unlit quirley stuck in the corner of his mouth. "Looks like rain."

"A storm," Josiah said.

"Maybe it'll go south of us." Scrap lit the quirley, and his first draw and exhale of the burning tobacco reminded Josiah why he had never taken up the habit in the first place. He couldn't abide the smell or the taste.

"Doesn't look that way."

"Nope, it don't." Scrap smoked leisurely,

but he seemed tense, watching Feders's tent, like Josiah. "I ain't never seen Feders, um, the captain, act so strange. You, Wolfe?"

"I try not to worry about Captain Feders too much. He's probably just adjusting to his new role. He's got some mighty tall boots to fill."

"Seems more than that to me. Seems to me there's a conflict between him and the major. You know anything about that?"

"If I did, it would be pure speculation. I'm not going to gossip about the captain if that's what you're looking for."

"Just wonderin', that's all. You don't have to go gettin' all hot under the collar."

"Didn't know that I was. Sorry." Josiah paused, looked away from the tent and back to the horizon. "You ready for this?"

"I've been waitin' for this all my life," Scrap said, pinching the hot ash off the end of the quirley, tapping it out on the bottom of his boot.

Just as Josiah was about to tell Scrap to leave his vengeful thinking behind and put his Ranger hat on, Major Jones stormed out of Pete Feders's tent.

"All right, Wolfe, good job," Jones said, walking past Josiah.

Every man stiffened, walked to the front of his waiting horse, and stared at the major for the command.

"Thank you, Major," Josiah said.

Scrap eased back, scurried silently to the end of the thirty-three-man line, and took his place in front of Missy.

A thunderclap rattled the sky in the distance, pulling Jones's attention to the horizon for a moment. "That's the last thing we need. It'll make tracking us easier. Not that the Comanche won't smell us coming. Isn't that right, Wolfe?"

Josiah ignored the question. It was possible that the comment from the major meant nothing, but to Josiah it rang of prejudice, and carrying that into a battle was as dangerous as swearing a hateful vengeance upon your enemy for crimes that may or may not have been committed.

"Should I get the captain's horse ready?" Josiah asked.

"No," Major Jones said. "He'll stay at camp and await further instructions. He'll have a small contingency of men to join us if the need should arise. But trust me, Wolfe, we won't need help from Captain Feders."

Josiah drew in a deep breath. He wanted to ask the major the same question Red Overmeyer had asked him: *Have you ever done battle with Indians?* But Josiah knew better. And he knew the answer was no, too.

Major John B. Jones had never faced a raiding party or fought with the Indians in their own lands.

Jones's lack of experience fighting Indians was a concern to Josiah, but no more than his own. Both men had seen battle before — just not like they were about to. The difference between the major and Josiah was simple: Josiah never looked forward to conflict, to the pure act of killing another man — whether the man was a Comanche or not.

But Josiah would kill if he had to.

Jones walked to his horse without saying another word, mounted the black stallion with the white diamond on his nose, and shouted a command for the rest of the Rangers to follow his lead.

There was a great rustle of spurs, boots, and long coats, as the thirty-three men did as they were told. As Josiah settled in Clipper's saddle, the only thing that seemed odd to him was riding with so many men, and being squarely behind Major Jones, second in command.

With a sharp command that echoed across the camp, Jones moved out, heading east, away from the coming storm.

Josiah followed, but as they took pace he looked back, and saw Pete Feders step out of his tent, a frustrated look on his scarred face. He tipped his hat subtly to Feders. The captain nodded, then turned and disappeared back inside the tent, his shoulders slumped, his disappointment obvious.

CHAPTER 27

Red Overmeyer cut away from the troop of men early on in the ride, long before they reached Lost Valley. He'd been sent out with another scout, a fellow named Ben Cheek, whom Josiah hadn't met, to follow up on the trail the Comanche had left behind after raiding the Loving ranch. There had been no sign of Red and Ben, or of the Indians, and Josiah was starting to become concerned as they made their way to the valley.

The trail was relatively easy to navigate, but as they drew closer to the nearly barren basin, the mountains rose higher, and the trail grew thinner and rockier, each step forward more precarious and worrisome.

Major Jones, who still rode lead, had proven to be an adept rider — not as skilled as Scrap, but skilled nonetheless — and he needed to be a good rider, considering the change in landscape.

Jones sat straight up in his saddle, alert

319

and fully confident. He was like a cat on the lookout for a mouse, ready to pounce, ready to kill. Question was, as far as Josiah was concerned, would Major John B. Jones play with his prey before he killed it for his pleasure, like a cat — and put them all at risk — or attack and get the deed over with as quickly as possible?

Honestly, Josiah was hoping that they wouldn't see one Indian, that the raiders were deep into Indian Territory, celebrating and planning their next raid. It was an offhand hope, and Josiah knew better than to share his thoughts with anyone, considering he was riding second, a sergeant and not a lieutenant, behind Jones. Encountering a marauding band of Comanche and Kiowa was something he was going to face sooner or later anyway; nobody knew that better than Josiah himself. Unlike most of the men on the ride, though, he'd signed up to be a Ranger, and not just an Indian fighter.

They were about sixteen miles from Fort Richardson, their destination for this leg of the search, and other than the trail the scouts had been sent on early in the journey, there had not been one sign of the Comanche or Kiowa.

The basin of the valley was filled with

mesquite trees, and the storm that had threatened earlier in the day had, thankfully, passed to the south of them, contributing a steady breeze but no rain. Clouds were quickly clearing away, vanishing as soon as they had arrived, fleeing east, and the air was suddenly turning muggy as the sun began to beat down and the heat of the day crept back in. July in Texas was never predictable.

Sweat beaded under the brim of Josiah's felt hat. His shirt stuck to his chest, and he tried not to pay any mind to the change in the weather, the feel of the day, but it made him sit up in the saddle. He was determined not to let the heat draw him down.

A redtail hawk spiraled overhead, riding an unseen circular trail higher and higher into the sky. It screamed from its place in the clouds, the air under its wings, happy to be flying. It surely wasn't hunting.

The ride had turned out to be far more comfortable than Josiah had imagined it would be in the beginning. Most of the men remained quiet, though the senses of every Ranger in the troop were heightened, on alert, every unknown movement questioned. Still, the rhythm of the horses, the draw of each breath, eased the worry, and proved to be salve for the weather and uncertainty that lay ahead.

Without warning, Major Jones brought the troop of Rangers to a stop. Josiah eased up next to him, uncertain what the problem was. He had seen nothing, had heard nothing to cause alarm on the major's part. Even Clipper seemed to question the major's decision to stop. The horse wasn't the least bit concerned about his surroundings, or at least, it didn't seem that way — and if Josiah knew anything, he knew what roused Clipper and what didn't.

"Is there something wrong, Major?" Josiah asked.

"Scout's coming."

Josiah turned his head to the right, then back to the left, and still saw and heard nothing. He didn't question the major. Not yet, anyway. Though he was curious how the major could be so sure of the scout's impending arrival. Josiah thought he had a decent set of perceptional skills, skills he'd honed since he was a boy in the Piney Woods. He would have been just as aware as the major — surely he wasn't that comfortable — on the lookout for Indians.

Before he could form another sentence in his mind, Red Overmeyer pulled up on the trail about twenty yards ahead of them, appearing out of a thick scattering of shrubby plants that Josiah didn't know the name of, or anything about. The man was on foot, his horse nowhere to be seen.

Josiah swallowed the question that had fully formed by then and decided he'd need to reconsider what Major Jones was good at and what he was not.

"Come with me," Major Jones said to Josiah. "The rest of the men need to stay where they are."

The major eased his stallion toward Red, and Josiah commanded the men behind him to stay put, then followed the major up to the scout.

"Looks like Lone Wolf is on the move," Red said.

"Lone Wolf. You're sure?" Major Jones asked.

"Mamanti, too. Painted for war. Word is there's about a hundred of them, maybe more. A day's ride from here, to the north. At least that's the report I got. No reason to question it."

"He's after revenge," Jones said. "His son was killed in a raid not long ago. I'm fully aware that Lone Wolf has a score to settle. War paint? That many riders? You're sure, Overmeyer?"

"Well, Ben Cheek is still out and about, trying to figure out what's going on. I didn't

323

see Lone Wolf with my own eyes, Major Jones," Red said, in his halting, German way of speaking.

"I suppose you didn't."

"Is this personal?" Josiah asked.

"I had nothing to do with the death of Lone Wolf's son, but I surely would have taken the shot given the chance," Jones answered. "Anytime a savage is killed, it's personal to them. Same with the hands at Loving's ranch. Those men had families, people that depended on them. We owe it to those families to bring the Comanche to their knees. This is Texas, not open territory where heathen lawlessness prevails. Man's got a right to work a ranch."

"Lone Wolf and Mamanti are Kiowa," Josiah said, dropping his voice to nearly a whisper. He didn't want to be coy or disobedient, and honestly the words had popped out of his mouth before he could stop them.

Major Jones shot Josiah a quick, disapproving look, and Josiah figured he'd best just shut up and listen from then on.

Red Overmeyer stood back, stepping out of the conversation, obviously trying to avoid any conflict with the major. The scout's gaze rose over the major's shoulders, to the outcroppings in the distance.

"A savage is a savage, Ranger Wolfe,"

Jones said. "You certainly feel the same way that I do, don't you?" The tone in Jones's voice was tight, past perturbed.

"There," Red said, interrupting the bawling out that was about to take place, pointing to a single outcropping, far to the north side of the basin's rocky rim.

Josiah and the major quickly followed the tip of Red's finger, dropping their disagreement — if it could be called that. Josiah might have a quarrel with the major, or with his views at any rate, but he didn't think it was wise just now to dispute the man's thinking about Indians or their status in the state of Texas.

Their vision came to rest on two Kiowa scouts, easing their way down into the valley.

"They haven't seen us," Jones said. "We need to silence them, make sure they can't report back to Lone Wolf that we're here, on their trail. Bring the troop forward, Ranger Wolfe. We're going into the valley. You take cover, Overmeyer, and circle back behind them in case they decide to run. Make sure Ranger Cheek is aware of my plans. I don't want him to get caught in the cross fire unaware."

Red's line of sight did not leave the Kiowa scouts. "You think that's a good idea, there,

Major Jones?"

"It's why we're here."

"To be killed by the Comanche and the Kiowa?" Red asked. "Been enough bloodshed if you ask me."

"Why would you say such a thing? Two of them against over thirty of us? They are sorely outnumbered and must not be allowed to get word back to their leaders. We have a claim to stake, a message that needs to be sent that change has arrived — a new battalion has set out after them and will not relent. They are subject to the laws of Texas whether they like it or not." Major Jones hesitated, his eyes brimming with anger. "Do you think there are more there than what we see?"

"Could be," Red said. "Those there could be decoys."

"No matter the number, we're Rangers, I tell you. Texas Rangers. And those are Kiowa Indians. Savages who brought death and mayhem to the Loving ranch and dropped blood upon the Texas dirt — without mercy, I might add. No mercy at all. Would you suggest, sir, that I, the duly appointed leader of the Frontier Battalion, should not engage two Indians, not bring them to their knees and force them to face the reign of justice?"

"I'm not suggesting anything, Major. Just be aware that these are Kiowa, Plains Indians, whose ways are foreign to us all — or almost all of us. The justice you speak of is white man's justice. It is a justice they care little about."

"They will or there will be war."

"There already is — for them," Red said.

Josiah kept his eyes focused on the two Kiowa scouts.

They truly seemed unaware of the presence of the troop of Rangers. That, in itself, made him nervous. He was more inclined to favor Red Ovemeyer's view that the scouts were not scouts at all, but decoys. But he also knew that the major's point was valid — at least to the major. They had stumbled onto their prey, and there was no letting go of it. Not until the confrontation was ended properly. Major Jones had made his intentions clear from the outset.

"You actually think there may be more than those two scouts, Overmeyer?" Major Jones asked again, as if he were reconsidering his next move.

"That I do, Major Jones. There may very well be more than two scouts. There very well may be a line of Kiowa and Comanche, joined together by one cause, hiding in the rocks, waiting for us to make a mistake."

"It does not matter," Jones said. "We are Rangers, I tell you. The governor would be less than pleased to hear that we did not at least detain the scouts. We do not have a choice."

"No, sir, I don't think we do. We surely are Rangers and have our charge. I will obey your command. But I will do so cautiously."

"My command sits directly on my own shoulders, Ranger Overmeyer, don't think I am not aware of that, too."

"I would never question such a thing." With that said, Red Overmeyer tipped his hat both to the major and Josiah and disappeared into the bushes from where he had originally emerged.

Major Jones watched Red, then started to say something, but Josiah cut him off. "They've seen us," he said, watching the two Kiowa scouts ride full-out down into the valley.

"Let's ride, Ranger Wolfe," Major Jones said, slapping his black stallion on the rump with the pair of gloves he held tightly in his hand.

Josiah had no choice but to give the rest of the men the order, and Clipper, too, as he galloped off after the major, deep into Lost Valley.

Whatever reservations he shared with Red

Overmeyer were left behind on the trail. He pulled his Peacemaker from the holster, chambered a bullet, and kept the six-shooter in his grip, ready at a moment's notice. If his reservations — and gut feeling — proved to be right about the Kiowa scouts being decoys, or lures, leading them into a trap where there was no escape, then he wanted nothing more than to be ready.

CHAPTER 28

The first shot rang out as soon as the troop of Rangers rode into the bottom of Lost Valley.

Major Jones had led the troop of thirty-three Rangers, at full speed, into the valley, and it was too late to realize that he and his men were surrounded by Lone Wolf and nearly one hundred and fifty fighting mad warriors. As Red Overmeyer had feared, the scouts were decoys, and Jones had led his men directly into a trap.

Once the Rangers were in the valley, the Kiowa circled behind them, quickly closing the way in — and the way out — of Lost Valley. There must have been another party of Indians a day's ride away — either that, or Red's scouting information was wrong — dead wrong.

Josiah was at Jones's shoulder, riding full-out. He had pulled his Winchester out of the scabbard and was firing as rapidly as he could at the Indians, alternating between his Peacemaker and his rifle, while Clipper maintained his speed. One Kiowa had already been struck down by Josiah's adept shooting, tumbling over a huge boulder as the warrior took aim at the oncoming Rangers.

The air was filled with the sound of horses' hooves pounding furiously on the hard ground, screams of pain and agony, yells of revenge and courage, all tainted with the smell of gunpowder, blood, sweat, and fear.

The major did not flinch, did not hesitate as they drove deeper into the valley, clearing the way with a constant barrage of gunfire. Jones remained cool in the lead, did not show one ounce of fear or regret. He quickly surveyed the circle of Kiowa that, at the moment, seemed impenetrable. "There," he shouted, pointing to a thin line of Indians near a shallow gully, full of scrub bushes and tender young mesquite trees. "We'll take our position there!"

They rushed as fast as they could toward the break in the circle, all of them pushing their horses as hard as they could.

The Kiowa were armed with breech-loading arms, carbines. If they had been armed with new-model Winchesters, the outcome would have probably been different. The bullets would have rained down on the Rangers more quickly, been more accurate, and taken more than a life or two.

As it was, the Ranger on the horse right behind Josiah took a shot to the leg. The young man, about Scrap's age, named Paulson, screamed in agony, drawing Josiah's attention away from shooting into the deadly circle of Kiowa, but he kept Clipper fully under control.

Josiah headed straight toward the gully, and saw the wisdom in Jones's decision — but for a brief second, he quit firing. He glanced over his shoulder just in time to see Paulson take another shot. This one hit the already wounded man square in the forehead. The force of the shot knocked young Paulson off his horse, and into the path of thirty oncoming horses. The other Rangers were running at a pace so fast that a few of them had no choice but to step on the Ranger. If the shot hadn't killed him, the trampling certainly would have.

Paulson didn't have time to scream; there was just a shot, a thud, and a rise of dust. Death was quick. That was the only mercy that could be found in the heat of the moment. Surviving took precedence. There would be time for sorrow and grief later.

Nobody knew that better than Josiah.

But Josiah screamed for the man without thought, screamed as loud as he could, his cry matching that of the Kiowa.

He shot in the direction where Paulson's fatal shot had originated. He couldn't tell if he hit anything, his eyes were tearing up from the rage and the dust, but he kept firing anyway. His heart was beating faster than it had in a long time — since Chickamauga, for sure. He could taste bile in the back of his throat, feel his emotions draining out of his body as the rage of battle numbed his senses and any of his immediate thoughts and concerns. All he wanted to do was live to fight on and make sure that his enemy did not. All he wanted to do was kill those that were trying to kill him.

The morality of the act, of the desire, of the emotion, was the least of his concerns. Paulson's death had ignited a stick of dynamite that had been stored and stowed since the end of the war. Josiah had hoped never to feel the insanity that a battle brings on ever again.

In a matter of minutes Josiah and Clipper crossed an animal path, hurried down a slight ravine, and were in the gully. Jones was just ahead of them, spinning his sweaty black stallion around in a circle, checking the area to make sure he'd been right in the choosing.

Bullets whizzed by Josiah's head, hitting the ground, piercing trees — it sounded like a hundred claps of thunder, hail bouncing off tin, or a hundred hard tinkles of a saloon player's piano. No matter, it was not a pleasant sheet of music, since gun battles were usually followed by a funeral march.

Josiah quickly scrambled off Clipper, leaving his trusted horse behind a tree. He started shouting to the other men who had followed suit and jumped off their horses after arriving safely in the gully.

"Form a line. There's long shots to be had, reload and keep firing until you get the order to cease," he screamed. "Hold the position. Hold the position."

Major Jones quickly joined Josiah, a pistol in each hand. Josiah paid no attention to the major at first. He was still watching the men ride into the gully . . . he didn't take a full breath or feel any relief until he saw Scrap Elliot ride in as the last. One of the men at the tail end of the troop looked to be wounded, a flesh wound in the right arm.

"Elliot," Josiah yelled as loud as he could. "Tend to that man."

Scrap nodded, dismounted in one swift, skilled motion, and was at the wounded man's side in the blink of an eye. He pulled the man off his horse and walked him back toward the spot where Josiah and most of the other Rangers had left their horses. It looked to be safe there, out of range of the Kiowa's carbines. At least for the moment.

Josiah made a quick count of the men. "Looks like we lost one man, Major Jones, and have another wounded."

"We're lucky then."

"That we are," Josiah said. "It looks like Ranger Paulson's horse has been taken down, too."

Jones exhaled deeply and shook his head. "Any sign of Overmeyer or Cheek?"

"No, sir."

"They have some explaining to do . . . but that's going to have to wait," Jones said. "We need to make a statement to these savages. They need to fear the Rangers, know we mean business." He stalked off then, joining the line and returning fire with both pistols, walking straight toward the shrubs where the first ambush shot had come from.

At first, the gully seemed the perfect spot for them to retreat to. Beyond a thin grove of trees where the horses had been stowed, there was a rising shelf of rock that rose so high, about twenty feet, that its shadow fell over the gully. The light was gray like evening even though the sun was beating down from a sky that was vacant of clouds now that they had run east. There was no way the Kiowa could take to the rim of the gully and fire directly down at the Rangers. And there was enough of a rise to the gully itself for the line of Rangers to fire over it, then duck back down for cover.

The only thing missing, the one ingredient that would have made Major Jones's choice perfect, was water. The gully was as dry as a steer's skull. The ground was hard and cracked, and it looked like no rain, or moisture of any kind, had visited the bottom of Lost Valley in a long time.

Josiah had not noticed the lack of water when he arrived in the gully, but as the gunfire between the Rangers and the Kiowa began to slow, he noticed the dryness of the area, and the potential problem this presented, since they were, for all intents and purposes, trapped, cornered by Lone Wolf, Mamanti, and their trickery.

The shots were long ones and intermittent now that everyone had settled into place — the Rangers in the gully, under the command of Major Jones, and the Kiowa shored up nearly in a full circle, except for the break that Jones had had the vision to see his men through to.

Off to the right of the horses was a spot where the men could gather and stand without fear of being shot. The only concern was scorpions or snakes, hiding in unseen crevices, waiting patiently for a bit of flesh to attack.

Major Jones and Josiah had pulled away from the edge of the gully and were discussing their options when Scrap joined them.

"Looks like that fella is gonna be all right. I got the bleedin' stopped, Major Jones," Scrap said. "He's on the ridge firin' with his good arm, achin' to get a kill or two for the pain he's in."

"Good work, Ranger Elliot," Major Jones said.

Josiah nodded in agreement. "How much water do you have?" he asked Scrap.

"Not a lot. A quarter of a canteen, if that."

"What about the rest of the men?" Josiah asked.

"I don't quite know," Scrap said to Josiah, a curious look on his face.

"Why don't you go check? See where we stand."

"Is there a problem, Ranger Wolfe?" Major Jones asked.

"If we're low on water, we're not in a good spot, sir."

Scrap started to interject a thought but saw a look in Josiah's eyes that warned him off. Instead, Scrap turned and hurried away, going all of the way to the end of the gully and talking to the last Ranger in the firing line.

"We will have to make do, then," Major Jones said. "Those savages aren't going to roust us out just because we're unable to quench our thirst."

"They will wait us out, if it comes to that," Josiah said. "One of the fellas said Cameron Creek is about a mile north."

"No one will leave this gully until I give the command. Is that understood, Ranger Wolfe?"

"It is, Major, but could it be a . . ." Josiah stopped, shut his mouth.

"A what? A mistake? I dare not think so. We have the savages right where we want them. Make no mistake, we will be victorious. Is that understood?"

"It is, Major. It is."

"Good. Come with me, Wolfe, we need to command the line. Rally our men, let them know victory is at hand. We will have these redskins on the run before nightfall."

Before Jones could turn and stalk toward the firing line, Scrap rejoined the two men — a worried look settled on his face.

"Most of the men are already out of water, Major. Some are suckin' mud tryin' to wet their lips. Most every man I talked to has had a loss, either a canteen or a mount. Looks like about a third of our horses are layin' out in the beyond, waitin' to be dinner for those damned Indians, or buzzards. I'd just as soon see a buzzard chaw up some dinner than those Kiowa. Water's bad, 'bout gone, though. It sure is. Could get right desperate," Scrap said.

A bullet zinged over Jones's head, and he barely reacted at all, glancing up causally like it was a fly instead of a bullet. It was almost like the major thought he was invincible, foolish as that was, or maybe he believed he was dressed in an iron suit.

Josiah thought he'd warn the major to duck down a bit, hunch his shoulders, but thought better of it. Jones surely knew he was mortal, not immune to the delivery of a bullet dipped in Lone Wolf's deep well of revenge. But he sure didn't act like it.

If Jones kept up his cavalier actions, Josiah was certain there'd be more than one casualty to report to Austin when the battle was over. And the major's career as a Texas Ranger just might be a short one.

CHAPTER 29

By dusk, the situation had gotten worse. The men were beyond thirst as the sun beat down from high in the sky — the heat inside the valley was almost unbearable. Deep inside the rocks, the air was unmoving, stagnant.

Finally, Ranger Dave W. H. Bailey, an eager young man with a head full of straw-colored hair and bright blue eyes, worked up the nerve and volunteered to gather up everyone's canteen and go find water — confronting Major Jones in a respectful, but forceful, manner.

"I still do not think that's a good idea," Major Jones said.

Bailey stood before him, his eyes pleading, showing no sign of intimidation or fear.

Josiah was standing next to Jones, anxious as well. He appreciated the backbone and fortitude that the young Ranger had mustered just to walk up to Major Jones unbidden and offer a plan that would relieve the troops of their thirst.

The major had not listened to anyone else, but for some reason, it appeared that Bailey was getting the message across.

"The other Rangers are starting to become desperate and very well might take matters into their own hands," Bailey said. "I don't mean to be disrespectful, and most of these fellas think you're the finest major they've ever served with, but thirst makes a man leery of just about everything, Major Jones, you gotta know that."

The Kiowa had dug into their positions, firing long shots consistently but not constantly, just enough to warn the Rangers that escaping from the Lost Valley floor would not be done with ease or without a serious fight. The shots came from various positions, a reminder from the Kiowa that they had the Rangers outnumbered at least three to one.

Jones looked on Bailey without anger. "The men are tiring and in need of relief, you say?"

"Yes, Major Jones, I do."

Watching the young Ranger hold his ground with Jones, Josiah stood back, more and more impressed by the second.

Major Jones reached up and tugged the

corner of his mustache, then turned to Josiah and said, "Once the first star shines, have another man go with Ranger Bailey to refill the canteens. The light of day will not be gone then but will be dim enough to cover their movement. The trail back will be under darkness if the creek is just a mile out, but that shouldn't present a problem for any man we have here. Talent, I tell you. Bright, fighting talent. The Frontier Battalion will be legendary before the new year rises."

Josiah sighed silently, glad of the change in the major's decision. "I would like to be the one to go with Ranger Bailey, Major."

Jones visibly thought about the request for a second, his brow furrowing deeply, then made another quick decision. "Take Ranger Elliot with you and Ranger Bailey, then. The three of you should be able to carry back all of the water we need."

"I don't think it's necessary for Elliot to —"

"It's not a request, Wolfe," Major Jones said. He turned then, leaving Josiah standing there with Ranger Bailey, glad that they were free to go after water, but none too thrilled at the prospect of taking Scrap along with them.

The North Star pulsed in the clear evening sky, signaling to Josiah it was time for the trio to leave the safety of the gully. Bailey and Scrap had gone about collecting canteens and had as many as they thought they could carry back full, tied together and flung over the backs of their horses.

Josiah checked his Winchester and slid it gently into the scabbard. Clipper snorted, like he knew they were readying to leave. They were all carrying as many bullets as possible, ready for whatever waited for them in the shadows and beyond.

Josiah didn't know much about Dave Bailey, but while he readied Clipper and waited for the first star to shine, he had learned that Bailey had signed up with the Rangers just a few months before, in May, not too far off from where they were now, in Wise County. His folks had a small ranch just outside Decatur, so Bailey was aware of the land, of the ways of the wild in North Texas. Josiah was glad of that.

The desolation of Lost Valley made him long to see a pine tree and smell the decay of dropped brown needles littered on the ground. Anything that reminded him of home would be a comfort now. He was out of his element, had been since they departed Fort Worth. He tried not to even think about Lyle, but he wondered more often than not if the little child would know him when he saw him next — if Lyle would even recognize his own father when he returned home . . . whenever that would be.

There was no question that the three men were nervous, unsure of what faced them outside of the gully, but the Kiowa's plan was obvious: hold the company of Rangers in the valley until the lack of water drove them to madness, to foolish thoughts and behavior.

If the trio did not go as charged, then the lack of water would surely be all the men's undoing and every one of them knew it.

There was no man among the three who would allow a little nervousness to take down a troop of Rangers. They were bound by the deed, and there was no room for failure. The fate of the entire company rested squarely on their shoulders — more specifically, on Josiah's shoulders, and he felt every ounce of the responsibility.

More men had volunteered to ride to the creek, but Jones had tempered the requests, praising the three chosen Rangers, and allowing that every man on the floor of the valley was needed to ensure victory against the savage Kiowa. Jones may not have had a sure hand at fighting Indians, but he was full of bravado, and knew how to keep his men focused and motivated. That in itself was a skill that would keep some men alive and was more than likely why Governor Coke had appointed Jones to lead the Frontier Battalion in the first place.

Scrap was enthusiastic, darn near giddy, at the order to go after water with Josiah and Dave Bailey. Elliot had been acting rather obedient, or just plain docile, since they had arrived at the Ranger camp from Fort Worth. Even more so when they left for Fort Richardson under Jones's charge. It was an odd and extremely noticeable change of behavior to Josiah, and when the opportunity arose, he planned on asking Scrap exactly what the hell was going on.

The boy's unfamiliar demeanor contributed to Josiah's unease about the three men going on the journey. He thought that two men would be enough, that they could carry all the water needed and that three men would likely draw the attention of the Kiowa — but he was not going to question Jones openly. He would do as he was told, his own compliance a little bit of a surprise to himself.

After getting a last-minute speech from Major Jones on bravery and the necessity of their triumph over the marauding Kiowa, the three departed the gully on horseback.

They eased north along the high shelf of rock, riding low in the saddle, hiding in the shadows as much as possible, aware of every sound, every shot in the distance, as the Rangers and the Kiowa continued to trade them in the valley.

Dave Bailey led the way on his horse, a young paint that looked a little too spirited to remain quiet the whole way, but the horse remained reined in by Bailey's firm hand. Scrap and Missy held the middle, and Josiah and Clipper brought up the rear.

They had all expected to encounter a volley of gunshots as they left the company of Rangers and headed for the creek, but surprisingly the way was clear of Kiowa. It was either an oversight or Lone Wolf and Mamanti were fully aware that the way to water was open and had another trap lying in wait for the Rangers. The Indians knew the landscape — that much was obvious — and delighted in trickery, taking advantage of the white man's lack of knowledge about their ways.

Josiah thought about both possibilities and

kept his concerns to himself. The Kiowa were not stupid. If the trail to the water was open on purpose, it was because they were allowing the trio to get far enough away from the camp to not have immediate help from the other Rangers.

Josiah rode steadily behind the two young Rangers, his eyes and ears open to the presence of anything that seemed out of place. He wasn't sure he would recognize such a thing, but he had to try.

Scrap and Bailey remained quiet, heading north with the purpose of saviors, their quest for water almost holy in its scope. Bailey showed no regrets and plenty of skill when it came to driving the paint along the trail as quietly as possible, folding himself expertly into the shadows of the rocks that surrounded them.

Dusk fell quickly.

All of the light was nearly wrung out of the blackening sky, like a wet cloth twisted and flipped, any moisture gone from the strength of the day. The bright sun was just a memory, but there was no breeze and still plenty of heat — left behind as a reminder of its long presence.

On horseback the mile passed by nearly in the blink of an eye. A thin, steady trickle of water, about six inches wide and as many inches deep, ran due south in Cameron Creek.

The run of water was like music on a quiet night, soft and welcome to the ears, its rhythm so familiar that it brought a smile to each man's face.

Almost simultaneously upon arriving at the edge of the creek, the three of them dismounted and scrambled for the water. Josiah's throat was so dry and parched, he felt like he had just walked through a high desert at noon and stumbled onto an oasis that turned out to be real, not a figment of his imagination.

The water was crisp and clean, cool to the tongue, but even more of a salve to the spirit. It was the best-tasting water that had ever passed through Josiah's lips. They were halfway through the journey to bring relief home to their fellow Rangers and had not seen hide nor hair of a mad Kiowa.

After refreshing themselves, they set about filling up the canteens.

"Phew," Dave Bailey said. "I sure expected to see some redskins along the way." He was smart enough to hold his voice low, but it still carried on the night air.

"Me, too," Scrap said.

"We aren't home free, boys," Josiah interjected. "Kiowa could be watching every move we make. I won't be at ease until we're back with the company."

"I just wish it was Comanche we were fightin'," Scrap said, filling up his fifth canteen. He walked the full ones back to Missy and threw them over the blue roan's back.

"I'm achin' to fight a Comanche myself," Bailey said.

"Don't pay much mind to Elliot, he's been carrying a score around with him as long as I've known him, and he's blind about the consequences of settling up."

"I'll keep that in mind." Bailey stood up from the creek, his knees a bit muddy, and lugged another load of canteens to his horse.

"One more trip and we ought to be about ready to head back, right, Wolfe?" Scrap said, tossing an empty canteen into the water.

Josiah didn't answer. He'd eased his hand to his Peacemaker. A twig snapped in the distance, and his bet was that it wasn't a critter coming to taste the same water they had just enjoyed so much.

"Wolfe?" Scrap repeated.

Josiah brought his finger up to his lips and motioned for Bailey to stop as he headed back to the creek. Both of the young Rangers reached for their six-shooters and did as they were commanded.

The night was clear, and the moon had risen high into the sky, a few nights past full. The light it cast down onto the earth was still bright enough for them to see a little way into the distance. Like most creeks, this one had trees standing as close to the bank as possible, surviving, growing, contributing to the shadows dancing on the ground.

Adding to the unease Josiah felt was the unpredictability that Scrap was exhibiting. A shot in the dark could lead the Indians right to them — and they would surely be outnumbered.

They all froze, their guns ready, and didn't breathe until they saw the maker of the noise, a raccoon and three of its kits, trailing down to the water to wash their paws.

Josiah sighed loud enough for the other two men to hear.

Scrap chuckled, and Dave Bailey shook his head and went back to work filling the canteens.

It didn't take long before their chore at the creek was finished. The three men mounted their respective horses and headed away from the creek, back toward camp, their thirst quenched, and their task nearly completed.

Following the same trail, they rode a little faster, but not so fast as to make a lot of noise. Still, not trying to draw attention to themselves did little good.

By the time Josiah spotted a Kiowa warrior sitting on horseback, watching them from the top of a ridge to their right, it was too late.

Chapter 30

A great horned owl fled from the top of a dead oak tree, the shadow of its wings trailing quickly over the trio. There was no quick beat of a wing — the owl was silent in its flight, a predator whose survival depended on the element of surprise, just like the Kiowa. Unlike the owl, however, with the Kiowa, if there was one, there were always more. Josiah could hear his own heart beat faster and knew the only chance they had to make it back alive was to outrun the warrior and his hidden comrades . . . if that was possible.

"We have to make a run for it," Josiah said, urging Clipper forward, up past Scrap.

Both men, Scrap and Dave Bailey, nodded in unison, and they all spurred their horses at the same time. A cloud of dust kicked high up into the air as they lit out from the creek, toward the safety of the gully in Lost Valley.

Josiah and Scrap shot quickly past Dave Bailey and his paint, but there seemed to be a problem. Josiah had been concerned about the spirit of Bailey's horse, and that turned out to be a genuine concern. The paint spooked, spinning, rising up on its hind legs with a loud scream, and tossed young Bailey to the ground.

The thud echoed up the trail like a distant clap of thunder. But Bailey didn't scream, didn't yell, he rolled away from the frantic paint and tried to scramble to his feet. The only weapon he had near him now was the six-shooter in his holster, and it had flown out when the paint spooked. Bailey had obviously forgotten to strap his gun, a dangerous mistake. His rifle was still in the scabbard — and the horse bolted off in the opposite direction, disappearing quickly in the darkness.

Josiah knew Scrap could have handled the horse, but Bailey didn't look to have the skills, or the steel mind to get past his own fear of the moment.

Josiah spun Clipper around to go back to help Bailey, but the one Kiowa warrior who had been standing on the ridge had multiplied into a party of six — and they'd cut off the trail.

Like they were riding lightning, all six

Indians descended down the trail and circled Bailey, their screams of war and terror overtaking the fear and troubles of the young Ranger and his errant horse.

Two of the warriors chased after Josiah and Scrap, shooting their rifles with deadly intent. Both of the Rangers scrambled behind a pair of huge boulders, jumped off their horses, and immediately returned fire.

The Kiowa took cover and continued to shoot, pinning Josiah and Scrap in between the rock shelf and the boulders. If there was a way out, they couldn't see it.

"Don't look," Josiah said directly to Scrap, ordering him not to watch what was happening to Ranger Bailey.

But the boy couldn't help himself — the color had drained completely out of his face as he watched, along with Josiah, the four Kiowa toss Dave Bailey to the ground. Bailey fought as best he could, but he was overpowered, and one of the Indians had already started to cut him up — pierced him with a knife in the throat — not stabbed him but brought him to his knees, forcing him to submission.

Bailey pleaded for his life, but his pleading fell on ears that did not understand the language of fear and did not care to learn. They had their own language, their own emotion, and it was clear that a single mind existed — the flock had captured their prey, and now it was time to take pleasure in the success of the capture.

The next thing they did was cut his tongue out, silencing Bailey forever.

Then they went after an ear, cutting slowly, making it very apparent that the Kiowa intended to enjoy Bailey's suffering and kill him in inches instead of all at once.

A bullet pinged off the rock about a foot to the right of Josiah's face.

A spark jumped out of the darkness, hitting him just under the eye. It felt like a piercing insect bite, and he had to look away. His eye watered up, and he couldn't zero in on Bailey, couldn't see what was happening, and for a moment, it was a relief.

Scrap tried to get a shot off, but he had to pull back and duck down. The two Kiowa had them thoroughly pinned in.

"I'd put him out of his misery, if I could," Scrap said.

"There'd be no crime in that killing," Josiah answered, wiping his eye so he could see better.

"We just can't let 'em do that to Bailey, Wolfe. He's a Ranger, damn it." Scrap's face was as pale as a dead man's, and sweat was pouring off his forehead from under his hat.

His fingers twitched, and his frayed nerves were more than apparent.

Josiah didn't know what to expect from Scrap, knowing full well how certain situations could trigger bad memories in some people — including himself. Scrap's family had been massacred by Comanche, and though Josiah wasn't sure what the boy had seen when the family was slaughtered, he was certain that Scrap watching the Kiowa torture Bailey was like watching his own family being cut to pieces.

Another bullet pinged off the rock, not far from Scrap's head this time.

Scrap gripped his rifle and stood up, screaming, firing repeatedly as quickly as the Winchester would chamber a round. "Die, you goddamn savages, die, goddamn it!"

The sound was deafening, and hot empty cartridges flipped about in the confines behind the rock without regard for Josiah. One landed on Josiah's forearm, burning his skin and leaving a quick blister, even though he'd swatted it away as soon as he felt it burning him.

Josiah reached up, then, rising off his knees in a short leap, and used the force of his forward motion to pull Scrap down, out of harm's way.

The shock of Josiah's action made Scrap loose his grip on the rifle, and it went spinning across the ground.

Scrap yelled out again in anger when he hit the ground, cussing like a soldier set loose on an enemy town. "Die, goddamn it. Let me kill the bastards. Just let me kill them, goddamn it!"

By the time Josiah made his way back to the ledge of rock so he could see what was happening to Bailey, his throat was dry, and he wished he was anywhere else other than where he was. He brought the barrel of his rifle over the edge first, following it with his sight.

He felt more helpless than he'd felt in a long, long time.

Bailey was still alive, weakening, the life draining out of him as quick as his blood, as the warriors went about slowly cutting off the other ear.

It was hard to see with everything that was going on; smoke from rifle fire clouded Josiah's vision, and the moon was bright but not bright enough to see the eyes of the Indians at the distance they were at. But it looked like there was blood on the Kiowa faces, like they were . . . eating the parts of Bailey's body they were cutting off.

Josiah fired a shot wildly, then looked

away. He had heard of such things, Indians gutting a man and feasting on the parts, but he'd never seen it. He hoped his eyes were playing tricks on him.

"He ain't dead yet, is he?" Scrap said.

Josiah shook his head no.

"Damn it, Wolfe, what are we going to do?"

"Stand our ground."

"But Bailey . . ."

"He's a dead man, and if I make it out of here alive, I'll have to answer for his suffering." Josiah drew a deep breath and dropped his head in defeat. "Even if we go out there in blazes, Bailey's near dead now. No tongue, no ears. Hard telling what they've sliced. It wouldn't be a life worth living."

"You're givin' up on him!" Scrap screamed as he raised up again, as unconcerned of the bullets flying as Major Jones had been in the gully. "You can't just give up and let Indians get away with a slow goddamned murder. I won't stand for it. No, sir, I won't." Scrap jumped up, trying to get over the rocks and out into the fray.

Josiah pulled him down again and saw that tears were streaming down Scrap's dirty, angry, enraged face.

"The only way we can help Bailey now is to get out of here alive and get the rest of our company on the trail of the Kiowas. You know that as well as I do." Josiah thought about slapping Scrap across the face to get his attention, to bring him out of his rage of past emotions, but he decided that wouldn't be the thing to do. Scrap had a right to his anger.

Instead, Josiah fired the Winchester in the direction of Bailey, just in time to see another Kiowa ride up out of the woods.

There was no mistaking who the Indian was. It was Lone Wolf himself.

Lone Wolf had counseled peace with the white man many times. He'd even sat at the feet of Custer in the late 1860s. But once his son was killed, returning from a raid in Mexico, Lone Wolf had sworn vengeance on the white man.

The Indian chief was dressed in a war bonnet, the feathers stark and white, glowing in the moonlight. His bronze skin shone, too, and it was almost like the Indian chief was stepping out of some ghost world and into the present one — the one riddled with screams, the smell of blood and gunpowder, vengeance and war floating in the clear sky like some invisible storm that could only be felt, not seen.

Lone Wolf sat atop a pure white stallion, no saddle, bareback, Indian-style, certain on the horse like he was attached to it.

The Kiowa chief charged toward Ranger Dave Bailey, who was being held up on each side by two blood-smeared warriors. At the last second, the warriors dropped Bailey and jumped back out of Lone Wolf's path. Bailey's eyes were rolled back in his head — either dead already or in shock. His face was nothing but mutilated meat and blood.

The chief was spinning a tomahawk over his head, and when he was at Bailey's side, he let loose of the weapon, burying it solidly in the Ranger's skull, bringing an end to his suffering with a crack that was the worst sound Josiah had ever heard in his life.

Lone Wolf pulled back on the horse, and it stopped, rising up on its two back legs, whinnying wildly, snorting and frothing at the mouth.

The chief screamed, "Tau-ankia," at the top of his lungs, and sent the name of his dead son echoing across the valley, an announcement that, finally, blood had been spilled in return and revenge had been delivered to the white man. It was not an end, though, but a beginning, of that anyone who knew anything about Indians and killing could be sure.

The Kiowa chief screamed his son's name again, "Tau-ankia," then rode off, leaving the tomahawk fully engaged in Ranger Bailey's cracked-open skull. His body was still now, crumbled like a useless kill, left for whatever would have it.

Scrap yelled in return, "No!" and without any warning, he scrambled over the rock, jumping off, firing his rifle in midair, and continuing to fire as his feet hit the ground running.

Josiah had no choice but to fire, too, giving Scrap as much cover as he could, but he had to make another decision quickly. Scrap was running toward Bailey's body, out in the open, unconcerned about taking cover, and Josiah could continue to shoot, or go after the young Ranger.

He chose to go after Scrap.

The thought of losing another man because of an error in judgment was too much to consider.

The warriors that mutilated Bailey's body had retreated, followed after Lone Wolf, but they were still returning fire, still turning and shooting as they fled into the darkness of the valley.

Josiah tore out after Scrap, running as fast on the hard ground as he could, shooting with his Winchester in one hand and the Peacemaker in the other.

The constant explosion of gunfire was

deafening, drowning any thought of fear or regret that was hiding just under the surface of Josiah's mind.

Mostly, he was shooting into the dark, toward powder flashes, toward anything that moved. If there was anything or anyone other than the Kiowa in the darkness, then they faced the risk of certain death — shoot now, ask questions later. Josiah had no choice now that Scrap Elliot had fully given in to his rage.

It had been a concern that Josiah had about Scrap — similar to the one he had about Bailey's horse — that the boy wouldn't be able to contain himself when he was faced with fighting Indians. The boy had said as much on the way up from Waco. Josiah wished he had listened to his gut and forced Major Jones to reconsider bringing Scrap along, but it was too late for that kind of thinking. Most assuredly too late.

They were about twenty feet from Bailey's body when a Kiowa warrior jumped out from behind a huge boulder and tackled Scrap, sending his rifle flying.

Josiah swerved and stayed on his feet, though he lost grip of his Winchester, and it slipped up in the air — but he was able to grab it before it fell totally out of his grasp.

The Kiowa had a long-blade knife in his

right hand, and he and Scrap were wrestling on the ground — Scrap on the bottom, holding the Indian's wrist, thrusting his knee into the crotch of his attacker, to no avail. They rolled and fought as Josiah regained his footing and brought his rifle up to aim — but in the darkness and dust, it was impossible to gain a shot that would kill the Kiowa and not bring injury to Scrap.

Scrap rolled over on top of the Indian, and the Indian thrust Scrap off him. Scrap tumbled backward, and the Kiowa scrambled to his feet.

Josiah fired off a shot and missed the Indian. They were standing about ten feet apart, but the dust and the darkness, and the uncertainty of footing, contributed to the missed shot. Josiah didn't panic, but prepared to fire off another round without thinking about it.

Scrap was able to right himself quickly, but not before the Kiowa could throw the knife.

The knife somersaulted in the air, its target sure, and the thrower an expert, full of experience. There was no nervousness or panic on the part of the Indian.

At first Josiah didn't know what had hit him. The force of the knife slammed into his left shoulder so suddenly it was like being struck by a heavy rock that had dropped, unseen, out of the sky. But rocks don't have points and sharpness — aren't honed to kill at the first touch.

The blade hit, point first, and sliced deep into Josiah's skin and muscle, coming to rest against bone. The hit sent him spiraling backward, and he dropped his rifle as the pain exploded down his arm. He screamed, but nothing came out of his mouth. The cry was distant, a voice he barely recognized as his own.

He heard a shot then, saw part of the Kiowa's head disintegrate — and saw Scrap run toward the warrior, unloading all of his bullets into the Indian's body — at least three shots to the heart.

The Kiowa shook like he'd been hit by six different men coming at him from different angles. Spasms quaked the savage from head to toe until he collapsed into a heap of unmoving nothingness, with Scrap standing over him, making sure every bullet had hit its mark — that the attacker was good and dead, his own revenge as complete as Lone Wolf's.

Josiah slid down the back of a rock, felt his pulse quicken, could feel his shirt quickly becoming soaked with blood.

He tried to say something, but it lodged

in his chest, the energy flowing out of him so quickly that the words couldn't make it to his throat and past his tongue.

Scrap hurried to him. "Damn it, Wolfe, don't you die. You hear me. Don't you die on me, goddamn it."

The knife was still stuck in Josiah's shoulder, the point nearly sticking out of his back, but the shoulder blade had stopped the trajectory.

Beyond Scrap's face there was nothing but the darkness that Josiah could see. Nearly every last ounce of light had been sapped out of the moon, and it didn't take long before all of that light was gone, too. Seconds. A heartbeat.

Blackness was fluttering around Josiah's face like a flock of buzzards trying to lift him up and take him away — to ride with them into the sky, into the heavens at least, far away from the battle.

It was then that Josiah knew he was hurt bad, and he could only hope that if he really was approaching death's door, then Lily and his three little girls would be on the other side, waiting for him with open arms.

CHAPTER 31

A bit of light trickled into the corner of Josiah's eye, and as he roused back to consciousness, the burning he felt in his shoulder was like no pain he had ever experienced before.

The bounce of the ride caused him even more discomfort, since it was obvious he'd been tossed over the back of a horse — his horse, Clipper. He was not so lost in the darkness that he couldn't figure out what was going on. Still, he didn't even have the strength to raise his head. There were two things that Josiah knew, though, two things that he was sure of. One: He wasn't dead, at least not in the presence of angels with faces he recognized. And two: The knife was gone, pulled from his flesh while he had taken leave of the physical world, when he'd passed out from the shock of everything that had happened.

There was a slight matter of disappointment he'd have to deal with at some point, disappointment that he hadn't died, hadn't felt the presence of his lost loved ones — but he was glad to be alive. Glad that Lyle still had a father who breathed. Whether he was still to walk on the solid earth toward Austin was another question.

He smelled of whiskey and vomit and tasted both, too, once he became more aware of himself.

Clipper was running full-out, being led by a rider that Josiah determined, in flickering images, had to be Scrap. If it were a Kiowa, he would be dead, unaware of being led anywhere, there was absolutely no questioning that. The Kiowa would not show one ounce of concern, not under the leadership of Lone Wolf, not under the clouds of a war that most likely arrived in the guise of an act of trickery in Lost Valley.

Scrap leaned forward in his saddle, and Missy, the blue roan mare, shined like a rare jewel in the moonlight, her sweat-covered muscles heaving toward home as she, too, ran full-out. The purpose of speed was not lost on Josiah, but all he wanted was for his pain to stop, for the world to quit moving.

One second he was fully aware, then the next he was away from the world — again — but when both horses finally roared to a stop, he was certain that he knew where he was at. He was back in the gully, back in the company of Rangers, safe, as far as he knew, but not sound yet. He was far from sound and close to death if his injury went unattended.

"Man hurt," Scrap yelled. "Man hurt."

There was a mass of men scrambling around Josiah, faces flashing in and out of his blurred vision: Jones, Red Overmeyer, Ben Cheek, as they pulled him gently from Clipper and hurried to a spot close to the rock shelf.

Coal lamps burned so brightly they hurt his eyes. Once on the ground, on a soft pile of bedrolls, Josiah was able to take a deep breath. The world had stopped moving. But unknowingly, unconsciously, he screamed out as loud as he could. The deep breath hurt like he had been stabbed all over again, like the Kiowa warrior was standing over him and grinding the hot metal blade into his flesh, then pulling it out again.

Red Overmeyer, who had been back out on the trail scouting when the attack had happened, pulled a flask of whiskey off his belt and handed it to Major Jones. Jones leaned down and lifted up Josiah's head, and put the flask of whiskey to his lips.

Josiah shook his head no, grimacing the

whole time.

"Take it, man, it's the only way you can ease the pain," Jones demanded.

"He can't die, Major." It was Scrap, standing behind Jones, looking down at Josiah over the major's shoulder.

"You did everything you could, Elliot, now stand back. I've seen men survive worse wounds than this, but if infection sets in he'll be in for a battle like no other. We need to get him out of here. We need to get out of here."

Jones urged the bottle of whiskey closer to Josiah, and at the next strike of pain caused by nothing more than breathing, he happily took the whiskey this time.

The alcohol burned the back of his throat since he was still unaccustomed to the effect and taste of whiskey, but it didn't matter — the pain was creeping away and a comfortable retreat to darkness was working its way to his consciousness.

His safety, the care of his own well-being, was completely out of his hands. The strength to decide what was to come next was gone from his concern. He would have to trust Jones and Elliot and the rest of the Rangers to decide his fate. It was not a happy compromise but one he had no choice but to make. All he wanted now was to sleep. That would rid him of the pain and the nightmare of seeing Ranger Bailey die a slow, miserable death, in his fresh, and active memory.

If death was to come to him, Josiah sure hoped it would be a fast death, in the form of a quick bullet to the head, not a lingering battle with infection like Jones had suggested, or even worse, a death like the young Bailey had experienced.

Josiah woke up to find himself securely tucked into a litter that was being pulled by a horse.

His shirt had been removed, and his shoulder had been bandaged in fresh linen. He could feel the skin pulled tight, and he knew he'd been stitched up. Somebody in the camp had the skills of a weaver or basket maker; there wasn't a doctor that Josiah knew of among the thirty-three men.

It was still dark out, still night, and since he was being pulled, facing away from the rear of the horse, he could see the starry sky stretching out beyond him. He had no idea what direction he was heading, or where, for that matter, he was being taken, or why. All of the stars looked blurry, his normal navigational aids taken from him along with his strength.

Scrap rode easily next to him, keeping pace with the litter. "I see you're awake, there, Wolfe. Hold up, Overmeyer, we need to get him some water."

The litter came to a quick rest, jolting Josiah enough that a sharp, stabbing pain coursed though his shoulder. He bit his lip and forced the groan of pain back where it came from. Thankfully, there was no more blood rushing out of the wound, but he sure could smell the whiskey that had kept the knife strike area sterile.

Scrap stopped Missy then, hopped off, and hurried to Josiah. "Here you go," he said, easing a canteen to Josiah's ready lips.

Josiah drank like he'd spent the entire last day walking through a desert. He was parched, weak, and more uncertain now than when he was brought into the camp after the attack. "What time is it?"

"It's late," Scrap said. "Long into the night. The Indians stopped shooting, and we had to double on our mounts since they killed nearly a third of our horses, but Major Jones thinks we can make it to Fort Richardson. We sneaked away. But I think the Indians ran off. I think we scared 'em, showed 'em we were there to fight to the death. That's what Jones told us, rallyin' us to leave that valley. I think it'll be haunted,

I sure do."

"They're gone?" Josiah's voice was raspy, like his throat was full of sand. "The Kiowa and Lone Wolf are gone?"

"Looks that way."

Red Overmeyer came up behind Scrap, his face long and drawn. "Good to see you awake and talking, Wolfe."

"What about Bailey?" Josiah asked.

Scrap gave Josiah another drink and looked over his shoulder furtively at Red.

The scout shrugged and said sadly, "We dug the boy a shallow grave with our Bowie knives and drinking cups. It was the best we could hope to do, that and cover it with rocks. The major said some fine words over the grave, and one of the fellas had a Bible on him. Not sure that the boy is safe on his way to the Lord's side or not, but death had to come as a relief for the poor fella. There's surely a special place in heaven for that one . . . all things considered."

"And a special place in hell for Lone Wolf," Scrap added.

Josiah nodded, not so much in agreement, but he understood the anger and rage the two Rangers held concerning Bailey's death.

Scrap pulled the canteen away from Josiah's lips — most likely it was the same water they'd gone after, the same water that had been the cause of the attack — and took a drink himself, looking off into the distance . . . obviously still remembering Bailey's trials.

Josiah wanted to be angry, but he just couldn't find the strength. As it was, he noticed Lone Wolf's tomahawk dangling off Scrap's belt. "You should have buried that tomahawk, too," he said.

"I plan on returning it to that savage someday," Scrap answered. "I plan on giving it to Lone Wolf myself, just like he gave it to Dave Bailey."

The rising sun brought the last set of the night's hidden worries to a quick end. If there were Kiowa tracking them, they weren't apparent or arrogant enough in their approach to allow the Rangers knowledge of their presence.

For the most part, it looked as if the trail to Fort Richardson was free of any treacherous creatures, save a badger or a scorpion. If a fellow was stupid enough to put his boot on without shaking it upside down first, or put his hand blindly in a hole — both of which Josiah had seen done in the past — then there would surely be a cost, no matter the trail — the present or the past. Overconfidence, or just plain ignorance, never ceased to amaze him.

As it was, they were nearing the front gate of the fort, and Josiah would be glad for the arrival. He wanted to be free of the litter and stand on his own two feet. There was still a great deal of pain in his shoulder, but his tolerance was growing, as was his appetite, which he considered to be a good sign.

Being bound in the back of a bumpy litter was not a pleasant way to travel. Thankfully, most of the trip had been spent in a whiskey stupor. He had an ache in his head that felt foreign, that had nothing to do with the injury. He was sure it was the aftereffects of the alcohol, since he was not usually a drinking man. The temptation would be there to continue a taste for whiskey, though, if the pain from the Indian's knife persisted.

Scrap whistled an unknown tune softly and kept a keen eye on Josiah. The boy's face was drawn tight though, like there'd been a change in his features, a wrinkle added to his brow when he looked over his shoulder in search of a threat. His rifle was out of the scabbard, settled across his lap, ready in an instant if the Kiowa had set another trap, felt emboldened, and attacked from an unseen spot on the ridge to their side.

It would be a long time before they both forgot Ranger Bailey and what had happened in Lost Valley.

CHAPTER 32

Major Jones stood before his men and several of the soldiers of Fort Richardson, including the commanding officer, Morton Steele, recounting the events at Lost Valley publicly for the first time.

It was the first time Josiah had seen Steele since arriving at the fort. Morton Steele was a tall, gray-bearded man who was, in his own right, a military legend. He had been a fierce commander with the Texas Brigade, and Josiah had served under him for many campaigns against the Yankee fighters in the War Between the States.

But it was not Steele who commanded the attention at the moment. Major Jones did. "It is beyond doubt that Lone Wolf is on the warpath," he said solemnly. "They were all well armed, carrying improved breech-loading guns, matching our .50-caliber carbines bullet for bullet. Those men carrying Winchesters fared better and probably made up for the ways of the Kiowa and their abundance of numbers and treachery. The days of bow and arrows are over, I tell you. The Kiowa were well mounted, and painted, and decked out in gay and fantastic style."

It was a small crowd, but the men were standing elbow to elbow, and Josiah was in the back of the tight room, a supply office of some sort, leaning against the wall, sweat beading on his forehead.

There were plenty of unopened crates carefully stacked alongside the inner walls of the room. The contents were unknown, but the crates were stamped in fresh ink, stating only that ownership belonged to the United States Army and nothing more. An iron gate covered a door that led into an armory. The door was closed and the gate thoroughly locked.

The smell of war was in the air.

It had been more than a day since they'd arrived at the fort, and the doctor, a short, bald man who looked like he ate more than he doctored, had redressed and re-stitched Josiah's wound. There was a small infirmary inside the fort, a narrow room with six beds, all but one of which was full, mostly with men with a cough that was thought to be contagious.

Josiah was weakening, not getting stronger, but he'd had the sense to decline the doctor's instructions to take the bed. He had seen the way an unseen sickness could kill a room full of people — specifically Lily and his three girls, who grew so weak and drained that they just faded away. He wasn't taking the chance of infection, knowing full well that it would be a fight he would have little chance of winning. He was surprised the doctor had suggested residence in the infirmary. But then, Josiah had scant trust for doctors, or preachers for that matter. Both had had little to offer him in the past when the need arose for their presence.

Instead of retreating to the infirmary, Josiah had chosen to stay in the livery, tucked in his bedroll in the corner, far away from everyone, except his horse, Clipper.

Now, stowed against the wall in the back of the supply room, he was waiting to speak to Major Jones about his further plans.

The first sign of infection was beginning to show in the long cut in his shoulder, a narrow red snake that was tender to the touch, and there was much to worry about, but he had decided, once he'd regained the capacity to think, that he was not going to die in some unknown fort among a cadre of unknown men. And he was not going to let anyone see, or know about, the infection.

He held the men of the fort in high regard. How could he not? They would fight next to him without question, but he refused to die among them. He refused to die among strangers.

If he was going to leave this world, and there were surely moments of pain and weakness when that was a real and sincere possibility, then he was going to go home and see his son, hold him one last time and look into his eyes . . . or die trying. It was that simple.

"We were victorious," Major Jones continued, speaking loudly to the crowd. "The Frontier Battalion proved its worth in one short span of time. If we had not confronted the Kiowa, they would have run roughshod into Parker County and delivered their furious brand of savagery to countless innocent men, women, and children. Ranger Bailey was just a boy himself. Can you imagine the terror they would have inflicted on a child?"

Red Overmeyer eased up to Josiah. "He sure does tell a grand story and rouse a crowd, doesn't he?"

"His version is what matters, and it's not that far from the truth," Josiah said in a low whisper. "We were outnumbered three to one, and lost two men."

"Two good men," Red added, nodding. "And you and another wounded."

"I count myself lucky to be alive."

"You look about half-beat, even now."

"It's hot in here."

"More than that I would say. You're not up to much else but gaining some rest, and healin' that wound."

"We'll see. I'm standing, able to put one foot in front of the other. That counts for a lot."

Major Jones seemed to be winding down his speech. "We have faced a quarrelsome enemy. One that should be on the reservation at Fort Sill and not be painted up for war. But Governor Coke, in his wisdom, put us on the path north to chase them back and show our strength. Never forget that, Rangers. Never forget that we ran them back."

A few men shouted in agreement, then the entire room erupted into a victorious rant, full of shouts and whistles. Survivors blowing off steam, soldiers readying for another battle in the stormy days ahead.

Men all around Josiah were glad-handing one another, slapping each other on the back, but he did not feel any joy. None at all. It would be a long time before he would be able to free himself of Ranger Dave

Bailey's last moments on earth — even though the thought of war, of returning the pain and blood put on him, was a temptation he thought worth exploring. If Lyle had left this world with Lily and the girls, then Josiah knew most assuredly that he would have no reason to return home . . . ever. Vengeance would be his home, just like a lot of the men standing in the room with him.

"You done a fine thing in the valley, Wolfe," Red said, almost as if he could read Josiah's thoughts.

"A good Ranger is dead."

"But you and Elliot brought the water back with ya. You knew it was a risk, that sneakin' to the creek might be your last act. I had a small flask of whiskey on me when I arrived back at the gully, but it sure wasn't enough to quench the thirst of thirty men."

"You ever see the Kiowa kill a man?" Josiah asked. His voice was thin, and sweat dripped down his cheek.

The crowd of men was parting, leaving the room, trailing past him in a loud rustle of boots and laughs. Josiah kept an eye out for Major Jones.

"Why do you think I'm here, Wolfe? I know what you saw. I know it all too well." Red Overmeyer's eyes were hard and cold, serious and sorrowful at the same time.

Jones came walking toward Josiah and Red, speaking with Morton Steele, a tight, pleased smile settling across his face.

"Excuse me, Major Jones," Josiah said, putting his hand out to stop Jones. "May I have a word with you, sir?"

At first a look of anger flashed across Jones's face, until he recognized Josiah. The major stopped, told Morton Steele that he'd catch up with him. Steele nodded, then said to Josiah, "I am glad to see you are on the mend, Wolfe." He stuck his hand out to shake. Josiah accepted it and was not the least bit surprised that the man had a tight, squeezing handshake, even though Steele was probably over seventy years old.

"I would hope to have a chance to sit and discuss the old days if you have the health and desire," Morton Steele said in a slow drawl. He was a true Texas gentleman.

"I would like that, sir," Josiah answered.

Morton Steele nodded, then walked off, joining the rest of the men leaving the supply room.

Major Jones remained. "Certainly, Sergeant Wolfe," he said, "I, too, am happy to see that you are standing. I had thought you might be a third fatality."

"Thank you." Josiah had turned away

from Red, but the hulking German man stood there, as if he wanted to be included in the conversation. "I'm sorry, Red, but I'd like to speak with Major Jones privately."

Red started to say something, then turned and stalked off.

Josiah lowered his head, took a deep breath, then raised his eyes to Jones, making a strong contact. "I would like to take leave of the Rangers until I heal, Major."

"I don't think that is a problem, Wolfe. The facilities here are more than adequate. Word has been sent to federal troops concerning the incident at Lost Valley. I think it will take a little time to prepare for what's coming. In the meantime, I think our presence here will be of use by helping to keep the Kiowa in check."

"No, I don't think you understand, sir. I want to go home. To Austin."

Major Jones looked Josiah up and down from head to toe. "You think you can make that trip, Wolfe, in your current state?"

"I have a son, Major. I would like to see him," Josiah said, not blinking, not allowing one quiver in his voice.

Jones nodded. "I understand. You have earned the right to take leave as you see necessary. I am sure that sitting here watching all that is about to commence would be a distraction to your healing — and to your heart. I want to send a message to Governor Coke anyway and inform him of our victory . . . and our losses. If you would be courier to that letter, it would be greatly appreciated."

"I would be pleased to do so, sir."

"I will also have a letter for Miss Pearl Fikes. You do not have any objections of delivering that letter for me, do you, Wolfe?"

"Why would I?"

"No reason that I know of," Jones said. He stroked his V mustache with his index and middle finger in one swift motion, then smiled briefly. "When you get to Austin and once you are ready to return to the Rangers, I want you to contact Captain Leander McNelly. It is being discussed at the moment in Austin that a company outside of the regular battalions be formed, a special force, if you will. Anyway, I think you would be a good addition to that company if it comes about. I will recommend you highly."

"Thank you, Major Jones, I appreciate that." Josiah turned to walk out of the supply room.

"Wolfe?"

Josiah stopped. "Yes, sir?"

"It wasn't your fault."

"What is that, sir?"

"Bailey's death. I agreed that you all should go to the creek and get the water. It was my command that sent Ranger Bailey to his death. That and the horrid situation that preceded it, rests squarely on my shoulders. I will never forget what a good Ranger Dave Bailey was and how good a Ranger he might have been had he lived," Major Jones said.

"I will never forget him either, sir."

Major John Jones nodded back. "You won't be traveling alone, Wolfe. I want you to take Ranger Elliot with you."

Before Josiah could protest, Major Jones strode by him, with a glare warning him off of saying another word, then hurried off to the group of men that followed after Morton Steele.

Scrap was nowhere to be seen.

CHAPTER 33

Scrap did not say a word to Josiah until they'd been on the trail for nearly three hours. "The last thing I wanted to be doin' today was escortin' you back to Austin. There's more of a fight comin' with those man-eatin' savages, Wolfe, and I'm gonna miss it."

They had stopped to water the horses at a bend in the Brazos. The river was familiar now, almost a constant companion in the entire trip north, as it would be going back home.

Clear blue skies stretched out before them as far as the eye could see. The weather would not be a hindrance, at least for the foreseeable future, and that was something Josiah was glad of.

There was very little he could do to alleviate the pain. It didn't matter if Clipper trotted or ran full-out, he was in misery. He chose to run full-out. Not because he was in a hurry, but because he was outrunning the infection that was invading his wound, using every bit of strength he had to see his way back to Lyle.

"I didn't ask Major Jones for you to come along," Josiah said.

"Well, this here partnership is gettin' a little trying."

"Go back," Josiah said.

"What?"

"Go back to Fort Richardson and tell the major I didn't want you to come along. Go get yourself killed, if that's what you want," Josiah said.

Scrap had the same clothes on that he'd worn for the previous few days, except now they were clean, and seemed tighter on his lanky frame. He was standing on the edge of the river, his canteen dangling in the water, filling it as full as he could get it. He stood up, albeit a little slower than he might normally have, probably for fear of busting out of his britches.

"You're blamin' me, ain't you, Wolfe?"

"Blaming you for what?" Each word took a concerted effort to speak. Josiah's canteen was full. He was just waiting for Clipper to finish drinking.

"For what happened to you. For what happened to Bailey," Scrap said.

387

Josiah didn't answer immediately. Silence hung in the air between the two men like a lead curtain had fallen straight out of the sky. Somewhere in the distance, a mockingbird ran through its routine of bird songs and calls: a redtail hawk spiraling upward; a nervous titmouse chattering about the lack of seeds in summer; a crow calling to its family, lost somewhere in the mottes, all different stories from the beak of one bird.

Josiah wished the mockingbird would shut the hell up, but the similarity to his state of mind was not lost on him. Jones had claimed responsibility for what happened, and it would have been criminal if he had not . . . but he had, fair and square like a good commanding officer should. That part of the ordeal was done. The rest of it would have to work itself out, like the infection in his wound and the scar that was forming on his chest, just at the shoulder.

"Now's not the time, Elliot," Josiah said, not looking directly at Scrap. "You're not bound to me."

"I'm followin' Major Jones's orders."

"And I'm overriding them. If you don't want to return to Austin with me, then leave now. I got enough problems to work out. The last thing I need to be doing is wasting what is left of myself arguing with you."

Clipper popped his head up from the river, water dripping out of his mouth. Josiah climbed on the horse's back, settled in, and reined him away from the river. He urged the horse to run and headed south, leaving Scrap Elliot standing there, his mouth agape with nothing left to say, yet again.

The temptation to stop in Fort Worth was great, but as far as Josiah was concerned, there was not enough time. He feared the comforts of Callie Melhaven's boarding-house would be too enticing to leave. Allowing himself to be healed up there would, no doubt, be wise, and he knew he would be well taken care of. But he also knew the grand house, with its turrets and fresh green paint, could be his last stop. He could sink into one of the many feather bed mattresses in the empty rooms and never stand back up on his own two feet. And, no offense to Callie Melhaven, her house was the last place he wanted to die.

He didn't want to die in a bed that wasn't his own, without ever seeing his son again. It was that simple. He wasn't going to stop until he got home. If he could ward off death with nothing more than pure thought and desire, then he would do everything he could to hold Lyle again.

Josiah wondered, though, as Scrap joined up with him, what had become of Mae Johnson. There was more than one possible outcome for the girl that Josiah could think of. Either she had taken to Callie's care and cleaned herself up, contributing wholly to the boardinghouse, or she had run off, either back to the Reservation in Waco or Hell's Half Acre in Fort Worth, taking up with what she had left behind.

Or she might be sick, dying or dead, the syphilis eating at her strength day by day. He chose to put that thought out of his mind, to hope that he'd been wrong and she wasn't infected at all, and to satisfy himself that he might not ever know what happened to her. He liked Mae, in an odd sort of way . . . but unlike her last statement to him, he could never love her, not the way she needed him to. He doubted that kind of love truly existed . . . the kind that would bring pure happiness and comfort to a girl like Maudie Mae Johnson. She carried her fair share of nightmares. There was no outrunning them — no love deep enough to banish them away forever. Josiah Wolfe knew that was the truth of things, as sad as it was to know.

Scrap lagged behind, intentionally keeping his distance, not broaching a conversation of any kind with Josiah.

At times they ran straight into herds of cattle heading north, and like the city of Fort Worth, they avoided contact with the cowhands and trail bosses as much as possible, easing off to the south, riding as close to the Brazos as they could. There was a nervousness in the eyes and voice of every trail boss they talked to when avoiding them wasn't polite or possible.

The news of Lone Wolf and the attack in Lost Valley had traveled fast.

At Josiah's urging, he and Scrap agreed not to tell anyone of their encounter with the Kiowa, about their own experience in the valley, or that they had been there at all. It was a difficult task for Scrap, but he held his tongue, much to Josiah's surprise and relief.

Josiah seemed to settle into the ride, the pain constant but expected. It sapped his strength but did little to dent his will. The infection, if it was that, didn't seem to be growing any worse. Nor did it seem to be getting better.

Nighttime came and went with him and Scrap splitting watch. Josiah took it first.

As they edged past Fort Worth toward Waco, their concern returned that they might encounter the posse that had chased them out the last time. Thoughts of Liam O'Reilly and *El Puño* returned to the forefront of both Josiah and Scrap's minds. They had talked about both men at the campfire on the first night — but had come to the conclusion that Lone Wolfe and the Kiowa were far more dangerous. Still, you had to give a couple of snakes a healthy dose of respect. They could strike when you least expected it, especially if you thought them tame, or just sunning out of sight.

Long into the second night, after a hard and nervous day's ride, as they rounded Waco, Josiah broke into a heavy sweat and the pain in his shoulder throbbed so hard inside him he woke up screaming.

Scrap came running from his spot on a ridge. "You all right, Wolfe?"

Josiah could barely speak. The fire had nearly died, wasted down to a bed of orange embers that gave off some heat, but not enough to keep a man good and warm. The night was cool and moist, and the air settled into Josiah's lungs heavily. Clouds covered the moon, though it was nearly gone, shadows chewing it down to a thumbnail.

Josiah had covered himself with a couple of thick blankets, but without thinking, he threw them off himself.

"What's the matter, Wolfe?" Scrap said, stopping just off to Josiah's right, within reach.

"I'm all right," he said, shaking his head. He sat up and wiped the sweat from his forehead. "I think so. I really do."

"You look as pale as a white stallion."

"Feel that way, too. But better somehow." Josiah eased out of his shirt. There was a little redness around the stitching, but just as quick as the pain had come, it was gone, too. "I think the infection might've worked itself out."

"Infection? Are you crazy? You should have stayed put if you was fightin' an infection. We could've stopped in Fort Worth and let Aunt Callie tend to ya. She would have been glad to see us, and we could have saw Mae."

"I doubt Mae'd be to glad to see us," Josiah said.

"You. She'd have been glad to have seen you!"

"No, in her eyes I rejected her. But maybe one of these days she'll come to understand that you killed Clem Dawson because you didn't have any other choice. You thought you were saving her."

"I was."

"I know."

"How am I ever gonna get to tell her if we act like Fort Worth don't exist?"

"I want to get home," Josiah said.

"You nearly died tryin'."

"I would have. Will, if I have to."

A robin chirped in the distance, the first sign of morning even though the horizon was still dark.

"Well," Josiah said, standing up, "We might as well get moving."

"Might as well. We're not that far now."

"Nope, not that far at all."

A relieved smile fell across Josiah's face as he made his way down to the river to clean himself up.

CHAPTER 34

The streets of Austin were crowded with a mass of people coming and going at mid-morning. Heavily loaded wagons and a Butterfield stagecoach were trailing each other out of town, west toward Arizona. Horses grunted and groaned, clopping along on a street that hadn't seen rain since Josiah had left town and even before that.

Women in their finest regalia — tall hats, parasols, velvet dresses that fell all the way to the ground, covering every inch of skin even though it was already hot as a fresh campfire — walked down the boardwalk, escorted by gentlemen in clothes just as fine. The noise and commotion seemed awfully loud to Josiah, but he was glad for the change of scenery, glad to be off the trail, and even happier to be as far away from Lost Valley as possible.

Scrap rode next to him casually, his eyes darting here and about as they passed the front of the state capitol, a three-storey limestone building with a small dome jutting up from its center, built in the early 1850s. The city still felt foreign to Josiah, and he hardly considered it home, even though the house that was now his was only a few blocks away.

Josiah turned down a street that angled off toward Republic Square, and Scrap followed along, though he pushed Missy up nose-to-nose with Clipper with a curious look on his face.

"I thought you said you lived a block off the railroad."

"I do."

"You're going the wrong way."

"I've got a stop to make."

"Don't you think you need to get home so you can get rested up?"

"I'm not going to die, Elliot. Not this time. And you can ride along with me, or you can hightail it back to Fort Richardson now. I'm in Austin, you did your duty," Josiah said. "I'm in no need of an escort."

Once the fever he'd been carrying broke, the pain seemed to fade, but it never fully went away. It spiked in intensity every once in a while, enough to remind him that he had been stabbed less than a week prior, and that the true healing would take time.

He knew he wasn't out of the woods as far as infection went, too. But for the moment, he was capable of riding a horse, capable of thinking and doing for himself — and now that he was back in Austin, there were a few things on his mind that he wanted to tend to before going home.

"Suit yourself, then, Wolfe. You and my pa's old bull sure would have gotten along, because you're both stubborn as hell."

Josiah smirked, a half smile crossing his face. He said nothing and continued to ride, his eyes on a constant search for a woman who looked familiar — a woman who was more likely to be found in another part of town, standing behind the bar at the Paradise Hotel — but he had to look. He had to hope beyond hope that Suzanne del Toro had returned to where she belonged, just like he had.

There was hardly anything left of Clive Werner's livery. Charred timbers stuck straight up in the air like a forest had once stood there and the only thing remaining was pillars that were once tall trees — or in this case, beams that were weakened and useless, all black and limbless from the fire.

It still smelled of fire and ash, but the smell of burned human flesh had long since been pushed away by the wind and time.

"I wonder what the heck happened there," Scrap said, tying Missy to a post just outside the sheriff's office, next door to the livery.

"A fire."

"You told me about this when we first met up."

"Yes, it happened right before I headed north," Josiah said, finishing off securing Clipper next to Missy. He started to pull his Winchester out of the scabbard, but stopped when he heard a voice behind him.

"You've no worry about that, Ranger Wolfe."

Josiah turned around to see Deputy Walt Pence walk out the front door of the sheriff's office. Pence had seen the skull, pointed out the hole in it. Josiah had liked him when they first met, even though Pence was young, like Scrap, but old enough to grow a mature, unwaxed mustache. "Good to see you, Pence," he said, walking up to the man and shaking his hand heartily.

Pence stepped back. "You hurt?"

"I'm all right."

"Sure he is," Scrap said, making his way to the two men. He shook Pence's hand. "Scrap Elliot. I'm a Ranger, too."

"Figured as much," Pence said. "You fellas come down from up north and that scuffle with the Kiowa?"

"You heard about that, huh?" Scrap said, a thin smile flashing across his face.

"Isn't nothing to be proud of, Elliot. We lost a few good men," Josiah said.

Both Pence and Scrap nodded, though the smile disappeared from Scrap's face instantly.

Josiah pushed past Pence. "It's good to see you, friend. Is Sheriff Farnsworth in his office?"

"Yup," Pence said. "I didn't mean no harm, Wolfe. It's just that everybody is talkin' about the Rangers outnumbered three to one and runnin' off Lone Wolf. I thought you might have been with them."

"No harm taken, Pence." Josiah glanced over at Scrap. "I won't be long," he said.

Scrap had started to join him, but stopped dead in his tracks. "You're the moodiest damn fella I ever met, I tell you."

Josiah ignored Scrap and pushed inside the door. He walked down a short hall and found Sheriff Rory Farnsworth sitting at his desk, his feet propped up, reading a newspaper — which fluttered quickly to the floor when he saw Josiah walk into the office.

"Wolfe," Farnsworth said, bolting to his feet. "You're the last person I expected to see walk through that door." He rushed to

Josiah and shook his hand. "You're a real bona fide hero according to the newspaper."

"I beg your pardon?"

"The fight with Lone Wolf, it's all here." Farnsworth hurried over and picked up the newspaper, then thrust it at Josiah.

He read the top of the piece in the newspaper quickly: "Local Rangers Fight Hand to Hand with Lone Wolf — And Win!"

"That's not true," Josiah said, handing the paper back to the sheriff.

"You don't want to read the rest of it?"

"Not if it's a story and not the truth. I 'spect I'll have to go over to the newspaper and set them straight."

"You're saying you didn't see Lone Wolf at all?"

"We saw him. Sure we did. But the fight wasn't with him."

"But you were wounded. I can see that."

"I'm no hero. Neither is Elliot out there. We lost two good men. One of them, Dave Bailey, suffered greatly. That wasn't a story. It's a pure, cold, hard fact, and his death is something I saw with my own eyes. That is true. I can't forget it. But none of us fought hand-to-hand with Lone Wolf, and every man there did his part. No one was a standout; none of us wants notice for that fight."

"None of you but Major John B. Jones,"

Farnsworth said.

"He's got his reasons for promoting the bravery of the Frontier Battalion. Reasons I understand, but might not like."

"Doesn't matter what you think now, Wolfe. Every man in town will line up to buy you a drink at the Silver Dollar. I wouldn't be surprised if you got a letter from Governor Coke himself."

"That's not my concern."

Rory Farnsworth sat down behind his desk. He looked shorter, almost overtaken by the ornate hand-carved oak piece of furniture. There was hardly anything on the top of it save the newspaper and a few law books that looked like they had never been opened. The spines were pristine.

"Why are you here, Wolfe?"

"What'd you ever find out about that fire?"

"Not much. Never did find those two boys you spoke of. Clive Werner didn't know a damn thing about them, so I'm of the same mind you are. They set the fire."

"What about the body? You ever figure out who it was?" Josiah was certain of one thing that he had not been when he left: Whoever it was, it was not Juan Carlos. Not that that eased his concerns about the old Mexican. The last sign of him had been the appearance of the black stallion outside of the boardinghouse in Fort Worth. Where Juan Carlos was now or what had happened to him since was anybody's guess.

Farnsworth shook his head no to Josiah's question about the body. Not a hair in his perfectly waxed mustache even moved. "No, I sure wish we could. Buried the bones in the cemetery and can't even put a name on the cross." He opened the desk, dug into the back of it, pulled out a small brown envelope, and handed it to Josiah. "Do you have any news of the old Mexican?"

Josiah took the envelope, a question forming solidly on his face. "He saved my behind again, then disappeared. What is this?"

"We found that when we moved the . . . skeleton. That, and a few buttons were all that was left," Farnsworth said. "I think the person was dead, though, before the fire. I think the person was shot in the head, put there, and the fire started to destroy the evidence and the identity of the poor sap."

Josiah emptied the contents of the envelope into his hand. A small gold chain with a gold cross attached to it fell into his hand. The cross had been blackened by the fire, so he rubbed the ash off of it, exposing two words etched into the gold: *"Paraíso espera."*

Josiah closed his eyes, felt his hand tremble. He remembered the cross, had seen it before . . . the night he had lain with Suzanne del Toro in his arms, naked, after a round of lovemaking. It was the first time he had been with a woman since Lily died. He had asked Suzanne what the words meant, and she had whispered, "Paradise awaits." Then they had made love again.

He took a deep breath and opened his eyes, stared directly at Rory Farnsworth, and said, "I'm going to hang on to this for a little while."

He didn't wait for the sheriff's permission. He stalked out the door, the cross buried in his fist, certain of where he was going next.

CHAPTER 35

Of all the places he should have gone, home was the last place he should have headed. He had a letter to deliver to Pearl Fikes from Major Jones, and he had been charged to make contact with Leander McNelly and Governor Coke. But those tasks would have to wait.

Lyle came first at the moment. After that, there was Suzanne del Toro's killer to deal with. The thought of Suzanne being dead enraged Josiah — but he was conflicted. He was happy as all get out as his little house came into sight, happy as all get out to think of seeing his son. He reined in Clipper and eased the horse to an easy trot.

Ofelia was sitting in a chair on the front porch, and she stood straight up as soon as she recognized Josiah. A broad smile crossed her face as she hurried down the steps, her squat little body moving forcefully, like a boulder rolling down a hill. The smile disappeared quickly, transitioning to concern and care in the blink of an eye, as she came to a stop by the gate.

"Señor Josiah, what has happened to you? Are you hurt?"

Josiah eased Clipper to a stop, climbed down off the saddle, and tied the horse to a post. "I'll be fine," he said, stopping to wait for Scrap, who was about twenty yards behind him.

Ofelia's hand was over her eyes, shading the bright sun, as she stood there and stared at Josiah.

He took a deep breath and looked past the Mexican woman. "Where's Lyle?"

"He is down for a nap. Shall I wake him?"

"No, I will." Josiah didn't move toward the gate though. He was still waiting. As odd as it was, he didn't feel like he was home.

The clapboard house was not near as fancy as Callie Melhaven's grand house in Fort Worth, but it was where he intended to live for the foreseeable future. But he would have preferred to have been standing in the front yard of the little cabin in the Piney Woods. That would always be home to him. Always.

Scrap eased Missy up next to Clipper, a frown set solidly on his face. Josiah had not said anything to Scrap about what he had learned inside the sheriff's office or what his plans were, and that hadn't set well with the young Ranger.

"Well, Wolfe, this here is the end of the road, I take it. Nice house."

"Not so fast, Elliot," Josiah said.

"What? I did what I was asked. I want to get on back to Fort Richardson and be with the rest of the company. I'm mighty tired of playin' nursemaid."

"I'm not asking you." Josiah ignored the sharp remark. He knew Scrap well enough to know he was just trying to make him angry so he would get his way. "We have some business to tend to here in Austin first."

"With who?"

"*El Puño.*"

"*Santa Madre de Dios.* Holy Mother of God," Ofelia said, genuflecting, making the sign of the cross. "He's a bad man, Señor Josiah. Mean and loco."

Scrap stared at Josiah, not paying any attention to her at all. He wouldn't even look the woman in the eye, or acknowledge her presence in any way.

"The man that sent Clem Dawson after Mae and us? The one you think that vermin Liam O'Reilly is ridin' for now?"

"The very one," Josiah said.

"Why didn't you say so?" Scrap asked, climbing off his horse. "Let's go get 'im."

"You need to calm down."

"Why? Why in the heck would I want to do that? We're Rangers, we can get 'im, right?"

"We have a few things to do before we go rushing in after him."

"You know where he's at?"

"I have a good idea," Josiah said.

Before Scrap could say anything else, something drew his attention away from Josiah.

Josiah followed Scrap's gaze past Ofelia, and to the porch. A little boy was standing in the center of the doorway, dressed in his nightclothes, wiping the sleep out of his eyes.

The sight of Lyle took Josiah's breath away. It never ceased to amaze him how much his son looked like Lily.

"Papa?" Lyle said.

Josiah smiled then, his eyes welling up with happy tears.

He ran past Ofelia, leaving the conversation with Scrap behind, and scooped up Lyle with his good arm, hugging him like he hadn't seen him in a hundred years.

"Here you go, señor," Ofelia said to Scrap, as she slid a bowl of steaming *menudo* in front of him.

Josiah had introduced Scrap to Ofelia, but it was obvious that Scrap wasn't going to leave his prejudice toward Mexicans at the door. That was not a surprise to Josiah, but it was a disappointment.

"Thank you," Scrap said, staring down at the bowl. He tore a bite of bread off the loaf and dipped it into the stew tepidly. "I hope it ain't too hot and spicy."

"It probably is for you," Ofelia said. Her lip turned up, and she stalked away. She wasn't going to be rude to Josiah's friend and fellow Ranger, but it was clear she didn't take too kindly to being treated like dirt in the same house in which she lived.

Josiah shot Scrap a look that warned him to shut up and just eat — but Scrap seemed either oblivious or like he just plain didn't care.

"I need you to do me a favor, Ofelia," Josiah said.

Lyle was sitting on his knee, watching every move, listening to every word, never taking his eyes off Josiah.

"What is that, Señor Josiah?"

"Do you know Juan Carlos? Juan Carlos Montegné?"

Ofelia stopped, wiped her hands on her pure white apron, and said, "Why do you ask, señor? Juan Carlos is a man of the *sombras*, um, shadows."

"He is a friend, an *amigo*. I need to get word to him that I have some bad news, and I need his help, if I can get it."

"He's the last person you need help from," Scrap interjected.

"Eat your food," Josiah snapped.

Scrap shrugged and went after another chunk of bread, eating furiously. He'd obviously decided that the *menudo* wasn't too spicy after all.

"Can you do that for me, Ofelia?"

"*Sí*, I can do that. I have family south of Republic Square, down in Little Mexico. They will help me to find him, señor, if he is around."

"Good. I need you to do this right away."

"Pat-a-cake, Papa. Play pat-a-cake?" Lyle said, clapping his hands together.

Josiah looked down and smiled at his son. He was tempted to tell Lyle no, that he had other things on his mind, other things to do, but he didn't have the heart.

He was glad to be home. Happy to see

Ofelia, happy to smell the smells he was accustomed to and eat the food that he knew. The thought of going after Emilio del Toro — at least confronting him, questioning him about Suzanne's sad fate — was something he didn't want to do but knew he had to.

He would wait, though, give himself a day to gain a little more strength, perhaps hear back from Juan Carlos, and get Sheriff Farnsworth and his men organized. There was no way he was going to the Paradise Hotel alone, or with just Scrap.

If Emilio was The Fist — this *El Puño* that everyone seemed to fear so much — then Josiah was going to be ready. Good and ready.

He wasn't about to ride blind into a dark valley again. Not this time. He had a score to settle . . . if his hunch about *El Puño* was right.

Ofelia had disappeared from the house, and Josiah was certain that she had gone on the errand he had sent her on.

Evening was coming on, the light outside turning dim and gray. Scrap was cleaning his rifle, readying himself for the next day. Josiah was on the other side of the room, staring out the window, with Lyle sitting happily at his feet.

"You're bein' awful quiet there, Wolfe," Scrap said.

"Got a lot to think about, I guess."

"Your shoulder hurtin' ya?"

"Not much. Enough to know it's there."

"You're lucky."

"I suppose so."

"You know this man, The Fist?" Scrap asked.

"I've met him. I didn't know it then, though, that he was so powerful."

"So he won't be expectin' you to know what he's up to now?"

"That's what I'm hoping."

Silence settled between them as Lyle played with Josiah's boot, giggling, fighting off sleep.

Josiah was getting a little nervous about Ofelia's absence, since he had little experience in readying his son for bed, but he could do it, and he knew he would have to stay next to the bed Lyle slept in until the boy was fast asleep.

"Could you do me a couple of favors?" Josiah asked Scrap.

"What?"

"I have a letter from Major Jones that needs to be delivered to Pearl Fikes and messages for Governor Coke and Captain McNelly. Can you deliver them for me?"

"I guess so."

"I don't want to leave Lyle again, until I have to. I really appreciate it."

"I'm not sure I could leave a place like this," Scrap said.

"What do you mean?"

"A little house, a son, food on the table. It don't look like a bad life."

"I'm not used to it. This living in the city is all new to me. I like to hear the coyote yip at the moon. The train still wakes me. But I 'spect I'll get accustomed to it all. If I'm around long enough. Rangering is still something I plan on doing. Don't know much else other than that. I can't quite see putting on a badge and working for Rory Farnsworth, being a deputy in a big place like this. I'd feel all squeezed in," Josiah said with a sigh.

"Well, if it was me, I'd get rid of that Mexican and get me a real wife," Scrap said, putting down the rifle and going after his six-shooter to clean.

"A woman is the last thing on my mind."

Scrap cleared his throat. "For some reason, Wolfe, I don't believe you. I don't believe you at all."

CHAPTER 36

The outside of the Paradise Hotel was quiet. No one had come or gone since Josiah, Scrap, Sheriff Farnsworth, and five of his deputies had taken up their positions along the street, on the rooftops, and in the alley that ran alongside the hotel.

Ofelia had failed to find Juan Carlos the night before, but just like she was asked to, she had put out the word that Josiah needed his help. Scrap had delivered the letters to Governor Coke and Pearl. She had sent back a message to Josiah that she was disappointed that he didn't deliver the letter in person, and that she hoped to see him soon. He quickly put Pearl out of his mind, for the moment at least, as much as possible. The task from Jones to see Captain McNelly would have to wait, too — what he was about to do had nothing to do with being a Texas Ranger, but everything to do with justice being served.

Josiah would have felt better if he'd known what had happened to Juan Carlos, but as usual, he had no clue where the old Mexican might be. He sure hoped his friend hadn't fallen onto bad times, been captured by Emilio's men or something worse.

The inside of the hotel was quiet, too. No piano music floated out into the morning air, and there were no angry cardplayers shouting about being cheated. Nothing stood in the street but silence . . . as if the day was anticipating something bad coming its way and it wanted to be ready. It was an hour after sunrise, and the heat from the clear skies was settling in for another hot July day.

Most all of the windows in the hotel were open, the curtains as still as stone walls since there was no breeze.

Footsteps on the boardwalk echoed upward to Josiah's position, garnering his attention.

He looked down in time to see Emilio del Toro heading for the front door of the hotel, dressed like he was ready to see a banker or going for an outing in his Sunday best, whichever the case might be. He wore all black — a long coat, slouch hat, shiny boots without spurs — and carried a cane, which made him look like a fine gentleman instead of the wicked man *El Puño* was reputed to be.

Scrap was at Josiah's side and brought his rifle up over the edge of the roof before Josiah could gently knock the barrel back out of the way. He shook his head no and watched Emilio walk casually inside the Paradise Hotel, as if he didn't have a care in the world.

"I'm going in," Josiah said.

"Are you crazy?" Scrap said. "I could have ended this with one shot."

"Man's got a right to speak for himself," Josiah said. "Proof is yet to be had."

"He ain't gonna admit to killin' nobody."

"I'm going in," Josiah repeated. "I'll do my best to keep in view of the windows, but if you hear a shot, give the signal to Farnsworth."

The sheriff was across the street, the same side as the hotel, on the roof of the building next to it.

Before Scrap could object again, Josiah scrambled behind the false front of the building and made his way down to the street level. He hesitated, not allowing himself to come into full view, then situated himself and double-checked his weapons: two fully loaded Peacemakers, a Bowie knife, a stingy gun similar to Mae's up his sleeve, and another, shorter knife inside his boot. He was carrying his Winchester in full view, unconcerned about hiding his intention to protect himself.

Ofelia had bound his shoulder after putting some of her remedies on it, plants ground into paste that smelled like the south end of a north-facing cow, but it dulled the pain so it was almost unnoticeable. The fight at Lost Valley seemed like a long time ago.

Josiah took a deep breath and walked across the street in the same manner Emilio had entered the hotel, as if he didn't have a care in the world.

The barkeep, the same skinny Mexican who had been there when Josiah first went looking for Suzanne, looked up, startled, when Josiah walked inside. Josiah closed the door behind him with a hearty shove so it would announce his arrival to anyone on the first floor of the building.

He strode right up to the barkeep. "Tell Emilio that Josiah Wolfe is here."

"He is not here, señor," the barkeep said.

"Don't lie to me, I just saw him walk in." Josiah brought the Winchester up and settled it in the crook of his left arm, resting the barrel there stiffly, ready at a second's notice to fire.

"There's no need for a weapon, Ranger Wolfe," a voice said behind him. It was a familiar voice . . . Emilio, The Fist, *El Puño*.

Josiah turned to his side, so he could see both the barkeep and Emilio. "I'll be glad to hold on to it," he said.

"Suit yourself." Emilio walked to a table just off the bar and sat down. "To what do I owe the pleasure of this visit, Ranger Wolfe?"

Josiah walked to the table but remained standing, luckily still in Scrap's view. "I'm hoping you'll tell me that your sister has returned from her travels, that you're no longer concerned about her welfare. I sure would like to see her."

"Ah, I wish I could tell you that she is here, señor, but I have not heard one word from my sister since I spoke with you last. I am very concerned about her."

"Surely," Josiah said, easing his hand into his pants pocket, "you have acquaintances in other towns that you have contacted about Suzanne's whereabouts?"

"Indeed, I have."

"Like Waco?"

Emilio looked at Josiah curiously, sizing him up. "I have business in Waco, yes. So?"

"And beyond?"

"What business is it of yours?"

Josiah pulled his hand out of his pocket

and let the gold cross dangle in front of Emilio. "Does this look familiar?"

"It looks like the cross Suzanne wore around her neck."

"Paraíso espera," Josiah said.

"Paradise awaits," Emilio said, standing. "Where did you get this?" He reached for the cross, but Josiah pulled it back and pulled the Winchester out of the crook of his arm, pointing it directly at Emilio's chest.

"Not so fast, señor," the barkeep said. As he reached under the bar for a gun.

"It is all right, Raul, Ranger Wolfe won't shoot me. He believes in the law and in giving a man a fair trial."

"You're right about that, Emilio. Or should I say, *El Puño?*"

"Ah, you know of The Fist. *Eso es bueno.* Now I would like to know how you have come into the possession of my dear sister's necklace? The one she treasured so much?"

"It was found on her body. What was left of it after somebody set fire to the livery."

"No. You're saying my sister is dead?"

"You don't appear to be too broken up about it," Josiah said, fully aware that the barkeep had not moved from his position, the pistol still in easy reach, just as the barrel of the Winchester was aimed at Emilio.

418

"And why should you be? All of the business that you shared with Suzanne is now yours. A reach that stretches from here to Fort Worth. Now, I think we need to step outside, and you need to have a talk with the sheriff."

"You are mistaken, Ranger Wolfe," Emilio said. He did not appear to be the least bit nervous or concerned about his welfare.

"You are claiming that you did not kill your sister?"

"Oh no, señor, I am not claiming that at all. You are correct. I killed her, then hired two beggar boys to set fire to the livery. Your friend, Juan Carlos, tried to warn her of my intention, but he was too late. I separated them, got to her before he did. Her touch was too soft. No one feared her, our business was drying up, being overtaken by others. I could not let that happen."

"What then," Josiah said, his pulse slowing as he pressed firmly against the trigger of his Winchester, "am I mistaken about?"

"That I will go with you," Emilio said. He nodded slightly and the barkeep pulled the gun out from under the bar. The window shattered, a bullet careening though it, catching the barkeep just under the temple before he could get off a shot at Josiah.

Josiah dove to the right and fired a shot

that wounded Emilio.

Sheriff Rory Farnsworth rushed inside the Paradise Hotel, followed by his deputies with guns blazing. Emilio was hit at least five times, throwing him to the floor in a bloody heap.

Josiah had slid under a table and nearly came face-to-face with Emilio, his eyes wide open, frozen in surprise, death taking him in a moment that he had not prepared for.

As Josiah stood up, he came face-to-face with Scrap.

"How about next time, I get to go in, and you do the shootin'?" Scrap asked.

"I'm just glad you shot when you did. Another second and I might've had a problem," Josiah said.

"I saw the barkeep raise the gun on you and figured if I waited to hear a shot and gave Farnsworth the signal, you'd be a dead man. I wasn't about to look that little boy of yours in the eye when he's a grown man and tell him I hesitated and that's what got you killed."

"How about there isn't a next time you have to take a shot to save my hide?" Josiah said with a broad smile, slapping Scrap on the shoulder, saying thank-you in the best way he knew how.

EPILOGUE

Josiah made his way up the hill while Ofelia and Lyle waited behind in the wagon. He could hear his son laughing as Ofelia tickled him, occupying Lyle while Josiah departed, to fulfill a deed that only he could.

It was one of those rare, perfect days in July, when the heat wasn't so unbearable you couldn't stand to be out in the sun, and the air so thick you couldn't breathe. There were a few clouds in the sky, and a nice, gentle breeze snaked its way through the cemetery.

A scattering of oaks stood over a fresh grave, and Josiah walked slowly to it. He kneeled down in front of the bare white-washed cross, took out his knife, and went about carving Suzanne del Toro's name into it. There was no prayer, no perfect words, just the act of letting the world know that a woman named Suzanne had existed. The wood was soft, probably pine, and the task took little effort. But it was harder than he'd thought it would be. Suzanne — Fat Susie — would always have a special place in his heart. Not only had she been there to catch him when he'd stumbled out of his grief over losing Lily and his family, but she had shown him the way back to the living, shown him a moment of tenderness and honesty. And for that he would always be grateful.

He wished things could have turned out differently. In another place, in another time, Josiah knew deep in his heart . . . that he could have loved Suzanne del Toro, loved her like she deserved to be loved. But that was not to be.

He finished carving her name, and it could be easily read by anyone who would take the time to look.

As he wiped his knife and slid it back into its sheath, he had the feeling that someone was standing behind him. He stood slowly, turning . . . hoping that Juan Carlos would be standing there, waiting with a smile, approving of what he had done.

But there was no one there, nothing but tombstones and broken dreams.

The employees of Thorndike Press hope you have enjoyed this Large Print book. All our Thorndike, Wheeler, and Kennebec Large Print titles are designed for easy reading, and all our books are made to last. Other Thorndike Press Large Print books are available at your library, through selected bookstores, or directly from us.

For information about titles, please call:
(800) 223-1244

or visit our Web site at:
http://gale.cengage.com/thorndike

To share your comments, please write:
Publisher
Thorndike Press
295 Kennedy Memorial Drive
Waterville, ME 04901